IT WAS PAST ELEVEN O'CLOCK WHEN DAWN LEFT THE CLUB AFTER HER SHOWER. . . . Close to her apartment door she felt vague inner stirrings, like anxiety or dread. End-of-the-day frame of mind, she told herself. She let herself in and groped for the light switch. . . .

He stood between her and the front door—unshaven, disheveled, and menacing.

Dawn screamed, spun, and raced for the back door. Her second scream was cut short by his hand over her mouth. His other arm circled her waist. . . . She kicked and squirmed, and tried to turn her face so she could bite his fingers.

He held her with arms as strong as steel bands.

She lunged with all her strength. She couldn't break free! Weakness washed up her spine. He had her! Oh, God, what was he going to do?

Books by C. K. Cambray

Where is Crystal Martin?
Personal
Conditioned to Death

Published by POCKET BOOKS

CONDITIONED TO DEATH

C.K. CAMBRAY

POCKET BOOKS

New York   London   Toronto   Sydney   Tokyo   Singapore

An *Original* Publication of POCKET BOOKS

POCKET BOOKS, a division of Simon & Schuster Inc.
1230 Avenue of the Americas, New York, NY 10020

ISBN: 0-671-70515-6

First Pocket Books printing May 1992

10 9 8 7 6 5 4 3 2 1

POCKET and colophon are registered trademarks of
Simon & Schuster Inc.

Cover art by John Nickle

Printed in the U.S.A.

For Monica,
with love

CHAPTER

1

The ringing phone dragged Dawn Gray up like a net from a sea of deep sleep. She rolled toward the bedside table, trying to blink away the night's debris. The clock radio digitals read 5:45 A.M., Tuesday. An hour and a half before the alarm would beep her into a new day. With waking came uneasiness. She didn't like early or late calls. Good things never happened between midnight and seven.

She grabbed the receiver and squirmed up, half propped on pillows. "This is Dawn Gray," she said.

"Dawn, it's Karl, over at the club."

Karl Clausman, the equipment manager, always opened South Harmon Aerobics, Pool, and Exercise. By the time the day manager welcomed the public at six, the lights and heat or air conditioning were already on and Karl had begun his daily free-weight session, toning his massive upper body. "What's up?" she asked.

"You better get over here right away. You got trouble."

Dawn cleared her tightening throat. "What kind of trouble?"

"You'll find out when you get here. I can't talk."

"Why not?"

"The cops just got here."

"What are the cops doing over at SHAPE?"

"I called them. Now I gotta let them in." Dawn now caught the anxiety edging all of Karl's words. "I sure hope your car starts," he said before hanging up and leaving her to get dressed.

Her Honda was legendary for not starting. Once a car had traveled over 200,000 miles, as hers had, every new day it ran was a gift from Nippon—never mind little things like balking now and then. This gray February morning the Honda did start, coughing and heaving like a flu victim. The New England cold dug into Dawn's fingers and toes. Where was the greenhouse effect when she really needed it?

As the Honda tunneled through the darkness she promised herself if SHAPE ever eased well over into profitability and her co-owner's share of the black ink amounted to real dollars, she'd buy a brand-new car, the first in her twenty-nine years. Paranoia or intuition whispered that the emergency behind this journey was going to affect that modest little dream, and maybe much else besides.

She wondered if she had ever expected peace of mind to be part of co-ownership of what had begun as a rather run-down operation nearly two years ago. If she had, that hadn't been the case. She'd found plenty of anxiety and no peace at all. It numbed her sometimes to think of what she had taken on. And of course she wondered if it had been a wise thing to do. Peter Faldo, her partner, had talked her into making the commitment. He had persuaded her that the money coming to her from her late mother's estate would work better for her if she invested it in the foundering South Harmon Fitness Center than if she cautiously plunked it into CDs. Peter added that her co-ownership would also provide her with employment and counterbalance the emotional upheavals resulting at the time from her breakup with her lover, Sam Springs. She sighed. It wasn't the first time in her life that she had allowed herself to be persuaded to act against her own interest. That was one of the big problems with being Dawn Gray.

She was just too malleable.

Swinging around the corner onto Walnut Street, she saw a police cruiser's flashers first, three blocks ahead in the SHAPE parking lot. The blue-white light exploded in bursts against the front of the redbrick building. High glass panels in the front wall framed the staircase leading up to the second-floor entrance and registration desk. Three stories, thousands of square feet, it was surely a presence on the street—and in her life as well. Despite her growing anxiety and fresh memories of the club's demands, she felt, possibly for the first time, a little swelling of pride because SHAPE was more than half hers.

One cop stood by cars belonging to early birds. He was gesturing that they'd have to wait in the cold awhile. The other cop she saw through one of the glass panels. He stood talking with Karl Clausman at the head of the stairs. She no longer noticed the cold as she locked her car and crossed the lot. To the cop waving at her to stop she called out that she was one of the owners. He nodded her ahead. A pale Karl introduced Officer Griffin. He smelled of Brut and wore long sideburns. Somber shadows shaded his blue eyes. "We have a fatality here, Ms. Gray," he said.

Anxiety sent her heart thumping against ribs.

"In the women's Jacuzzi." The cords stood out in Karl's thick neck as he made a face. "I found her."

"We'd better go down there again," Griffin said. "The morgue people will be here in a few minutes."

On the way down the interior stairs Dawn aimed an inquisitive glance at Karl. "Eloise St. Martin," he said. "Looks like she passed out and drowned."

"We didn't pull her out," Griffin said. "She'd been underwater a long time. It was way too late."

Dawn groaned. This was every bit as bad as her worst fears. Apprehension flooded in, sharpening her senses.

She smelled yesterday's sweat, the distant pungency of pool chlorine. Discolorations on the wall-to-wall and ceiling tiles grew increasingly vivid. In the women's locker room the scents of stale body powder, soap, and deodorant were oppressive.

Shower tiling opened out onto the Jacuzzi terrace. Stainless-steel tubes curved down like question marks into the still water. Quite on its own, one of her arms found its way around Karl's coconut-sized left bicep. This wasn't her line—at all! She advanced more hesitantly than the men. Karl's bulk tugged her forward. "The pumps were going when I found her," he said. "I turned them off."

Eloise St. Martin lay face down under four feet of water on the bottom of the wide bath. On the edge of the lowest tile terrace her left foot rested. Its reddish callus pads were separated by a high narrow arch. Her buttocks on which she had devoted so much thinning energy remained—forever now—a bit chunky. Hips, back, and shoulders were trim. Strands of her long black hair, buoyed by bubbles, rose and waved in ghostly currents. Her whole body was winter white and so very still.

Sorrow rose up in Dawn, as overpowering as an eruption. She felt light-headed. She needed to cry, but at that moment the tears didn't come. She clung to Karl, needing his bulk. Griffin mumbled regrets and got out a notebook. He asked Karl to give him the details about who had drowned and how he had found the body. With the club securely locked for the night and no doors forced, it seemed Eloise had been in the Jacuzzi all night. Grateful for relief from the pitiful sight, Dawn hurried upstairs to a computer terminal and opened the woman's file to get her address and phone number for police records. File opened, she hesitated for a moment. Some additional entries caught her eye, but she ignored them. They had nothing to do with the recent tragedy.

They couldn't. She sent the personal data document to the printer and tore off the sheet.

When she got back downstairs, the morgue crew had arrived and was pulling the body out of the water. She chose to wait in the locker room while they "checked her out," as the female member of the team said. At that moment sitting down on a long bench seemed like a good idea to Dawn. She heaved heavy breaths and tried to gather her thoughts. In time she heard the paramedics chatting about water in the lungs. "Passed out and went under, looks like," the woman said. Her partner added, "No bumps or bruises. Too much heat, not enough time to get out."

In time Eloise's body was covered, moved to a stretcher, and carried away past the clustered early birds who now knew why their workouts were being delayed. Among those held up was Beth Willow, an employee. Dawn waved her in ahead of the others. Slight of frame and petite, Beth made up for her lack of strength with tremendous energy. In her six months of employment, she had never refused to do a job or messed up a given task. She was a jane-of-all-trades without whom Dawn would have felt lost. Her wide-eyed face was shadowed by the hood of her down parka. "Dawn, you look . . . awful," Beth said.

Dawn nodded. "A drowning can do that, I guess."

Beth nodded. "It's all so dreadful!" She shook her head, first in sympathy, then in puzzlement. "But why didn't anybody see her?"

"We'll worry about that later. Right now go down to the women's locker room. Put up a rope and a sign that the Jacuzzi's closed. The police will want to check it all out."

Beth nodded and looked at Dawn appraisingly. "Don't look so worried. It was an accident, wasn't it?"

"Of course. But that can be trouble, too."

Dawn badly needed to talk to her partner. She could have used Peter's support right about then. But Griffin had more questions and a kindly warning about health and safety board representatives who sometimes showed up after unhappy events like this. Finally he left. Dawn looked at her hands. They were trembling. She needed coffee, food, something in her stomach. But not yet. First she had something to do.

She grabbed the phone and dialed Peter's number. She got his answering machine. Damn! It seemed he had spent the night away from his condo again—a rather common occurrence; he was fond of the ladies. Right then she found that rather annoying. She left a message, asking him to call her at once.

She made a note in her day planner to send flowers in the name of the club to Eloise's funeral. She understood the woman had no immediate family. Dawn knew more about her than about the average club member. It had been necessary to talk to her when she filed a complaint last month and then to take the necessary steps to deal with the problem. She pressed her palms against her face. The poor, poor woman! Dawn recalled the high curve of Eloise's immersed arch. She groaned and felt tears burning her eyes. She sobbed in solitude.

Later, red-eyed but calmer, she strolled around the club and whispered the terse details of the misfortune to the eight staff members on duty. Thinking of a lawsuit, she asked them to refer any questions about Eloise's death either to her or to Peter. Only in this lawsuit-crazed country could a person weep for the dead one moment and dread the Ghost of Negligence Past the next. She recalled that the Jacuzzi room was plastered with signs warning against using the bath alone and limiting immersion to five minutes. Fine. But the big question remained unanswered.

Why had the club closed with Eloise still in the Jacuzzi, dead or alive?

She found the schedule sheets and checked last night's crew. Who was the manager? Lucy DeMott. Normally she was as steady and reliable as the tide. Last night, too? She found her phone number in the staff computer files. It was now after eight. Lucy had closed SHAPE at midnight.

Without wasting a second, needing to find some answers, Dawn dialed Lucy's number. The phone rang and rang until it was finally picked up, a husky hello greeting Dawn.

"Hello, Lucy? This is Dawn Gray at SHAPE. I hope I can talk to you for a few minutes." Right then a swell of inadequacy washed over Dawn. Peter should have been doing this. He was the brash, ambitious one. He spoke assertively and took SHAPE more seriously than she believed she did. He would have been forceful and probably more effective with Lucy. But he wasn't around. . . .

"Sure, Dawn. What about?"

"About closing up last night. You were on duty, right?"

"Yep."

"You want to run through the routines, what you did?"

"Sure. Why?"

"Just—do it. Okay?"

"No problem. First thing was—"

"Hang on a sec, Lucy. I don't want to hear about the written procedures. I need to know what you *really* did. I'm aware no manager really goes through all that rigamarole."

"I pretty much follow the rules, really." Lucy ran through it all. When she got to pool, sauna, and Jacuzzi, she said, "And I checked them all. Made sure everybody was out. Made sure the sauna heat wasn't on and the Jacuzzi pumps were off."

"And they were? The pumps, I mean."

"Sure. Then I went on to—"

"That's enough on routines. You're sure about the Jacuzzi, Lucy?"

"Nothing much to be sure about. It was still and

7

empty. Okay? Hey, what's going on? Why all the questions?"

Dawn imagined Lucy in her nightgown, maybe with a cup of instant in hand. Blond and big-boned, she could model for the Spirit of Fitness. In fact, Peter had used a photo of her in her leotard and headband on one of the club membership-drive posters. "Karl found Eloise St. Martin drowned in the Jacuzzi when he opened up this morning."

"Dear God. Oh, I'm so sorry!"

"So you see why—"

"Of course I see. But how did she get in there? The building was deserted when I locked up. I was the last one out."

Dawn hesitated. "Then I guess she hid somewhere because she wanted to have the place to herself—avoid the crowds, do something illegal—and then she had some kind of accident and drowned."

Lucy's laugh was coarse and abrupt. "Are we talking about the same Eloise? She was afraid of her own shadow. She'd just as soon check into Motel Massacre as stay at SHAPE alone in the dark."

"The morgue crew examined her when they pulled her out. She seems to have simply"—Dawn found herself shrugging—"drowned."

"Well, it doesn't sound right to me. I think you know what I mean, Dawn. The club had some problems a little while ago. Right? And Eloise was mixed up in them."

"Well, yes, but—"

"If I were you, I'd quit talking to me and call Zack Keyman." With that final bit of advice, Lucy hung up.

Dawn stared at the receiver. As if from a great distance came the faintest alarm, like seabirds moving to safety ahead of a far distant hurricane. Zack Keyman had worked at the club. He had caused . . . trouble, and she had been forced to deal with it, and with him. Looking back now, she saw that it could all be seen as rather ugly. Just for a moment imagination gripped her in its gauzy fist. Suppose Eloise hadn't drowned accidentally. Of course she *had*, but . . .

She hung up and began to pace the office. Come on, she told herself, shake that nonsense off! The pep talk didn't work. She knew because a hard lump, like a hunk of six-topping pizza, had settled into her stomach.

Eloise had been Zack's first accuser.

CHAPTER
2

Peter was in his usual take-charge mood when he got to the club at nine-thirty. He ran a hand through his curly hair, his actions quicker than normal—and the man moved fast all the time. Not the kind of metabolism Dawn had first expected from one so tall and solid. "He moves as though someone's after him," Jeff Bently, the new massage therapist, once said. If anything chased Peter, it was the wish for success and the prosperity that went with it. The expensive wool suit and French silk tie he wore today well reflected both his good taste and the money he needed to support it. He spoke enviously of whiz kid computer millionaires. "And there're millions in fitness, too, D.G.," he said. "Just not as many, that's all. That's why we have to hustle. Hell, I'm already thirty-five!" To the soaring balloon of his optimism and tendency to take risks she tried to serve as ballast, keeping the enterprise afloat, neither soaring too high toward risk regions where the club didn't yet belong nor allowing it to be dragged down by the sand of excessive safety.

If she erred, it was on the side of agreeing with him too often, not pushing her own viewpoints hard enough. Nonetheless, up to now they had done well as a team. After dismissing Eloise's death with a quick "Hey,

tough break!'' and drawing a cringe from her, he identi-
fied the most important fallout items from the tragedy.
He held up two thick fingers. "The law and the press."

Within minutes he was on the phone to Milton Glassman, the club's attorney. He flipped on the speakerphone so that Dawn could help respond to the
attorney's abrasive questions. If a suit was to come, it
had to be from the "negligence angle," Milton said in
summary. He was cheered to hear the victim was single
and parentless. "You could have lucked out, Healthies.
Stay quiet. No statements. Refer any questions to your
lovable shyster. You'll get my bill. I'm running tight this
A.M. Be cool."

As Peter hung up, Dawn said, "He's even softer-
hearted than you about all this. A woman *died,* for goodness' sake.''

"Nobody asked my permission for her to die, D.G. I
wouldn't have given it. But now we gotta deal with it."

"Okay. Sorry."

"The press . . . the press . . ." Through slitted eyelids Peter gazed around their office at the two desks, the
personal computer soon to be upgraded to become the
center of the club's work station, filing cabinets, the
vendor giveaway posters framed and hung to brighten
the walls: Lifecycles, Nike sneakers, free weights, food
supplements, all hawked by men and women with off-
earth lats and pecs. "If any reporters call, we level with
them: accidental drowning. Maybe she had heart failure
or something. We don't know. The point we make is
that the club is safe. We think she broke the safety rules
and paid the price. Then—"

"But we really don't know for sure what happened."

"We know it was an accident."

"I'm not even sure of that. I talked to Lucy DeMott
who was on duty last night. She said maybe we should
talk to Zack—"

"Come on, D.G.! Zack's history around here. We
took care of the lady's complaints by taking care of

Zack. I don't even want you to dream he was mixed up in the drowning. It was an accident. Guaranteed. Now, can that stuff, okay?''

"Sure." Dawn knew her face was red. Zack's firing was a sore point between them. Her resurrecting it wasn't doing the partnership a favor. She had been out of line, and Peter had put her in her place. Her imagination, with Lucy's help, was running wild. Groping for some perspective, she realized how important the safety rules were throughout the club. She went to the computer and wrote a memo to the staff: "In the wake of the recent tragedy . . ." She made a strong plea that in the weeks to come all written rules be reviewed and implemented to the letter to avoid a possible repetition of "the sad accident." She scheduled three brief meetings with the morning, afternoon, and evening staffs during which she would have Peter, ever the more forceful personality, pound home the message. Then she set out on a one-woman tour to review the posted safety notices.

She went down to the first level, underground, to check out the eight racquetball-squash courts. In use whenever the club was open, they needed to be fully booked to keep the income per square foot up—never a problem. She peered through the small window in one of the court doors. Two housewives wobbled after a blue ball, pausing and panting to giggle out the score. After working hours would come the serious men, each armored with a pro-signature glove, who played in speechless concentration, goggled like Martians. They didn't need to read the posted notices about eye injury. She hoped players hadn't ignored the posted Red Cross notice on quickie CPR. Everyone who joined had to sign a release protecting SHAPE against sudden failures in the human machine. Just the same, if someone went down clutching his chest . . .

One class was going on in the larger of the two aerobics studios. That was progress. When they had first taken over the club, the daytime hours were dead. They had worked hard to change that club-wide, with some success. Help arrived from changing American lifestyles: fewer strict nine-to-five jobs, increasing shift-related service jobs, and more consulting. More people had free time during the day.

She took the elevator up to the Olympic-size heated pool—a big drawing card, for which the rates were accordingly adjusted. It was a money-maker, though upkeep cost a fortune. She checked the signs: No Diving, No Running, No Bottles, No Drugs, No Alcohol, No Swimming Solo, No Roughhousing. She moved on to the Instructions on the Use of the Facility where lap and open swim schedules were clearly posted. Deck use rules for summer, too, had survived without defacement. Outside, snow had drifted against the Thermopane windows. Condensate dripped down the wide glass expanse. In her day planner she made a note to arrange to have somebody study that energy loss. The present structure seemed inefficient to her.

Body bronzers were keeping the three machines in the tanning center busy. And Peter had thought they wouldn't be successful! One of the very few times she had persisted with him. She deserved the small swell of smugness: her tenacity had put a few more dollars in the till.

She wandered through the women's locker room. Police lab technicians were finishing up in the Jacuzzi area. Under their direction Beth Willow was laboring with scrub brush, mop, and bucket. Some of her dark hair had spilled free from a wide bone barrette and waved in front of her eyes. Dawn's memory flashed to Eloise's floating strands. She groaned softly. Steadying herself, she called to Beth. "Hey, want to take a break in a few?"

Beth looked up, startled. The labor had brought color to her pale cheeks. Her bright violet eyes burned with energy. Dawn noticed, really for the first time, that

Beth's heart-shaped face was delicate and well made. The loosened hair enhanced an exotic appearance that was normally quite unnoticeable.

"What time is it?" Beth asked.

"Lunchtime. Join me? I'll treat. I want to finish checking the safety notices first, though. Meet you at the bar in twenty?"

Beth nodded her assent, then resumed mopping with a zealot's enthusiasm. She really worked too hard, Dawn thought.

The third club level held the two Nautilus circuits. The general rules for operating the machines and the principles behind the system were clearly displayed, along with warnings about abusing them. She paid close attention to all the disclaimers that protected SHAPE. Next she checked out the rowing machines, exercise bikes, treadmills, and StairMasters. All were marked with advice to quit at once in case of shortness of breath or discomfort. She asked Allen, a phys ed major from the local college who was filing aerobic record cards, to go over all the disclaimers with a yellow highlighting marker.

"Eloise, huh?" he asked.

"You got it."

"That was a total down, boss."

Dawn nodded and moved on. No problems with the pocket billiards and Ping-Pong tables. Not easy to be fatally injured there. Finally there was the half-size basketball court. Guys pushing middle age, pretending they were seventeen again, regularly blew out their knees on it. But that didn't happen because SHAPE was negligent. That was macho.

She walked over to the atrium banister and looked down three levels to the well of plants and ferns thriving below in the generally humid club air. She felt the hum of activity in the building, even at midday. Pride surged. She and Peter were actually *doing* it, making a success of SHAPE. Against all odds, it had seemed at first. But they had persisted and worked hard—something both of them knew how to do, thank goodness. Now, despite the loans they had taken out and the interest and principle that came off the top every month, they were truly on the verge of making real profits. Even with the dreadful business of Eloise's accidental death threatening, if they kept their wits and their luck held, they would make it.

At lunch—chicken salad on rye, no-salt corn chips, and a glass of buttermilk, all whipped up by Gene at the food and liquor bar off the reception area—Dawn chattered to Beth. Over the weeks since her employment, Beth had gradually become a friend. Today her slow, understanding smile in the face of her employer's nervous babbling reminded Dawn that one of the rules of friendship was a willingness to listen. She clamped her lips shut in mid-sentence and smiled. "Shut up, Gray! Give Beth a chance to get a word in. I'm sorry, really."

Beth's smile widened still further. Her teeth were white and even. "So you're a little keyed up today, Dawn. Small wonder. Nothing like starting the day by being blasted awake by a phone call. Never mind a corpse in the Jacuzzi."

"You don't mind cleaning up after the cops?"

"Uh-uh." She wrinkled her pert nose. "Let's change the subject." She winked a violet eye. "How you doing with our new massage therapist, Mr. Oat Granola."

"Jeff Bently? Oh, we've had some friendly chats."

"Did you ask him to go out?"

Dawn studied the end of her sandwich. "I thought I'd give him a chance to ask me first."

"He's gentle and sweet," Beth said.

"You sound interested."

"Not my type, Dawn. I'd probably do better with the guy you used to live with, the way you describe him."

"Lordy. Heaven help you. Sam Springs certainly

wasn't gentle or sweet. He was a wild man—*is* a wild man."

"A doer, a mover and shaker. Not a granola man. A gobbler of kielbasa and fries." Beth was grinning. "Anyhow, I think Jeff'd be nice for you. You need a social life. All work makes Jane—and all that."

"I'll consider your advice, Ms. Willow."

"You should, because I'm right."

They gathered up their paper plates and cups and put them in the trash. "Oh, I meant to tell you earlier," Beth said. "I saw somebody in the club yesterday that I thought was permanent history."

Dawn licked mayonnaise off her finger. "Who?"

"Zack Keyman."

Dawn froze. Him. She felt herself pale. She wanted to tell Beth she didn't want to know that. She wanted to forbid her having seen him. She wanted him never to have been inside this building again. Never! Because if he had been . . . No, no! Eloise's death had been an *accident!* To Beth she said only "If you see him again, let me know." She turned away to hide her bloodless cheeks.

Later that afternoon she was relieved to hear that Suzette Gagnon, who led the five-thirty Tiger Aerobics class, had called in with the flu. Dawn would take the session in her place. She enjoyed filling in from time to time. Today, as she squirmed into her leotard, shorts, and leg warmers, she particularly relished the upcoming energy discharge. She sorted through her tapes, made two years ago when she had been dubbed Big Beat Sweat Queen by one exhausted but appreciative class during the early months of her co-ownership. In those lean days she had led all three sessions, the evening hour-and-a-quarter ones back to back, with only fifteen minutes between. Her resting pulse had been forty-two then, and there hadn't been a sag on her anywhere.

As she led the Tigers through their warm-up, she studied her body in the mirror among the heaving shapes of nine-to-fivers. On the threshold of thirty, her machine looked to be holding up just fine. Her long legs were still solid, thanks to frequent late-evening workouts. Her former twenty-three-inch waist had widened maybe an inch in the last year. So she was aging a little. Being five feet nine let her get away with being slightly top-heavy. Her firm shoulders were wide and slightly sloping, her neck long and unblemished. She was lucky to be well proportioned. Even time wouldn't change that. One of the many gifts from Mom and Dad, may they both R.I.P. Beneath the maroon headband her smiling squarish face boasted two dimples; above, her straw-colored hair shone with health and determined brushing. She felt the loss of a little flexibility from her less rigorous exercise schedule, but she would loosen as the workout got under way. If she needed confirmation that her appearance was holding up, she found it in the covert glances of the three men among the dozen women in the class. They liked having her in front of them now, but they wouldn't much after the routine stretched into its last half hour.

"Let's start out with a little running in place, gang," she called out. "I'm going to ask you to keep the beat. It'll get a bit stiff. Try your best to keep up with me. That way you're sure of getting your money's worth." She dimpled. "But then, you are the Tigers, aren't you?"

By seven o'clock the Tigers had turned into pussycats. Dawn was panting a bit herself. She flopped on a bench and pulled on her leg warmers. Cooling down, she headed for the locker room. The shower felt great. Dried and dressed, she peered into the Jacuzzi room. The bath had been refilled. Beth was an angel. She took down the ropes and Out of Order sign. This wasn't the place to mourn the loss of Eloise St. Martin.

She went upstairs and did some paperwork. Beyond the expanse of entryway glass, snow squalls swirled like dervishes. Fatigue descended suddenly—the price for

17

toughing out what had to have been her worst day in memory.

By the time she got into her Honda, the wind had died and the snow had steadied into a slower but determined descent, haloing the streetlights and muffling the city sounds. The Honda had front-wheel drive. She had no problem getting under way. She tuned in to a country music station. Lightweight tenors wailed about eighteen-wheelers and truck-stop mommas. Despite being tired, she couldn't relax. She kept looking in the rearview mirror. She felt she was being followed. At a light she turned and looked behind her. Through the snow it was hard to see anything but scattered headlights and masked roadside shapes. She just couldn't tell. . . .

Not until she was inside her apartment did it occur to her that, if someone had been following her, she shouldn't have come here. Possibly whoever was behind her—if there had been anyone—now knew where she lived. She told herself to stop it. Her imagination was running wild, released by stress and fatigue. She knew she ought to eat something, but she had lost her appetite wondering what, if anything, lurked outside. She went to the window and looked out. The world was a wash of white. She couldn't even see across the street. She threw the dead bolts on the hall and backstairs doors, then put on the teakettle. She paced her small quarters, waiting for the water to boil.

After the breakup, she and Sam had divided up their modest possessions. She had intended to replace her share, thus ridding herself of their unpleasant associations. But her resources hadn't been equal to that task. All her spare dollars went back into SHAPE. So she still slept on the bed they had used during their eighteen months together. He had promised her a honeymoonlike trip. That first promise she had believed. It took months for her to realize that Sam scattered promises the way a goldenrod spread pollen—and with about as much follow-up. She halted her descent into the whirlpool of recrimination, guilt, and what-ifs that still swirled up periodically in her consciousness, even though the breakup was already two years past.

She took a cup of tea to her rocking chair, its wide curving back covered with artificial fur. She had bought it at a tag sale, enchanted by its inspired grossness. It had slid off the Honda's roof on the way home, and its hairy fabric had been torn. She had covered it with a flowered quilt. Somehow for her it was more comfortable than the most expensive ergonomic wonder. She usually put on earphones and listened to loud 1960s rock tapes to get her mind off Sam and their past. Tonight, though, with something in the air, she couldn't bear to cover her ears. And there was "no loud playing of radios or TVs" after nine o'clock, according to the strict canons of the Harnishes, superintendent and wife, whose fundamentalist orientation was marvelous for apartment house upkeep but deadly for small talk.

She sat in silence, cup and saucer on her lap. In time she began to sniffle. Poor Eloise! She used a Kleenex, took a deep breath, and put her head back. Howling wind woke her at 2:00 A.M. She looked out the window into a swirl of northeaster. Was somebody still out there watching her? Chasing away the discomforting thought, she crept off to bed and pulled the covers over her head.

CHAPTER
3

With snow removal lagging and commuters taking reckless chances, the drive to work was tortuous and tiring. Dawn had just arrived, taken off her parka, and traded boots for shoes when the phone rang. Thinking she hadn't even had time for a cup of coffee, she lifted the receiver.

"My love, this is Hector."

Her heart thumped. Oh, God, still! She wanted to tell herself she had ended it, though she hadn't told him. "H-hello there."

"I got back from Singapore day before yesterday. I had more business to take care of here in the city. But it was you I was thinking of—in Asia as well as here." His voice, with its vague Slavic inflection, played down her spine like a wooden hammer on a xylophone. She didn't like her reaction. It told her she still had a long way to go before she reached indifference. The temptation was still powerful. "We must meet somewhere as soon as possible. I need to hear in person your reaction to my offer—don't say anything now. Tell me when we can meet—today."

As before, she was swept along by his demanding personality. "There's been some trouble here at the club. And the weather . . ." She was dismayed to hear the hesitancy in her voice. "With all the snow I'm not sure I can get around."

"Rudolfo can handle any weather. We'll come by and pick you up. Let me have a time. I have a busy day ahead. You're my first priority, Dawn my love, give me a reason to get through it."

"Hector . . ." Damn her pounding heart! She wasn't leading the Tigers. She was just talking on the phone!

"A time, Dawn. Now."

She imagined Hector Sturm angling the receiver away from his ear. His free hand would be beating time in the air. He wasn't a patient man. She had seen him on the phone often enough, frequently from a tangle of dampened sheets. She drew her breath in sharply at those memories, as piercing as assassins' knives. What he had done with her then! What he still seemed able to do! Reading her own reactions was no mystery. The problem was changing them. "Three-thirty," she said. She shouldn't!

"Excellent! I'm looking forward to hearing your decision. Though I'm certain I know what—"

"But I have to be back at five-thirty. I'm leading a session."

"Come now, Dawn," he scolded.

"I'm leading a session." She hung up gently. He didn't like hearing that. "Deals poorly with rejection," she muttered. For that reason she had a very hard time getting it together to reject him. And was she crazy to want to? Hector, Hector. Nearly twenty years older than she—and all the lover a woman could want. She got up and started moving around to get her mind off . . . all that.

At ten SHAPE's accountant paid her and Peter a visit. Ketty was thin, nervous, and smart. She handled her fan-folded computer printouts with swift fingers, her gestures crisp and economical. After presenting all of SHAPE's financial details, some of which Dawn didn't clearly understand, Ketty sat back and said, "To sum up, then." She grinned. "Next month you start making money."

"All right!" Peter bubbled.

After Ketty left, Peter hit Dawn with half a dozen club-related schemes, from more sponsored weekend trips to hiring a full-time consultant to recruit members for cholesterol and stress control. She imagined the promised profits, no matter how generous, flying away on little green wings. She assumed her negativist stance in an effort to hold him off. I must not be so easily persuaded, she warned herself.

After nearly a half hour she made Peter angry with her refusals. His neck reddened, and he loosened his tie. "A nice word for you, D.G., is 'stick-in-the-mud.' A better one is 'pain—' "

"One of us has to be conservative. It sure isn't going to be you."

"You have to take risks to succeed!" he protested loudly.

"We've taken some. We'll take more. We just can't take every one that comes along."

Peter shoved a hand through his curly hair. It sprang back, unaltered. His dark eyes were wide, even hostile. "Do you know I have a timetable for success, D.G.? For the success of Peter L. Faldo. And I am behind schedule. Get that? I don't have time for you to drag me down."

"Oh, stop!" She got up and turned away from him. Without looking back, she left the office. She hoped he would think she had left in anger.

She knew she had departed because, in the face of his persistence, she would have changed her mind.

"Come back here!" he called.

She fled at a speedy walk, refusing the indignity of running. Having not run, she would nonetheless hide until Peter's boiling ambition returned to a slow simmer.

She walked up to the third level, to the room with the

new sign: Massage Therapy, by Appointment Only. She knocked and Jeff Bently called, "Come in."

Jeff was in a yoga position, twisted like a root in the middle of the floor. At six feet five, he had a lot to twist and untwist.

"Am I interrupting something?" Dawn said, smiling.

"The flow of vital restorative currents; the surge of balancing fluids."

"Maybe I should be wearing a raincoat."

Jeff squirmed into a cross-legged sitting position. He wore John Lennon glasses, and his brown hair was shoulder-length. He was forty-something. "Not necessary. We're talking internal bodily processes. No mess. No ugly cleanup." He gestured at a woven mat. "Go ahead. Grasp at straws."

"Story of my life, Jeff."

"I doubt it."

She sat. She wasn't really sure why she had come to see him. Keep busy, she told herself. Forget Peter's ambitions and Hector's desires. "How's it going here?" She waved around at the room decorated with anatomical charts featuring skeletons, organs, pressure points, and the flow of energies according to the principles of Chinese medicine. The smaller adjacent room's door was ajar. Its sign read In Session, Please Wait. "Is this going to be a successful enterprise for you, Jeff?"

"I've got two one-hour sessions booked this morning. Both repeats. You saw my literature?"

She nodded.

"Designed it myself. I do a little art. And now that I have this central location, I'll be running some small ads in the free papers." He smiled. "It might just work."

"I'm glad. It gives the club still another dimension."

He got up. "I'm sorry to hear about what happened to Eloise. You want to talk about it, Dawn?"

She shook her head. "It's not going to hurt SHAPE, I don't think, though it was a terrible tragedy."

He looked at her appraisingly. "I think you have more to say than you're letting on."

She was startled by his insight. About to reply, she was interrupted by being paged on the intercom system. There was no phone installed here yet. "Gotta go," she said. "We'll talk later. Promise."

"Only if you decide to open up."

On the way to the phone in the Nautilus area she realized her excursion to Jeffland hadn't gone so well. She wasn't sure what she had expected from the man. Tuesday certainly hadn't been a good day. Wednesday was proving to be only slightly better.

Then she got some good news. The caller was Officer Griffin, who had quizzed her about Eloise's death. He reported that a police doctor had looked over the body. Water in the lungs; no bumps, bruises, or contusions. "The woman got too much heat and went under. Nobody was there to pull her out."

"She shouldn't have gone in alone. It was against the posted rules."

"Like all the fun things in life," Griffin said. "Have a good day."

How soon three o'clock came! She wasn't sure if she dreaded or anticipated her rendezvous with Hector. She stood inside the entryway in her parka, heart pounding. Now and then she wiped away the condensate with her sleeve to clear her view of the parking lot.

At precisely three the stretch BMW swept in, seemingly impervious to the elements. It was white and elegant, save for a few slush slugs clinging to the rocker panels. Its passenger compartment windows were smoked, so she didn't see Hector till he swung the door open from the inside. She slid in beside him. "My sweet!" His arms were around her. For a moment, as his mustached lips slipped toward her, she thought of holding him off, explaining. Then he kissed her, the familiar, gentle pressure stirring memories that flew up shining like fireflies.

She had met Hector Sturm when, after a knee injury

a doctor recommended SHAPE as a good place for light rehabilitation. Seeing him as she first had, dressed in new designer sneakers, shorts, and shirt, she hadn't been greatly impressed. He was thin, with a runner's ropy legs. From a distance his dominant features seemed to be high cheekbones and a thick sandy mustache. Then she saw his piercing black eyes—and her indifference faded like fog. Those eyes bored into hers without restraint of any kind. They boiled with strength and power. She stood, clipboard in hand, mouthing drivel about rehab session lengths and repetitions, transfixed by that gaze like a speared antelope. When he asked her to go out for a drink there was no way she could say no.

In defense of her weak will, she had broken up with Sam and been utterly manless for thirteen months. As well, she had spent every waking hour struggling to get the club off the ground and half of her sleeping hours worrying about it. If she needed further enticement, Hector's wealth and commanding presence had provided it. Let's hear it for older men! she sang as he indulged her with lobsters and Vouvray. Who cared that he was the same height as she? He took her to Rhode Island for the weekend. Somehow he arranged for them to stay in an old mansion atop a cliff overlooking a sea that obligingly turned gray, stormy, and romantic for their benefit.

In robes borrowed from the owner's collection, they cuddled by the high, wide windows and gazed down at surging white breakers and long tongues of foam. He confessed that after meeting her he had broken up with the younger woman he'd been seeing for some time. Dawn wasn't to feel guilty, he told her. That earlier relationship had already begun to sour. While a capable paramour, the woman simply wasn't stable. "Nor were her breasts as large and lovely as yours," he whispered before sliding his head down to pay her nipples moist, earnest tribute.

Once an almost-married woman, she had thought Sam

loved her thoroughly; there was little more for her to know. Then Hector had opened her eyes to her ex-lover having failed in that field as well as all the others. Call it tenderness, patience, skill—goodness, who cared what name was put to that which, time after time, had her screaming, whimpering, and trembling, pleased from head to toe. Sloe-eyed and aroused, he praised her youth and her body—and made rich demands on both, which she met with a martyr's passion.

To one who had been raised to watch every penny, having to deny herself nothing while in Hector's company was as refreshing as a scented shower. "Your wildest wishes are made modest by habit," he murmured into the folds of her ear. The hair stirred on the back of her neck. She knew she could get from him whatever she wanted, so her contrariness bade her to ask for little—and so earned his approval. "A jewel who wants no jewels," he had said one day, offering her an unwrapped velvet box fresh from an expensive jeweler's hot hand. In it lay a platinum body chain, "measured to fit not in dull inches, but in spans of my loving hands." And there, above the warmest of her flesh, he bade her wear it—always—in secret tribute to his love. . . .

Rudolfo, whose face she had never seen, thanks to the translucent partition between him and the rear seat, drove icy streets with subtle skill. He remained waiting in a small lot while she and Hector rode the elevator to a private club penthouse in the heart of the city. There the weather had turned the antique furniture, paintings, and cut flowers—in February!—over to their solo use. Once she had a glass of wine in front of her, she knew what to expect. Hector wasn't a man to delay or temporize.

"I know you've been pondering my offer." He leaned forward over the immaculate tablecloth. She avoided his gaze for the moment. Her eyes fell to the gold links in his French cuffs. In the best taste, as was everything he did. "I want your answer. Now."

Her answer, of course, was no. The question, posed before his long business trip to Asia, was: would she agree to be his kept woman? "Mistress," they used to call such a woman. There were other, less flattering words for the arrangement. No matter the words, the proposition was tempting. Of course Hector was married in what she, the one hundred percent American naive one, had always considered the European style. His wife was his age and lived well in New York City. There urban delights occupied her time and much of his money. He had mentioned that she had "a young, virile friend" whom she helped out financially from time to time. In the face of this worldliness Dawn's small-town morality and unexamined sexual principles fell to pieces. She had told herself that when this moment finally came, she would simply say no into his expectant face. Instead she now said nothing, realizing silence meant vacillation. Oh, Lord, she *had* made up her mind.

"Your yes guarantees another trip to the Costa del Sol," Hector murmured.

"It does?"

"Of course, my love."

Oh, that trip! She had left the club for five days, to Peter's great distress. Hector needed to go to southern Spain on business. They had flown to Madrid, then down to Málaga. The waiting car and driver had taken them westward along the coast. He had reserved rooms in a paradise on earth disguised as a resort hotel called the Puente Romano in Marbella. There they had enjoyed an early-summer idyll. There, too, she glimpsed the extent of his wealth, gauged by the marble floors, the meticulously tended paths winding through cool groves of tropical foliage, the tennis courts banded with beds of blooms, the speedy delivery to their balconied suite of drinks and faultlessly presented meals. Into its bars Arabs winking at the Prophet's teachings strode with leggy Scandinavian women on their arms. Hector took her strolling along the quay at nearby Porto Banus.

There opulent yachts rode at anchor and white-walled buildings clustered into a bayside crescent backed by low hills. He rented a two-master and a skilled captain who was professionally deaf and blind to their fleshly carryings-on. That day she tanned private places for the first time.

Most fondly she remembered the Puente Romano Beach Club brunch buffet. The club boasted waterfalls and pools. Around them lounged Europeans speaking a handful of languages, the women topless. The food, served under a circus-size tent, was spectacular and without end: langoustines, beef, and salmon cut and grilled to order by chefs wearing toques and smiles; salads and aspics collared with vegetable purees; a dessert tray groaning with calories and scented by ground almonds. The wine flowed, all white and bucket-chilled, appearing magically at the slightest tip of Hector's head. They dined in shade, then moved out near the waterfall to sun. The wine went to her head. She tottered to the ladies' room and came back with her suit top in her beach bag. She sprawled in a chaise beside Hector, pleasantly aware of a few pairs of hot European eyes on her bod. He twined her hair with gentle fingers. "You are so . . . lovely," he said. Toward late afternoon, wined about out of her mind, she tried her high school Spanish on the head waiter. *"Aquí, está paraíso,"* she ventured. "Yes, madam," he said, his English flawless.

Now, here in this New England February, Hector was tempting her with sunlight and rich memories. The ice of her resolution reached in solitude crumbled under the twin suns of remembered Spain and his presence. She glanced at her watch. "It's getting to be time to go," she said. "My class . . ."

"We'll go, Dawn, after you answer me." His black eyes locked on hers. There was no looking away.

"I've been thinking a lot about your offer."

"And?"

"I—I need a little more time. Please." Why didn't

she tell him no? The answer *was* no. But it wasn't, really, until she said it.

"How much more time?" He touched her wrist where it lay on the tablecloth. She saw the displeasure on his face. She hesitated. "You're not trifling with me, are you?" he said. "You know I won't be—"

"I know," she said.

"One week. You may have one week for further pondering. Next Wednesday we'll meet again. As we did today. Three-thirty. This delay is foolish. I'm sure in the end you'll accept my offer. Not to do so would be"—he shrugged under a smile—"idiocy!" He held both her wrists in his hands. "I want very much for you to become a big part of my life. And it will be a grand life for us both!"

"Hector . . ."

He tilted up her chin with a gentle hand and looked far into her eyes—oh, he did know how! "My love, are you wearing your chain?"

Her hand, as though with its own mind, dropped to her waist. "Yes!" she breathed. "I put it on this morning."

His hands dropped lightly to her shoulders. His direct gaze spoke of unmasked desire and carnal knowledge. Her inner wilting before them seemed as correct as "please" and "thank you." Even as she rebelled against her recent eager submissions, she understood the strength of his powers—and their origin in her, the object of his passion. Man-woman, woman-man, somehow doubling back on each other, and in difference becoming whole. Neither had shown a lack of enthusiasm in playing those primal roles. Though they gussied them up with Spanish beaches and platinum chains, had they been naked castaways his touch would still have detonated her response. Despite herself, she brushed his lips with her fingertip. "My little blasting cap," she murmured.

"I have been called many tender things, my sweet." He kissed her hand. "But be careful with the adjective 'little.' '' He laughed, but beneath it she caught the edge of annoyance. "Were you referring to my stature or to my—"

"Not to anything specific. Just a term of affection, Hector. Good thing you're not *sensitive* or anything."

His gaze seemed to gather strength. "You're well aware by now of where and how I'm sensitive."

She couldn't stop her blush. And at her age, too!

He lowered his arms and hugged her hard. His lips moved close to her ear. "You're mine, you know. Without benefit of clergy."

"No."

"Oh, yes, Dawn. Mine now, and mine to have when you agree to my offer."

No, it would be a dead end for her. Kept, careerless, and cast aside—the three *k*-sounds of the dominated woman. She had to shake herself free. She had to tell him she couldn't accept his offer. She absolutely *had* to.

So why didn't she? *Why?*

"I want to hear you say you're mine," he murmured.

"No!"

He licked her neck. She pulled away. "That's not fair."

She saw the pulse of newly born desire rising and falling in his neck. She was dismayed to understand how well she knew him. His eyes told her he was thinking of raising the arousal stakes. She wasn't at all sure she could resist, should that happen. She tugged free. "I have to go lead my class."

"Stay and I'll be your class of one." Hector's eyelids had grown heavy. Pulse, now eyes—time to get out of there!

In the club elevator she allowed him to kiss her more deeply than was wise. It took a brief bout of championship wrestling to free herself once they reached ground level. She raced away, panting.

"Remember, you're mine!" he called after her.

No, I'm not! she said. But to her great dismay she spoke only to herself.

CHAPTER
4

Thursday morning Dawn bustled about the club. She rounded a corner heading back to the office—and glimpsed Hector in a Nike shirt and shorts. Her heart thumped and she retreated. Having returned to the city, he had apparently resumed his exercises and had come by the office hoping to catch her there, no doubt to chat—and to put on more pressure about becoming his designated housemate, the DH in the ball game of his love life. Got to avoid that, she thought. Turning toward a mirror, she glimpsed her face—flushed to full workout level. At that moment she knew she was as likely to agree to his proposal as to reject it. Yes, he was persuasive—and charming as well. She thought having seen him would surely shake up the foundation of her day. It didn't, and for the worst kind of reason.

There was another drowning.

A staffer rushed white-faced into the office with the news. "They're pulling her out now," he said.

"The pool was closed!" Dawn bolted up. Flu had hit the lifeguards. Not able to staff the published schedule, she had personally supervised the posting of signs in a half-dozen locations: Pool Closed until Further Notice. She paged Peter, and he matched her strides as they rushed to poolside.

Karl Clausman and Jeff Bently were hauling a woman's body out of the pool. Karl stood in the waist-deep water. His thick arms were around her thighs just above the knees. His massive upper body was taut with the weight. Jeff bent over, his hands around her wrists. They slid her face down up onto the pool deck. The corpse's back was to Dawn, its hair matted to the white back like black paste just above the suit's red yoke. Karl scrambled out of the pool. He picked up the body, held it vertically, head down. He wriggled it up until his arms circled the still chest. He began to squeeze rhythmically. Water surged from the woman's mouth as her lungs partially emptied. He stretched her out face up on the tiles and knelt beside her. Now Dawn saw who she was. She gasped. Nicole Thurston! Karl and Jeff began CPR, pausing periodically to check for signs of life.

There were none.

Dawn burst into tears. She told Peter to deal with the police and emergency squad. She ran sobbing through doorways and halls, twice nearly tripping. She hid in the office and wondered if she was going crazy. In time she stopped crying—and started shivering. Her hands trembled. A second death! Oh, that was bad enough. But that it was Nicole . . . She knew what that might mean. She would have to face Peter with it more aggressively this time and not let him shoo away what were now becoming solidly forming suspicions.

By the time Peter, Karl, and Jeff returned to the office, they had the facts in hand. Like Eloise, Nicole appeared to have entered an unattended pool and drowned accidentally. Several club members had seen her earlier that afternoon doing her Nautilus workout. Afterward it was her custom to do a leisurely twenty laps. A strong swimmer, she had ignored the warnings of pool closing.

"So . . . I don't think we're liable," Peter said in a husky voice.

Dawn shook her head wordlessly.

She knew it wouldn't go as easily for the club as it had with Eloise, accident or not. That afternoon a police detective arrived. Detective Morgan wore a perpetual scowl, the residue of "twenty years on the crime line," as he said. He asked permission to talk to club members and staff. After doing so he came back to the office to talk to Peter and Dawn. "So you got two accidents on your hands, huh? The cop doc took a quick look at lady number two. Drowned, sure enough. No apparent hanky-panky." His tape recorder was running. "What you think about that?"

Both Dawn and Peter made vague, noncommittal noises. She remembered her partner's advice after the first death: avoid the press and liability. Nonetheless, at their first private moment, she was going to remind him about what she suspected.

Detective Morgan persisted. His questions came from all angles. When he asked if Nicole and Eloise had anything in common, Dawn felt herself stiffen. Brash Peter handled that one. Just club members, that's all. One social and popular, the other shy and quiet. Nice ladies, both. In time the detective went away, thinking who knew what.

They heard then from Nicole's husband, a bank vice president. His voice was raw with grief. Dawn whiffed the will to revenge in his clipped words. His attorney had been notified . . . negligence . . . suit. She kept her composure. She asked that he please refer all details of the suit to Milton Glassman. Milton was alarmed enough to come to the club that afternoon to get the details personally and look over the scene of the accident. The *second* accident. What kind of club were they running here?

He took them both into their office. He was even more nervous and faster-moving than Peter. He looked like a sparrow hopping about after crumbs. His Adam's apple bobbed as he issued instructions, his paisley bow tie wriggling slightly in time. He said they should thank God the pool closing had been posted everywhere from the front door in. In his legal judgment a charge of negligence would never stick. Just the same, it would cost them some money to fight the suit. How was SHAPE doing for bucks these days?

By the time he rushed off, a hefty retainer in hand, Dawn's nerves were worn thin. Sometime that morning, she had to talk to Peter about the deaths, but not just then. She wandered around the club and found Beth Willow in the trainer's room. She had assumed the trainer's duties under her own initiative when the former trainer had walked out and not returned. She said she had started nursing school, but had dropped out. After that she had worked for a sports medicine doctor. "Kind of lumpy qualifications, huh?" she had said when she was hired. Dawn hadn't cared: Beth was cautious, knowledgeable, and quick to send members off for medical treatment when appropriate.

Beth was cataloging the supplies, entering the information into a laptop computer, heart-shaped face bent over the plasma screen. "Expensive little devil," she said. "But worth it. Dates from when I was a little more prosperous." She'd explained that she had last worked for a software company that issued yearly bonuses.

"Can I talk to you while you're working, Beth?" Dawn asked.

"Talk away."

Dawn smiled and told her friend about Zack and the two dead women. She explained that both of them dying was just too much of a coincidence.

Beth looked mildly startled. "I heard they both died accidentally. Did somebody find out something to change that?"

Dawn shook her head. "No, no. I'm just supposing. I want your opinion. Do you think I should insist that Peter take my suspicions seriously? If I'm right, well, we have to start doing stuff to protect the club's reputation.''

Beth's violet eyes narrowed slightly in puzzlement. ''Why do you want to talk to me about what you should do?''

''Sometimes I have trouble standing up to Peter, Beth. You know how he can be.''

''Pushy and ambitious.''

''Exactly.''

Beth tapped her small foot, matching the time by flicking the computer case with a fingertip. She was thinking. In time she said, ''You have a partnership, right?''

''Share and share alike, the good and the bad. Up to now it's been mostly bad. We hope to show a profit—''

''Then you have to take your suspicions to him. Your concerns are valid.'' She pumped a thin-boned fist. ''Don't be timid. Go for it!''

Dawn went upstairs and found Peter in the office. She closed the door and faced him. Before starting to speak, she waved him out from behind his desk. It was a power post, and she had a hard enough time confronting him as it was. When he sat in a chair facing hers, she said, ''Let's get right to the point, partner. I think you remember as well as I do what Eloise and Nicole had in common.''

He looked at her blankly.

''They both had trouble with the same guy.''

''I know,'' he answered.

''You knew from word one, Peter,'' Dawn reminded in a somewhat harsh tone.

He nodded wearily. He wore his troubles written in lines on his brow. On a good day it was smooth. Today's events had etched new creases. ''Zack Keyman, right?''

Zack had been one of the former management's better employees, it seemed. He had worked in the Nautilus circuits as an instructor-manager. His energy and unfailing courtesy had been important factors in his being asked to stay on when the club changed hands. Though short and burly, Zack was square-jawed and handsome, with green eyes and black hair. He clearly enjoyed working with women, hardly a unique preference among the male staff members.

A little more than a month ago Eloise St. Martin had asked to speak to Dawn privately. She complained that Zack had touched her against her wishes and made obscene proposals. Inwardly Dawn had cringed. Bang! There it was—the kind of trouble her personality was ill-suited to handle. She hated confrontations, but now she would have to confront Zack and ask him about his actions or be present while Eloise stated her charges to his face. As luck would have it, Peter had been out of town at the time, and so the matter was firmly in her lap.

She invited Zack into the office. He sat with his legs spread apart. His SHAPE uniform pants were a size too small. She could see the shape of his thighs and sex through the maroon fabric. His large perfect teeth were exposed in what seemed to her at that moment a sensuous smile. He was already making her nervous, and they hadn't gotten into it yet. "I've received a complaint," she started and then laid out all that Eloise had said.

She had expected denial. Instead, Zack said, "So what? I do it to all the broads. Mostly they say, 'Stuff it.' Either way, they like it."

"I doubt that, Zack."

"Hey, most of them are married. They haven't been propositioned since the ring slipped on. It's a Keyman bonus. No extra charge."

"You must know it's against club rules."

"Made to be broken. Right?"

"As a matter of fact—no!" She forced herself to meet his green-eyed gaze. "There's to be no sexual harassment in this club! I want you to apologize to Eloise."

"She's an uptight virgin, drying up on the vine. She should be so lucky if I really tried to put the make on her. She shoulda said yes instead of come crying to you.''

"Zack, listen to me." Dawn was aware her voice had tensed in the face of his macho chauvinism, which bordered on insolence. "You're a valuable employee, right? You've done well with the members—up to now. You have to do two things to keep your job. First, you have to apologize to Eloise. Second, you have to change your ways.''

"Like hell!''

"Zack, we want to keep you on the staff. Please don't curse at me. And please think carefully about what I'm asking you." Her heart pounded.

He opened his mouth, but she jabbed a finger at him, feeling like an actress. "Don't make things worse, Zack. You're right on the edge. Do yourself a favor and be quiet for once." She sent him on his way before he was able to draw her into a debate she knew she'd lose.

Dawn heard he later made a halfhearted apology to Eloise. As for changing his ways . . . two days later Nicole Thurston came to her with a similar complaint. With Peter still away, Dawn knew she had to handle the matter at once. Nicole, more aggressive than Eloise, told Dawn that if something wasn't done, she'd resign her membership and speak out publicly about what had happened.

Dawn had summoned Zack and fired him on the spot. At first he assumed she was joking. When it became clear she wasn't, his face reddened. He made large fists and clamped his arms against his sides to control the violent urges exposed by his savage expression. "You . . . can't! I need this job. I like it here.''

"You should have thought about all that before you offended Nicole.''

"Change your mind!" His eyes were wide now, slightly protruding.

"I will *not* change my mind, Zack Keyman!" In a way she was continuing her acting performance, seeing

37

herself as though through eyes set in the wall. She had gotten away with it up to now. All she had to do was finish. She took an envelope from the desk and put it on the blotter. "This is your pay up through the end of the day, plus two weeks severance. I'm leaving now. Take it with you, and clean out your locker. I don't ever want to see you around here again."

She attempted to pass him on her way to the door. She never really saw the arm that he suddenly threw around her neck. A bulging bicep pressed into the side of her neck. Vertebrae popped with the strain. "You're not firing me!" he growled.

Her legs turned rubbery with fear. She tried to speak, but the tubes and cords in her neck were dreadfully compressed. She flapped her arm like a wing against his side. "If you don't change your mind, Dawn, bad things are going to happen at SHAPE!"

She lunged wildly, momentarily relieving the pressure on her throat. She managed a squawking noise that had more effect on him than her blows to his side. He released her. She faced him, aware her face was scarlet. She panted. "Leave!" she croaked. "Leave right now!"

He rushed out, and she staggered back against her desk. *Bad things are going to happen at SHAPE....*

When she had calmed down, she realized that firing Zack was her first unilateral act: she hadn't gone to her partner for approval. If she had, she feared he would have talked her out of it. Damn her indecisiveness!

When Peter returned to the club and heard her story, he told her she had overreacted. As much as she wanted to deny he was doing so, he really did lecture her on acting without his approval. Their arrangement was a partnership. She ought to honor that all the time. He did. He went into great detail about how he would have handled the matter, had he been consulted. His solution involved getting Zack some counseling and offering both women greatly reduced membership fees. Well, what was done was done. He hoped Dawn, like Eloise and

Nicole, would forget about the problems with Zack, now that they were over. . . .

Holding Beth's encouragement in her mind, like a beacon toward which she advanced, she leaned across her desk. Instead of working into her case, she blurted, "I think Zack Keyman somehow killed both Eloise and Nicole. I think he did it for revenge. Down deep, Peter, I don't think he's a very nice person. Not a nice person at all!"

Somewhat drained himself, Peter wasn't about to be patient with her. "So you're back on that again? Look, the police said both women drowned by accident."

"My intuition—"

"Look, D.G., your intuition has been wrong as often as it's been right."

"What would you say if I told you Zack was seen in the club again the other day?"

Peter blinked. "That doesn't prove anything." He didn't sound convinced.

"Beth saw him."

Peter leaned over and took both her wrists lightly in his hands. "Trust me. There's nothing to it. Zack is history. Those women died by accident. End of story."

She wasn't convinced, and she *was* annoyed with him. She had the feeling that once again he was pushing her, using his more effective personality. He wasn't necessarily right. Really!

But she couldn't at that moment bring herself to oppose him any further. She left the club in a bad mood that the drive home through the cold didn't improve. She poured herself one of her rare drinks from a bottle of scotch with dust on it. It went right to her head. A while later she picked up the phone and called the police. She asked for Detective Morgan. She had a hard time getting through. When she heard his voice, he sounded harassed and tired. She had to remind him who she was.

"What can I do for you, Dawn? If you could make it fast, I'd appreciate it."

She told him about Zack Keyman.

"Got an address or phone for him?"

"No, his file is at the club."

"Get it when you can and phone it in."

She hesitated. "How long do you think it'll be before you can talk to him?"

"You don't deal with the cops much, do you? If you did you'd know we're spread thinner than piss on a rock. This is the era of the drug felon. To tell you the truth, chasing after this Keyman guy in connection with two accidents doesn't rate. Sounds like a real long shot, with no crime evident. When? I'll get to it when I can. That's the best I can do."

After hanging up, she again began to feel as though she wasn't alone in her apartment, as if someone was spying on her. She looked out her windows into the cold street. She scanned the windows of the apartments down the block. Some were dark. In the shadows anyone could be looking out at her. She drew all the curtains against any prying eyes and the cold. It didn't help.

She tried to read herself to sleep. A romance usually did the trick: gorgeous young women seeking true love at epic moments of history. Straining bodice laces and manly chests. Love! Escape!

She dug into her latest, but that night it didn't work. Amidships on the aristocratic British blockade-runner's sloop the faces of Eloise St. Martin and Nicole Thurston fastened themselves like alien leeches over those of hearty cockney seamen. She let the paperback fall to the coverlet. What would the two deaths mean to the club? How was she going to keep the balance of the partnership with Peter unless she became more forceful?

She stewed over the problems of SHAPE awhile; then her overwrought mind presented the face of Hector Sturm. She groaned as a host of memories swept in like an advancing army—all too many of them erotic and pleasing. Oh, no, she had decided. She simply had to tell him. If only he wasn't so self-possessed, so rich, such a good lover . . . If only *she* wasn't so easy to control and manipulate. She had to learn how to stand up for herself.

In the wee hours she slept. She awoke sour-mouthed but eager to face Friday. She dragged herself to the club, ill prepared. How much so became obvious when she was summoned to the front desk at the request of a new member. She nearly gasped when she saw who he was.

Sam Springs, her ex-lover.

Her stomach swooped downward. Seeing him unexpectedly knotted her emotions like badly handled yarn. His grin was ocean-wide. "Good to see you again, Dimples," he greeted warmly.

She groaned inwardly at the threadbare familiarity. "Sam," she said evenly. "What brings you to SHAPE?"

"I'm a member! I'm in on a family membership. Dinah took it out in her name." He giggled, that annoying sound she hadn't heard in two years. Time hadn't improved it—or him. "I didn't want it under my name. I figured you'd probably blackball me, Dimples."

She would have. She hadn't ever wanted to see him again. She hadn't laid eyes on him since the final confrontation and breakup that day in Dunkin Donuts. (She hadn't bought so much as a munchkin at any of them since.) She looked at him with an almost fresh perspective. The boyish face had gone a bit to flesh, but it still glowed with the energy that had once attracted her. From that energy sprang a high level of intensity that led to his success as an independent computer hardware salesman. He had once made a great deal of money very easily. He was tireless in pursuit not only of customers but also of pleasure, travel, excitement, and sports. He did things! Only in time did she understand that his energy was manic, balanced on the scales of his brain by equal swings to merciless lethargy nourished in the womb of depression. He proved expert at hiding his affliction from her, arranging solo trips when his mental balance beam tipped down to the dark side.

Even so, she had some hesitancy about making the major commitment of moving in with him. It was all too characteristic of the way she failed to run her life that she allowed him to persuade her that saying yes to his invitation was not only the economical but also the wise thing to do.

Only after they were together daily did she see the elaborate stage machinery behind his determinedly bright performance. His illness alone wouldn't have discouraged her. She would have stood by him; she had her tough side, in some areas. Nor would the parade of psychiatrists, counselors, elaborate tests and analyses, and their attendant expense have driven her to break her informal vows. It took Sam's threats and assaults to drive the wedge between them. Even so, the inevitable truth sank slowly enough into the stout oak of her tenacity. Only when several doctors convinced her that it was beyond Sam's powers to control his suicidal, hostile actions did she contemplate breaking up. Even so, it took his battering her on two separate occasions to truly make the point. After the second bruising she met him at the doughnut shop and ended it.

"So how's it been with you, Sam?" she asked.

"Since the hospitals, you mean?"

"I guess. How's your life?"

"Better than ever." He held up a finger—number one. "What a friend I have in lithium carbonate! Evens everything out for me." He made gentle waves in the air. "Smooooths out that ole debil psyche I used to have. No more trips to heaven; no more roller coaster to hell. It was kinda rugged for a while, getting it all back together. But I did it! Drugs are the answer! Couldn't have made the comeback without Dinah. Hey, honey! Come and meet Dimples!"

Ah, yes, Dawn remembered that bray across a crowded

room. How nice not to have it be a part of her life any longer. Dinah came at a trot. My, God! She was a red-head wearing an exercise suit made out of one of the new clutch-me fabrics. It was the perfect choice for her generous, trim figure. Her wide face carried scattered light freckles that suited the deep green eyes. The mouth detracted just a bit: too wide, but her teeth were straight and white. Dinah was a comely young woman, Dawn thought, realizing she felt no jealousy whatever. Reflex made her check out Dinah's left ring finger. Dinah and Sam weren't married.

Dinah's glance, though not stony, wasn't warm, either. It covered Dawn from top to toe. "Pleased," she said. "Sam still talks about you." She elbowed him lightly. "Too much, I think sometimes."

"Not to worry, babes. Dimples and I are history." Sam's face glowed with that familiar energy. "Just a coincidence she happens to own half this place."

Dawn's antenna swung around. "How do you happen to know that, may I ask?"

Sam winked—another old, annoying mannerism. "Secrets of the trade."

"What trade?"

He shrugged. "Later sometime, okay, Dimples? I'm a family club member here on a sort of half-business, half-pleasure basis."

His riddles always annoyed Dawn. "Do you mind explaining?"

"I'm working for Healthways, New England."

Dawn knew the organization: the largest group of health clubs in the region. They were franchisers, too. Kentucky Fried Physiques. "What do you do for them?"

"We'll talk about it later, before too long."

Dawn swallowed her irritation. To Dinah she said, "How long have you been members?"

"More than two weeks." Dinah's voice was low, without an edge. Dawn was getting the feeling her ex had done well to get her. "It's a lovely club, and I'm having a ball!"

Sam's arm slid around Dinah's shoulders. "Just wanted you to know I was around, Dimples. No sense you running into me and having a heart attack. One of these days, before long, we'll talk, right?'

"About what?" Dawn asked somewhat icily, tired of his double entendres.

Sam and Dinah swept off, arm in arm. "Business. We'll talk business," he said before tossing her one last wink.

CHAPTER
5

Normally Dawn spent a fair amount of the weekend at the club, getting caught up on record-keeping and odd chores, but after last week she couldn't bring herself to go in on Saturday. She needed an event to get her mind off SHAPE. She decided to give a small dinner party.

The guests would be Beth Willow and Jeff Bently. Dawn wanted to deepen her friendship with the petite woman and to express her thanks for all she did for small pay. As for Jeff, Dawn was attracted to him. What with Hector hovering in the shadows like a goalie-masked movie murderer, she needed to develop some kind of healthy new emotional relationship to help her resist the older man. And of course inviting guests gave her an excuse to cook. She had enjoyed that part of being Sam's POSSLQ (person of the opposite sex sharing living quarters). Unhappily he was one of those who ate to live, not vice versa. He had gobbled down her greatest meals with no more enthusiasm than her worst. The supremely fresh vegetable, the cunning dash of fresh herbs, went by him like major league fastballs. She sighed. Don't dwell on losses, Gray, she told herself.

When both Beth and Jeff agreed to come, she went shopping for a hearty winter meal that wouldn't damage her modest budget very much. Braised lamb shanks, she decided, with herbed rice and a big tossed salad. She even invested in a single Chilean tomato. Having traveled as far as an Arctic tern, it was priced accordingly. She thought of the old joke about the woman who asked for two dollars' worth of tomatoes, and the grocer said, "Why not take a whole one?" A bottle of Domestica from sunny Greece would provide modest elegance. She noticed artichokes were on sale. She bought three for appetizers.

Just before her guests arrived, she took off her sweater and turned up the apartment heat, for which she paid. She normally kept the place at about fifty-five degrees, wore wool, and never caught cold. She played her 1970s pop and jazz tapes low for background.

Jeff arrived first, bundled and booted, bearing a gift: herbal bath blend. "Just sprinkle in a tablespoonful when you're running the hot water," he said. "Balms the skin, soothes the mind."

"Mine could use a little soothing." She hugged him lightly. "Thanks."

Beth brought a bottle of sherry. They got into it at once. Dawn found out more about Jeff's background. He had been on Wall Street! Though he didn't come right out and say so, she suspected that he might have been an arbitrageur or some other type of wheeler-dealer. During the bull market of a few years ago he made quite a pile, grew disillusioned, and quit. Then he went to India and China to study herbal medicine, healing, and massage. He spent many of those months wearing a variety of religious and regional robes. Quite a departure from his Calvin Klein suits and ties. "My tastes live on in your partner, Peter," he said. "I know good clothes when I see them."

"Dress for success," Dawn said. "Success is what he wants."

"And what does Dawn want?" Beth's fair skin was rouged with sherry.

They made a game of planning her future that lasted

well into the meal. Like so many tall, slender men, Jeff had a huge appetite. Luckily petite Beth had a stomach to match her size. So the hostess didn't run short of food. No leftovers either, though. They finished off the Domestica, too.

By that time Dawn was gabbing about the effects of the last week at SHAPE on her nerves. Jeff suggested that he and Beth become Dawn's support group. Having to stand fast behind the club in the face of two fatal accidents was only part of the increasing challenge she faced. The rest was the tough job of counterbalancing Peter's whims and tendency toward wild risk-taking. Dawn realized that, indeed, she could use a little emotional reinforcement and maybe some folks with whom to share her problems. Jeff smiled. "And there can be only one name for our little group. Any guesses?"

They didn't know.

"I hereby charter us as the Dawn Patrol!"

Groans.

With a sly smile, Beth said she had to leave at ten-thirty. She hoped Dawn didn't mind; she didn't. After Beth left, Dawn made coffee and invited Jeff onto the twin rocker to drink it. They talked about the rocker and the mocha blend coffee. It was good, but she savored more the touch of their shoulders, the brush of Jeff's long brown hair against her ear. She drew out of him talk of his travels: Sri Lanka, Macao, the Chinese countryside. He had often been in physical danger, but he was modest about what he had to do to survive. She closed her eyes, enjoying his presence and the sound of his voice.

In time they got around to talking about their personal lives. She said she was completely unattached—almost true—and would do well to make new friends. He told her that his last few years had been so up and down "that no woman cared to keep up."

"You didn't know the right women," she said. She

turned to him. "Why don't you take off your glasses?"

"Why?"

"So I can see your eyes better." She grinned. Believe that one and . . .

He removed the glasses and dangled them between thumb and forefinger. His pupils were a rich dark brown.

"Nice eyes," she said.

"It's myopia that does it."

"Umhhh . . . She ran her fingertips across the shallow track left by the metal temple piece. He lightly held her hand and nibbled her fingertips. His tongue was a moist burr against the pit of her palm. "I'm glad you invited me over, Dawn."

"Were you hoping?"

"I'll never tell." He took her face in his long hands. "Yes, I will. I was going to invite you out for dinner. I'm not much of a cook. Then with . . . what happened at the club, I thought I ought to wait."

She looked speculatively up into his narrow, well-made face. "Is that the only reason?"

His shoulder twitched against hers. "I couldn't believe a woman as sweet and lovely as you could be available."

"My middle name—Dawn Available Gray."

His arms slid around her in a proper hug. She sighed and clung to him. "Watch out: I'm part barnacle," she said.

Midway into their second deep kiss, a buzzer ripped the air. Somebody at the downstairs door.

"I'm not home," Dawn murmured.

Jeff whispered, "I'm on special assignment to Simla, northern India."

The buzzer blasted again—and again. At last it fell silent, and Dawn turned her mouth up to Jeff's.

When the knock came, there was no mistaking who it was, even before the growling voice. "Ms. Gray, I seen your light, and this deliveryman won't give me no peace." Mr. Harnish, her fundamentalist landlord, to whom it would never have occurred that she might be entertaining a man alone. "Let's open up and get this over with, all right? Ms. Gray?"

"Yes! Damn!" She slid away from Jeff and checked the mirror for dishevelment. She opened the door. In front stood Mr. Harnish—bald, graying, veins curling like worms under the skin above his temples. Behind him . . . Oh, no! The deliveryman worked for a florist or possibly a flower grower, judging from the size of the box he carried. His arms scarcely reached around it. He had taken but two steps through her doorway when the perfume of fresh cut flowers wafted into the apartment's dry February air. He looked around and saw no piece of furniture broad enough to bear the box. He put it down on the floor with a grunt and eyed Dawn. "You got the record for the new year, cutie. Sign here."

Mr. Harnish eyed Jeff. "How long he stayin' here, Ms. Gray?"

"As long as I want him to. Okay?"

"Okay with me. Not okay with the Man Upstairs. According to the Word—"

"Not now, Mr. harnish. It's almost the twenty-first century. The Word is having some heavy going. Now please leave."

She closed the door behind the two men, turned, and found Jeff staring at the box. "We're talking four figures here," he said.

"Oh, don't worry about that." Dawn tried to lead him back to the rocker.

"You gotta open it."

"Why?"

He looked sharply at her. "Because it's not going to go away."

She knew who had sent the flowers. She untied the velvet bow and lifted the lid off. The scent of blooms was richer than spilled perfume. Her head swam with the cloying sweetness. She parted the paper on a vast heap of roses, mums, irises. . . . If she filled every container in the apartment, the bathtub would still overflow with the remainder. She picked out the card, put it in her pocket.

Jeff had put on his glasses. "You aren't going to see who they're from?"

"I know who they're from."

"I see."

"An admirer. I have an admirer, all right? But there's nothing—"

He rested his hand on the top of her head. "Shhh! It's a good time not to explain, Dawn."

He was polite enough to stay around for about ten minutes. He promised to see her again, but didn't say when. He left her with a chaste kiss in the doorway.

She managed to wait until his footsteps faded before she clenched her fists at her side, closed her eyes, and practiced her primal scream. She pulled the tiny envelope from her pocket and savaged it open: "Dearest Dawn: I swim in love for you. Come, Wednesday! Hector."

She rushed to the open box and drove her hands down into the stems and blossoms, intending to crush and twist them. Their powerful scent rose up like opium smoke. She staggered. Her arms trembled. She pressed the blooms against her face, bruised the blossoms until her cheeks were streaked with precious petal ooze and her own tears of bewilderment. . . .

An hour later, bathed and calmer, she turned on the radio. Soft reggae chirped in the background. She began to close the curtains. Another cold night. She looked down from her bedroom window at the snow-crusted street. A lone car sat with its lights off. The plume of exhaust told her the occupant wanted to remain warm. Whoever it was seemed to be waiting for something.

She stood motionless, watching for long minutes. The car didn't move. Nor could she make out its occupant or license number. The vehicle was a dark-colored sedan with body damage. In time she closed the curtains with unneeded energy and tried to persuade herself that she wasn't again feeling watched.

CHAPTER
6

Peter tossed the open letter to Dawn. The stationery was expensive vellum. The letterhead belonged to a big-time law firm. It told them SHAPE was being sued in connection with Nicole Thurston's death. Even though the club would turn the case over to Milton Glassman, there still was the matter of paying the man past the retainer he had already extracted from them. And if the suit should be successful . . . On the speakerphone, Glassman told them they didn't have to worry. Thurston didn't have a case. By the time it got to court and he worked his nonpareil legal magic, "You won't be payin' a dime, good people. Not one FDR."

At noon Dawn found herself with the phone in her hand, placing a call to Hector. She felt she ought to thank him for the flowers, no matter that they had dampened her evening with Jeff. Always when she dealt with him her motivations were ambiguous and unclear. She called his private number. Along that route a secretary never stood in the way of . . . was it love? Lust? Passion? Obsession? The sound of his slightly accented voice did its usual job on her spine. She managed to sound completely grateful for the blooms.

"And have you made your decision, my sweet?" he said.

"I thought I had until Wednesday."

"Is it that difficult a decision?" He was a bright man, and saw through her easily. "Whether or not to come away with me and be my love?"

"Wednesday. I'll see you Wednesday."

"If you insist. I'll send Rudolfo for you. You'll come to the pied-à-terre."

Even as she dreaded the rendezvous, she knew she'd go. She absolutely had to tell him she was refusing his offer.

Still agitated by her brief conversation, she was summoned to the front desk. Four women she recognized as longtime members, the precious kind who used the club during the day, had asked to speak with her. Phyllis Melaney, active in community affairs, had been appointed spokeswoman. She was warmhearted but officious. She invited Dawn to the bar area. They declined her offer of juice on the house. Dawn wasn't entirely surprised when Phyllis said, "We'd like to hear your version of the two drownings."

Before Dawn could get out a word, Madge, not a timid woman, either, said, "We girls have been talking it over. We wondered if"—she lowered her squeaky voice—"anything's, like, going *on*. You know?"

Dawn sipped her juice, hoping she looked calm and self-possessed. She cranked up her brightest smile. "I'm happy to tell you that the police have said both deaths were accidental." She spoke with a clear conscience. Even though she had her suspicions about Zack, Detective Morgan wasn't much interested in investigating what to him seemed verified accidents. Very likely Dawn was overreacting to the curious coincidence that both drowning victims had been Zack's accusers.

"Nicole Thurston was a friend of mine." Claudia Donelli's brows were raised in suspicion. "She could have given swimming lessons to Flipper the Dolphin. How could she have drowned?"

"I have no idea," Dawn said.

"We have your word, then, that nothing weird is going down?" said Samantha Dawson. Called "Stick" by the staff, she had heaved on weights by the hour for years, with no resulting increase in bulk.

Dawn raised her palms. "I don't know of anything going on, no."

Phyllis Melaney circled the others with a glance. "We've talked it over, the four of us. I guess you could say we're here to put you—the club, really—on notice. We're a little nervous. We're not panicked yet. But . . . if something else happens, we're going to want rebates on our memberships. In a few words: if there are any other 'accidents,' we're outta here!"

Dawn nodded, suddenly chilled. "I understand perfectly what you're thinking. After all, I'm an owner. When two people die in my club, well . . . I think you can understand why I'm a little nervous, too."

"There's talk that the club was negligent," Phyllis said. She cocked an eyebrow.

"Absolutely not!" Dawn said. "Both women broke the rules. Eloise used the Jacuzzi illegally after club hours, and Nicole swam with no lifeguards in a pool that I personally closed and posted. Uh-uh! We were *not* negligent."

Tiny Cynthia DeForrest, who seldom spoke to anyone, said softly, "People are saying Nicole's husband is suing."

Dawn swallowed. How fast bad news traveled! Good news came on snailback. "Our attorney says he has no case, for the reasons I just pointed out."

"I see," Cynthia said.

Dawn wasn't sure she really did. Nor was there anything more she could do to change the woman's mind. "I hope you all aren't going to walk out on the club, just like that."

"No," Phyllis said evenly. "If we go, we'll have a real reason."

"I assure you you'll never find one," Dawn said.

"Good." A chorus of positive chirps and smiles. There came a relaxation in the tension. Then the women were off together in their clique. No question they could make trouble if they chose to. Dawn felt that they were testing her mettle, but she wasn't sure what they expected her to do. Remove all doubt surrounding the two deaths? That she couldn't do.

Filled with misgivings, she wandered back to the office. In the back of her mind there determinedly lurked . . . Zack Keyman. She sorely wished the police would talk to him. Then her mind, if no one else's, would be at ease.

She became still less at ease as Wednesday arrived. "Come, Wednesday" indeed! She ran through scenarios in her mind, in each of which she told assertive Hector that she had had enough. It had been great, but the time had come to end their affair. Not only would she not become his little live-in lovebird, she no longer wanted to see him. Her hypothetical words changed, but the general theme didn't: let me go, lover. One thing was sure. If she got a version of all that out of her mouth, he wouldn't like it.

Rudolfo must have had a direct line to the Naval Observatory chronometer. As three-thirty came, right to the second, the big car swept up the drive. After getting into the rear seat, she turned back to the club, as she often did to survey her investment. Standing at the top of the entryway stairs was Beth Willow. Dawn waved, slightly embarrassed. Beth returned a gesture of what must have been puzzlement. As well she might. After all, Saturday night she had left the apartment early to give Jeff and Dawn time alone. Beth must be wondering about how curiously her friend distributed her affections. Dawn decided it was time to take the petite woman into her confidence. Maybe it would do her good to talk about Hector with another woman. Oops! By the time she met Beth again, Hector would no longer be part of her life.

Or would he?

Hector's pied-à-terre was a small penthouse atop a downtown apartment complex, within walking distance of the high-rise headquarters of the local captains of industry and commerce. He greeted her with a smile and a long hug. She was aware of his expensive cologne. His smooth cheek told her his barber had been there earlier to shave him. The cook had come and gone, leaving behind delicious aromas. He announced hot soup and seafood casserole. Wine, too, of course, one of the long-necked Rhine bottles—crisp, sweet, and undoubtedly expensive. Hector's exquisite tastes.

She studied his angular face, its familiar lines. She had grown to know him well. She saw a surprise twinkling in the black eyes. Dread and anticipation swirled in her heart. "We'll eat. Then I have an announcement," he said. His warm smile was infectious. Her mood improved, no matter her determination to refuse his offer and arouse his certain displeasure. They raised their glasses in a toast. The expensive crystal sang. Over the thin rim of her glass she saw his face hood itself with desire. She had come to recognize that expression. In private moments she gloated over it and the acts to which it led.

When their meal ended, he led her into the wide living room. Beyond its glass wall, she glimpsed the city's towers of power dusted with winter white. "The Schubert?" he said.

She shrugged. "If you want." She didn't know classical music. But one night, long ago now, he had played in the background what she learned was that composer's Quintet in C. At first it went over her head. But then had come the second movement overflowing with plucked strings and sorrow. Though untutored, she had begun to cry. For her there could have been no other response. He had taken her in his arms then, explaining the piece and praising her sensitivity. Since then it had carried unique meanings for both of them.

When he turned back from the CD player, she touched his face with her fingertips. "Tell your secret," she whispered. "I know you have one. And you can't stand to put anything off, even for ten minutes."

Hector nodded. He folded his arms and looked at her appraisingly, preparing to study her reaction to the words to come. "I've asked Marina for a divorce," he said.

Dawn's heart lunged against her ribs. "I—I didn't expect that."

"It's all fallen to ruin between us. There's no sense continuing the charade." He tried to read her face. "Are you pleased, my sweet?"

"That's all . . . between you two. What I think doesn't matter."

He frowned. "You don't think this might one day be important to us?"

She turned to him, met his intense gaze. "I hope with all my heart that you didn't do that because of me." He opened his mouth to speak, but she rushed on. "Because I'm not going to be part of your life anymore. I'm refusing your offer—to be your playmate."

He stiffened. "Don't vulgarize the potential of our relationship, Dawn. And think carefully about what you're saying."

"Think carefully? It seems as though that's all I've been doing. During a week when two women have drowned in my club I was thinking about you when I should have been concentrating on them. Oh, I thought plenty, Hector! And carefully, too. I've turned it all over and over again, looked at us every which way. My answer has to be no."

He looked at her in silence. She sensed him steadying his face against a tide of emotion while Schubert's string quintet tore into her own heart. Music for moments of anguish.

"Why?" he asked.

"Hector, that's just not where I want my life to go."

He asked her then what that direction was. She told him she wanted to move toward more personal control and self-sufficiency. The words escaped her lips with none of the eloquence of her mental rehearsals. She spoke in choppy phrases and broken sentences, half choking on her emotions. The longer she talked, the more feeble her hope of penetrating the shell of his will became. Trying to sum it up with some force, she blurted out, "The club's become the most important thing in my life."

"The club! What do you get out of it that's so satisfying, my sweet? Responsibility? Do you enjoy having had two women murdered there? Do—"

"Why do you say they were murdered, Hector?"

His brows arched in surprise. "Well . . . I'm no fool. To me it seems obvious. In any case, the deaths should carry a message to you."

She frowned. "What message?"

"That, for you, nothing good will ever come out of the club. That you should be looking elsewhere for a fulfilling future."

"Elsewhere?"

"Of course. In any case, do you enjoy the 'pleasures' that your responsibility for the club brings?"

"That's part of being an owner."

"If you let me care for you, your only responsibility would be pleasing us."

"Hector—"

"Do you enjoy the near penury that your rash over-commitment has brought? If you allied yourself with me, your money problems would be over, very likely for the rest of your life. How much money does SHAPE earn for your personal use each month, Dawn?"

She told him.

"I'll multiply that by ten, my sweet, and give it to you on the last day of each month. A payday of sorts, if that suits your style." He waved his hand around the penthouse. "You'll live here rent free, with no worries about food bills. And Ms. Nello will be just as happy to cook for two as for one. There'll be trips, too—business for me, pleasure for you. You'll enjoy the Bügenstock Hotel, high on a mountain above Lake Lucerne—"

"Please stop!" She sprang up and turned away. She paced to the wide window and looked down on rooftops. She pressed her hands to her face and drew shaky breaths. The music assaulted her raw emotions.

Hector went on. "And maybe the day will come when you'll finally develop a little greed, and I can have the pleasure of satisfying it." He was behind her, hands resting lightly on her shoulders. His lips were near her ear. "And, if you like, there can be the possibility of marriage."

She pulled away. "No! I don't want to talk about it anymore. I'm not going to do it! I want to leave here. Now!" She crossed the room toward the closet.

"Dawn!"

Hesitantly she turned back to him. His face was reddening, an unpleasant sight she had never before witnessed.

"You're being a fool! You toss away what other women would kill to keep," he hissed.

"I don't care!"

He came toward her, shoulders bunched with barely controlled rage. She thought distantly of Zack Keyman. He had raised his clenched fists at her. She threw up her arms to protect herself, panic squirming up amid inner turmoil. Then he was on her—but, oh, God, not to hurt her! His arms were around her, his lips against hers. Even now, sweet longings arose like distant echoes. With a great effort of will she turned her face away, but couldn't pull free of his embrace.

"Dawn, Dawn, you sweet young fool," he whispered, "can't you see I love you?"

He had never said that before! Not ever. Not during their most intimate moments. Not even when . . . Not at all. She sagged, and he enfolded her completely in his arms. "My love, my love!" His lips were on her neck.

She understood the pivotal moment had come; all before had been maneuvering, like the blue and the gray before Gettysburg. Not intentionally both of them had arrayed their emotional and rational regiments, keeping little in reserve. She had to be decisive now or the battle was lost.

She raised her arms and broke his hug. She shoved him away, using the strength of a conditioned body. "Hector, I can't! And the reason is that the club means more to me than you do!"

"The club. That damned club!" He was shouting, a loud bark that shook her like a hand. She hurried for the closet. "Can't you see it's doomed to fail, Dawn?" She grabbed her parka. "I do not accept your decision!"

He was bellowing, and it frightened her. "The matter is still open!"

"No, no, it isn't!" She fled for the door.

"We'll talk again, Dawn."

Her insides twisted. "Don't make us go through this again!" she cried. She tore open the door and threw herself into the hall. She stumbled toward the elevator.

"The club is doomed!" he called after her.

She jabbed the button, both fearing and anticipating his pursuit. She looked back. He stood in the hallway facing her, open arms outstretched in ongoing, permanent invitation. Schubert spoke for him.

She flung herself into the elevator and pressed her forehead against a cool metal panel. Before the door opened at the lobby level she was weeping at full strength. Out in the cold, she turned toward the limo still parked in the suite's designated space. Rudolfo started the engine. Exhaust puffed from the tailpipe as tears began to freeze on her cheeks. For a moment she thought the chauffeur was preparing to drive her back to the club. Then she realized that Hector had spoken to him on the car phone. The BMW swung from the space, out of the lot, down the block, and around the corner. No more rides for her.

She tried to convince herself she'd never enter that car again.

Two bus rides later she was at the club, out of sorts and uncommunicative. She wondered if she had truly done the right thing. If she had, was that the end between her and Hector? She knew the answer: only if he was willing to allow it. She feared his vast psychological and financial strength. He had the power to go to any ends to keep her in his life. He loved her! Oh, God, that had been a stunner. The supreme flattery and fright rolled together. If he truly loved her, would he passively accept her attempt to leave him, or would he take steps to keep her? And how far would he dare go? He could try to buy her, abduct her . . . Who could guess at the limits of his audacity?

She hung on until ten for her routine solo workout. At that hour the Nautilus circuits were closed to members, and that level of the club was virtually deserted. The action was on the basketball and racquetball courts below. Working out alone was one of the few perks Dawn allowed herself. As she heaved on the machines, she imagined for a short time that she was punishing Hector with the expended energy. How childish! She shouldn't forget the fine moments they had enjoyed together. And, heavens, he had said he loved her! Reviewing those words yet again, she wondered if he truly meant them or if he was launching a final assault on her defenses. But she did not believe he was so calculating. Hector was too self-assured and intelligent to be that cold-blooded.

CHAPTER
7

It was past eleven o'clock when Dawn left the club after her shower. She drew a deep breath through her nostrils—her own rough thermometer: when the fine hairs froze far up her nose, she knew the temperature was close to zero.

After four tries, her Honda coughed to life. The streets along the way to her apartment were largely deserted; folks were at home by the fireside. She tugged her mail out of the box. Dear Occupant . . . She climbed the stairs, thinking distantly of Hector's express elevator. Close to her apartment door she felt vague inner stirrings, like anxiety or dread. End-of-the-day frame of mind, she told herself. She let herself in and groped for the light switch. Even the flood of Sylvania wattage failed to relax her. She found herself making the rounds: kitchen, bedroom, bath, then back to the living room.

Zack Keyman stood between her and the front door—unshaven, disheveled, and menacing. "Dawn, I want—"

She screamed, spun, and raced for the back door. Horrid fright gave strength to her legs, even as it weakened the volume of her second scream—cut short by his hand clamping over her mouth. His other arm circled her waist. He pulled her brutally away from the door. Her panicked mind exploded with the recent memory of him nearly strangling her. She kicked and squirmed, tried to turn her face so she could bite his fingers.

He held her with arms as strong as steel bands. She could do nothing to help herself.

"Hey, don't be scared," he breathed into her ear.

She felt certain that this man had somehow drowned two women at the club. She lunged with all her strength. She couldn't break free! Weakness washed up her spine. He had her! Oh, God, what was he going to do?

"Calm down, baby."

Her heart slammed against her ribs like a hammer. His horrid hand bruised the soft tissues of her face, held it like a clamp. Glancing sideways, she glimpsed a blurred face carrying a puzzled frown. She began to tremble and hated herself for her weakness.

"Don't be scared, Dawn. I need to talk to you."

She grunted questioningly. Her panicked breath hissed damply from her nostrils onto his restricting fingers.

"Forget about screaming."

She grunted again. If he freed her mouth, she'd get off the loudest scream either of them had ever heard. He carefully eased the pressure just a bit. She filled her lungs, her nostrils dilating.

"You're thinking about screaming again," he whispered. "I'm telling you there's no reason to do that. None at all. All I want to do is talk to you."

Her knees trembled. Through the panic some thought found its way. He hadn't really hurt her—yet. If he wanted to, nothing she could do would stop him.

"No screaming. Deal?" His breath was rancid.

She nodded.

He freed her mouth, but his hand still lurked near her lips.

"What do you want?" she asked. Her voice was a shaky whisper.

"Like I said, I want to talk to you."

"About what? Will you let me go?"

"If you promise to behave, Dawn."

She should be forceful in this situation, not let him know precisely to what depths he had shaken her. "Promise me you won't hurt me."

"I do."

"Fine. Good, Zack." She stepped away and got her first good look at him. His unshaven face still carried a frown of puzzlement. He needed a change of clothes—and a shower. "First I have some questions for you. Answer them and then we'll get to yours." Was she going to get away with taking charge? Being bold wasn't her strong suit. She backed slowly away from him but held his eyes with hers. Her knees were nearly solid now. "I'll be honest: I'm thinking hard right now about calling the police, or going back to screaming. So keep your hands off me."

"You got upset over nothing." His handsome face tried to set itself into what was its normally warm smile. Handsome wasn't everything—not by a long way.

"I don't think coming home and finding a man in my apartment is nothing, especially when that man smothers me half to death and for all I know is going to cut my throat or rape me."

"Dawn, I never was thinking of any of that."

She waved away his nonsense. "How did you know where I lived? How did you get in here?"

"I been following you since you fired me." His weak grin gave way to a sullen glower.

"Why?"

"To find out where you lived. To figure out when the best time would be to come and talk to you."

Dawn took a deep breath and sagged against the kitchen sink. "That's . . . not quite the . . . sensible way to behave. How did you get in?"

"Came up the cellar stairs a half dozen times over the last week. Studied the lock. Kept trying different skeleton keys till I found one that worked."

A leaden feeling weighed her down. "I see. Don't you

think it would have been easier just to come up to me somewhere in public and—''

''You know damn well you wouldn't have talked to me!''

She closed her eyes and drew a deep breath. ''So what is it that you want to talk about? Make it quick; then you can leave.''

''I've tried to get other jobs, but everybody wants references. I knew you wouldn't give me a good one. So . . . nobody will hire me.''

''So? Why are you here—now—in the middle of the night? What do you want with me, Zack?''

''I want my job back.''

She looked at him, trying to read deeper than his sullen glower. At that moment she realized he was playing a game with far deeper levels of action than the obvious, like a chess master who sees further into a position than the amateur. The minor pieces were job and work, the major ones murder and revenge. ''You're not being honest with me, Zack.''

''I said I want my job back.''

''I suppose you're going to tell me you don't know two women died at the club over the past two weeks.''

The frown again. ''Nah, I didn't know.''

''I don't believe you.''

''So what?'' The frown was back, now possibly one of confusion. ''What does their dying have to do with me?''

She weighed the wisdom of keeping silent and safe against confronting him and testing her stubborn suspicions. She walked into the living room and picked up the phone. She kept a careful eye on him. She keyed a nine and a one, then turned to him. ''I'm about to finish dialing the police. I'm going to tell you what I think, then finish the call. You won't be able to stop me.''

''Dawn—''

''Don't try. Listen to me, Zack. I know you killed

Eloise St. Martin and Nicole Thurston!" She dialed the final one.

"I didn't!" His green eyes widened. "Honest to God, I didn't!"

"I know you did! You did it because I fired you. You did it to get even with me, them, and the club."

The police operator answered along with a tape beep. Dawn blurted out her name and address. "I have an intruder in my apartment. His name is Zachary Keyman—"

"Jesus! Dawn, you are a crazy woman!" He turned and snatched up his coat where he had hidden it behind the couch. He tore open the door and ran out. "I didn't kill anybody!" he shouted before slamming the door behind him.

Dawn sank slowly down to the floor. "It's all right. He's gone," she breathed into the phone. "But he should be arrested. He's a murderer—"

"One moment, please."

She was transferred to the precinct house. After a long dialog, with an understanding officer, she persuaded him that she didn't need a police visit after all. She took another ten minutes to give a detailed physical description of her assailant.

She jammed a chair under the kitchen doorknob, though she was sure she had accomplished her objective: frightening Zack off by letting him know she knew he was responsible for the two drownings. Soon he would be throwing clothes into a suitcase and preparing to flee the city one step ahead of the law.

After tonight he would be a fugitive. She could only hope that would keep him too busy to cause SHAPE more trouble.

Sleep? After the day she'd had? She lay under the blankets wide-eyed, heard the wind work its way around the corners of the apartment house. She groaned and thrashed, her mind replaying the long minutes with

Zack. It took nearly an hour for her to segue into recollections of the afternoon with Hector, which were scarcely more comforting. Past his declaration of love, the seductiveness of his propositions, and the conflict of their wills she had discovered a small nugget that was hers to mine and cherish. A nugget of true self-discovery, even, dug from the lode of her deepest personality: the club *was* more important to her than he. Past that, the club was personally significant in what she was coming to understand was the changing constellation of her life. In one way, that was a surprise. In another, it seemed inevitable.

The next day at the club she had a visitor: Detective Morgan. He had checked the precinct call log in connection with some other police business and had seen her name. "This Keyman guy was the one you talked to me about before, Dawn?"

After her rocky night, she wasn't in a patient mood. "The same one you said it would take you forever to get around to questioning, Detective Morgan."

"That wasn't quite what I said." His normal scowl was lightened by a twitch of grin in the right corner of his mouth. "Why don't you tell me what went on between you two last night?"

She did, while his little tape recorder ran. When she finished, he took a moment to scratch his head. "It's nice to see you don't hesitate to call somebody a murderer, when there don't seem to have been any murders."

"My intuition knows better, Detective Morgan." And, she reminded herself, so had Hector's.

"You can call me Monty. I'm not a formal guy. Keyman was upset by your accusations?"

"He ran!"

Morgan nodded. "If he shows up again at your apartment or here at the club, let me know."

"You're starting to believe me, aren't you?" Dawn said.

He got up. "Let's say Keyman's drifting up toward the surface of the dark sea of police attention."

Dawn smiled. "You have some lyricism in you."

He bowed slightly. "I'm a closet poet. According to the legal code, that's only a misdemeanor. Good day."

Just after lunch Jeff and Beth stopped by the office. "Second official meeting of the Dawn Patrol," Beth bubbled. "We've come to check up on your life and suggest a diversion for this evening."

Dawn's eyes swung at once to Jeff. He hadn't spoken to her since the frustrating night of the blooms. He winked back, but she wasn't sure what that meant. A pleasant warmth had risen up in her chest at seeing him. More strongly than ever she wanted to develop their relationship. Damn Hector and his three hundred flowers!

Their idea was to get together at Beth's apartment for the first session of their own private Truffaut retrospective, by the last one of which they would have seen all the films he directed, or at least all those videotapes that could be rented locally.

"I love French movies!" Beth smiled prettily. Her violet eyes lit her heart-shaped face. To Dawn it seemed her friend had commando beauty—it sneaked up on you when you least expected it. "Jeff will pick you up here at six. No working late tonight, boss. I'm going to cook Chinese for us—something I don't do every day, believe me."

When Peter came in, she went to speak to him at once. Before she could get a word in, he told her Glassman had taken a look at the Thurston suit. He stood by his position that very likely nothing would come of it. Luckily the press seemed to have ignored the two drownings. "We're home free, D.G.!" he said.

"Not until Zack Keyman's in jail," she muttered. She told him about Zack's terrifying visit to her apartment.

He sympathized with her fright but was certain no murders had been committed by Zack or anyone else.

In earlier months of their partnership, she would have heard him through in silence, though she disagreed. But yesterday's events as well as her nugget of self-discovery had shaken her inner status quo.

"Oh, Peter, you're full of it! You really are. I'm just too busy to go into the details of just why right now."

His eyes widened. "Well! What have we here?"

"I'm not sure, smarty. Maybe it's the death of patience."

"Meeting adjourned," he said.

At six Jeff came into the office bundled up. He suggested they walk to Beth's apartment, only seven blocks away. "It's a crisp, clear night," he said.

She agreed, glad for the chance to speak to him alone for a while. "Jeff, I'd like to explain about the flowers the other night," she said.

"You don't have to. Really."

"I think I do." She began what turned out to be a lame story filled with holes big enough for a 747 to fly through. But instead of shutting up, she made it worse by trying to back and fill, explain, amplify. She was completely bungling the narrative.

They were walking along a stretch of narrow sidewalk leading by shop fronts. The city maintenance crews had been busy. The snow dunes heaped outside her apartment house were not in evidence in this commercial area. For that reason, she realized later, it was easy for Hector's limo to whoosh up to the curb right ahead of them before she clearly realized what was happening.

Hector slid nimbly out the rear door and stood ahead of them on the sidewalk lit by storefront neon. He wore an expensive camel-hair overcoat and a Russian sable hat. He scarcely glanced at Jeff. His eyes burned at her. She slowed, hesitant.

"I really can't accept your foolishness, Dawn." He stepped toward her.

She saw now that his eyes were red and his normally

immaculate grooming looked frayed. Had he been crying over her?

"What foolishness?" she said.

"Your toying with me like this before you come around to doing what you ought—coming away with me."

In the cold she quickly felt her cheeks flush. "Hector, this is the club's massage—"

"I want you and I love you! I don't think you believe that."

"This isn't the time or the place to get into that again!"

"I bet this is Mr. Flower Power," Jeff said. "The signs of excess are everywhere."

"Don't joke with me, boy." Hector's glance moved briefly over Jeff's lanky frame. "More than ever now I'm not a man to be opposed." He grabbed Dawn's forearm. "My sweet, that I am performing like this must make you realize the truth behind what I say—and the sincerity and permanence behind my offer."

Her insides twisted. Over the months there was no question she had made a niche of sorts for him in her heart. Now it was all going so dreadfully askew. "Hector, no, please—just leave!"

He tried to whisper, grasping for a straw of intimacy. Wrought up as he was, his words emerged in a choked baritone. "I've opened a bank account for you. In my pocket are two tickets for Sint Maarten. I've been invited to use a friend's villa. When we return—"

"No, Hector. No! I told you: I'm staying with the club." She tried to shake her arm free.

His face twisted unpleasantly. "Haven't you gotten the message yet, Dawn? The club is finished!" He pointed toward the yawning limo door. "Your destiny lies there, with me!" He began to drag her toward the car.

"Hector, no! Let me go!"

She was never quite sure what Jeff did then. It happened so fast! There was a flurry of motion not unlike the movements she had seen on "Kung Fu Theater," only frighteningly quicker! Jeff's hands lashed out at Hector's neck—one, two, three viper-swift blows. The older man tottered. Then Jeff's long arms collared him and tossed him onto the rear seat of the limo. Jeff slammed the door. "Drive on, James!" he shouted. Then he gave Dawn his arm. "Let's go," he said.

They hurried on in silence. Dawn's ears were perked to hear Hector's voice baying after her. When she heard nothing, she glanced back. The limo sat unmoving. Whatever was taking place behind its darkened windows didn't involve physical pursuit, at least at the moment. She was only slightly ashamed that now she felt, among the wash of other emotions, the sweet swell of her desirability. Everything between her and Hector was swinging around, and that gave her hope that she would truly escape him.

"Want to talk about any of that?" Jeff said.

"It's what I was babbling about earlier. Wait till the whole Dawn Patrol is assembled. You'll hear it all." Her voice shook.

"Have it your way."

She glanced speculatively up at him and smiled. "You didn't study just religion in Asia, did you?"

He grinned. "Now and then I needed a brief diversion from high thoughts and mental discipline. I moved into a different discipline: martial arts."

They walked hand-in-hand the rest of the way to Beth's apartment.

Beth had made a hot garlicky Italian dip that she served with raw vegetables as an appetizer. Even though her toddies were mild, Dawn's went quickly to her head, which made it easier to tell them the story of Hector and Dawn. She covered everything from their first encounter, through the platinum body chain, right up to that evening. They were good friends: they listened and made no comments.

When she finally wound down, Beth said softly, "I can see his point of view: you sort of led him on and now you want to dump him."

Dawn shook her head. "No, it wasn't like that, Beth. What we had was real. It's just—well, everything changes."

Jeff took off his wire-framed glasses and cleaned them. "Hector doesn't seem like the kind of man who gives up—at anything."

"I'll say!" Beth had paled during Dawn's dramatic tale. "Maybe you should just go along with him. That's what I'd do." She giggled, somehow managing to look five years younger. "Not really. I'm getting mad at him on your behalf."

Dawn smiled. "Thanks. I guess. But getting mad at him, Beth, isn't a good use of your energy."

"Support anger," Beth said. "That's what it is."

They ate dinner, watched *Jules and Jim,* and played Trivial Pursuit. Beth didn't need to give them a tour. They could see all of her studio apartment from where they sat. It was stylishly furnished. Some of the furniture and wall hangings looked expensive. When Dawn praised them, Beth said, "Relics from the glory days of my computer career."

Jeff was too good at Trivial Pursuit. Dawn and Beth joined forces, and he still beat them. "Another nail in the coffin of women's equality," he said, straight-faced. Not until both of them sat on his chest and bounced did he recant. After an enthusiastic three-way wrestling match, their evening ended.

The temperature had dropped. Jeff and Dawn walked quickly back toward the club's parking lot. "I'm sorry you had to play a part in the Hector-Dawn saga," she said.

"No problem."

"Anyhow, thanks for . . . your help." She looked up

at his shadowed face. "I hope you maybe—understand me better?"

"You have a lot of loose ends in your life, Dawn. They need to be tied down or snipped off, it seems to me."

"What does that mean for the two of us? Together, I mean."

He adjusted his collar and hunched his shoulders against a gust of bitter wind. Her nostril thermometer said it was at least five below.

"Hard times ahead," he answered.

"What's that supposed to mean?" She was a bit annoyed with him.

"You have Hector and you have SHAPE, or half of it anyhow."

"And?"

"You must know more trouble is about to land right in your lap."

"It is? How can you be so sure? I think the worst is over."

"I don't."

"Why not? Did you also learn fortune-telling in the East?"

"Intuition, I guess. Nothing I studied formally."

"You think Zack is going to come back and—kill somebody else? I still think he killed both women somehow." She looked up at him, wanting an answer.

He shook his head. "It's not something there's any sense in talking about now."

"Jeff!"

"Want to jog the rest of the way? I'm freezing."

In bed that night she thought about trouble. Right then it wore Zack Keyman's face. She had forgotten to call the locksmith and have him change the apartment's locks. She couldn't help but think Zack was lurking about, ready to . . . what? She groaned and pressed her face to the pillow. She knew what.

Murder again.

The next morning at the club she saw Hector going through his workout. She busied herself elsewhere, hoping he'd leave without a repeat of last night's incident. It was so awkward having him as a member! An hour later she went to the bar for a juice. Ahead in the lobby she saw Hector. Facing him angrily was petite Beth. Dawn could tell by their postures and expressions that they were both upset, though she couldn't hear their words. Shortly he spun on his heel and walked off. Dawn hurried out to Beth. "What was that all about?"

Beth's high cheeks were red. "I decided to give him a piece of my mind about you."

"Beth! Was that wise? I don't think you should get involved!"

"I couldn't resist, I guess." She pressed a palm to her face. "I made him my enemy."

"On my behalf? Not necessary, Beth. Really."

"I guess I got carried away. Sorry!" She turned and hurried away. Dawn walked toward the atrium.

Below, Dawn saw Hector hurrying out of the club. She knew he'd be back—to see her. She had never seen him so out of control as he had been last night.

Today she felt much less flattered than frightened. She looked down toward the cluster of tropical plants at the bottom of the atrium. A shiver shook her, as though a breath of winter had penetrated concrete, insulation, and warm air to chill her. What in heaven's name was going to happen to her?

She was paged, and she hurried to a phone. The call was from Zack Keyman.

She closed her eyes, remembering his powerful hands on her. Earlier she might not have dared to take the call. Now . . . well, she thought it wiser to speak to the devil than to imagine what he might be doing. This particular devil had been busy. First he said he had seen an attorney and would be bringing suit to get his job back and for defaming his character by accusing him of murder. Likely he had gone to a public defender and hadn't quite gotten the jargon right. Unwittingly he delivered some good news: the police had paid him a visit and asked him questions. She had been behind that, so it would be part of the suit. Bad enough, she supposed. But he had worse in store.

". . . and so I called your partner, Peter Faldo. I told him what you're trying to do to me. That you're nutso. He said he's going to talk to you."

"Oh?"

"And that there's maybe a chance I could get my job back."

"Listen to me, Zack and listen good. There is no chance you'll be rehired. None at all! Got that? Tell that to your attorney!" She hung up.

Peter wasn't in yet. No doubt another evening of tom-catting. Lord, wasn't she getting judgmental? Her own personal life wasn't going to guarantee her sainthood, either. She was annoyed because she wanted to have it out with him regarding Zack. As her emotions calmed, she knew her resolve and energy would dim. She would be more likely to compromise her opinions or wishes. She knew herself well enough: Ms. Malleable.

Peter didn't come into the club that Friday. He called in to the desk to say he had a touch of the flu and was going to try to fight it off before it dragged him down. She called his condo, but he wasn't there. Clearly he wasn't fighting the flu alone. In a bad mood, she decided to stay and catch up on paperwork, then work out, both calculated to improve her frame of mind. About eight o'clock she took a break and found Beth in the trainer's room talking to a member about an effective diet and exercise program. She invited her friend for a glass of juice.

Strolling down to the bar, they had to pass the office. Out of the corner of her eye Dawn caught a glimpse of movement. She turned. She saw Zack Keyman disappear around a corner. She went after him, shouting his name. Beth followed. "What's all this?" she said.

"Zack Keyman has been forbidden to enter this building!" Dawn called over her shoulder as she sprinted toward the staircase. "What are you doing here!" she shouted down the stairwell. "Stop, Zack! Stop and talk or I'll call the cops!"

"Dawn! Relax a little, for goodness' sake." Beth's short legs were flashing to keep up.

"Not until—Zack, *stop!*"

She had lost sight of him. She asked two instructors to leave their groups and help her search for him. After half an hour they decided he had slipped out through one of the first-floor safety exits.

Still uneasy, she poured her concerns on a patient Beth. "I'm frantic, because I *know* he's going to kill somebody else."

"Dawn, you shouldn't be talking about murder. There haven't *been* any murders. Just two accidents. Forget your wild intuition and you'll be a happy lady."

Monday morning Dawn pounced on Peter the moment he walked in. She closed the office door behind him. "Zack Keyman!" she said to him.

"So he broke into your apartment. What else about him?"

"He called to tell me he's going to sue me and SHAPE. Then I caught him sneaking around the club the other night. He got away before I could find out what he was up to." She jabbed a finger toward her partner. "Peter, on the phone he said—I can't *believe* this, I really can't—you told him it was possible he could be rehired."

"I heard about his suit, too, D.G." At the small wall mirror he checked collar and tie alignment. "I was mollifying him, mostly because of your earlier overreaction—"

"My over—"

"You heard me. You flew out of control with your suspicions. Zack can be quite dim-witted in his way. You have to use that against him." He went on to cite instances of the man's outright stupidity. Despite her smoldering resentment she sat and listened to her partner make a case for the man, as though he wasn't a violent creep who clearly possessed a murderer's temperament. Peter then worked back toward the reasons why rehiring him might be a viable course of action. The longer he talked, the more flustered she became. Peter was full of it. Why didn't she tell him so?

As it was, she never got a chance.

There was another tragedy.

Karl Clausman knocked on the door, then threw it open. "Trouble in tanning!" he said. "We've called an ambulance."

They hurried down to the first level where the two tanning machines stood inside partitions. A crowd had gathered—the magic of bad news. "Oh, God!" Dawn breathed. The odor! Like that she remembered when, as a little girl, she had burned a few strands of her hair in a candle flame. It was the smell of burning flesh that had drawn attention. Bursts of conversation told her that a machine had jammed with someone inside. When its lid wouldn't open, someone had torn the line cord from the heavy-duty socket to kill the power.

The emergency squad arrived, bulling their way through the dozen onlookers. Using special pry bars, they made short work of the jammed latch. Dawn was aware she was sinking her fingertips into Peter's upper arm. The machine was long and narrow, a space-age razor clam of plastic and metal.

"Step back!" one of the squad men bellowed. "We're gonna raise the lid."

Some of the women in the crowd turned their faces away. Dawn couldn't. Her mind was a turmoil of dread bordering on panic. A squad man was ready with a blanket. The lid rose amid a chorus of groans and two screams. Dawn glimpsed patches of blackened flesh, then the squad man mercifully lowered the blanket. The two other squad men bent over the burned woman.

"She's still alive," one said.

"Where're the damned medics?"

In minutes they arrived, carrying a stretcher. "I'm going with them," Peter said. "Get everybody out of here. Close up this part of the building."

Dawn nodded. She was swallowing to battle back the nausea. He bent over and whispered in her ear. "You'll probably have to deal with the cops, too."

When the woman had been carried off, Dawn shooed everyone out. In minutes the news would be all over the club, causing the worst kind of stir. She checked the tanning log. Chantelle Carson had signed in—oh, God— two hours ago! She leaned against a wall and covered her face with her palms.

Abruptly the odor was too much for her. She fled for the women's room, gagging even before she reached the toilets. Emerging, sour-mouthed and sweaty, she wasn't in the best of shape. She went to the phone, dialed. "Beth . . . help?" she said.

Beth came down from the trainer's room filled with questions. One look at Dawn's face and a sniff of the air quieted her. "What can I do?" she said softly. They made a sign saying that the tanning salon was closed until further notice. Dawn used her master key to lock the door. She was shaking when they got on the elevator. Beth asked if she wanted company. At that moment she didn't. She wandered back to the office alone, staring dumbly back at the inquisitive glances of passing members.

She sagged into her desk chair. Overriding her inner distress and her concern for Chantelle Carson, whom she hadn't known personally, came one unadorned thought, as ugly as an open sore: Zack Keyman had struck again.

Twenty minutes later a call came through for her from Detective Morgan. "We got a call a little while ago. Phyllis Melaney thought we ought to know that somebody got burned over there. Considerate of her, don't you think?"

Phyllis. Leader of the Gang of Four who might now be on the verge of canceling their membership—and being very noisy about it. How could she blame them?

"I'd like to come over and talk to you, Dawn."

"You don't think the burning was an accident?" She knew how foolish that sounded, but had to say it anyway to this man who had assured her the two drownings were accidents.

"I'll be bringing a clerk with me and maybe somebody from the lab, if I can free somebody up. You keep everybody away from that machine, hear? See you in a few minutes."

Dawn sat down to try to compose herself. She had poor luck and was relieved when Morgan arrived.

As she led him down to the tanning area, Dawn hated to admit she was getting used to seeing his lined bloodhound face. Now among its creases she saw something new: a sparkle of interest in the deep brown eyes. Could there be something of Sherlock Holmes hidden under the tired bureaucratic shell?

He touched nothing, but asked her to describe the procedure for using the tanning unit. After she described it, he muttered, "Bad for your skin."

"You wouldn't dare say that if you had seen Chantelle!" Dawn found herself suddenly on the edge of tears, then beyond. She wept despite herself.

He grunted. "Let's get out of here. Lock up again. The lab guy can't get here until tomorrow." Back in the office, he introduced a stocky woman with black hornrims and a charming smile. "Miz Darlene Sopht will be copying your membership and staff lists."

"Well . . ."

"We could get a court order and all that, if we have to. If you just agree, it'll be a lot easier."

"Why do you want them?" she asked.

Morgan sat, leaned back, and interlocked his fingers behind his head. "So we can start checking."

"On what?"

"You gotta ask?" He grinned thinly. "This and that. You know."

"Why bother? Arrest Zack Keyman. Save the taxpayers' money."

He turned and surveyed the framed posters on the walls of the office, centering on the one featuring a muscular girl in a leotard. He spoke with his back to Dawn. "The woman who was just burned—Chantelle Carson. Was she one of the ones who complained about Zack Keyman's Russian fingers?"

"Well . . . no. There were only two. They're both dead."

He grunted. "You know, Dawn, I talked to your chum Zack."

"He said he had talked to the police."

"He's a certifiable nut, you know," Detective Morgan said.

"Of course he is. And—"

"But is he a criminal kind of certifiable nut?"

"I saw him sneaking around here last Friday night!"

The detective turned. "Now, that *is* interesting."

"I hope you also find it interesting that he followed me in his car and on foot, finally broke into my place, grabbed me, and nearly frightened me to death."

"Old news. You know it's time I had a chat with your partner. What say?"

Peter called in late in the day from the hospital. Chantelle Carson had died without regaining consciousness. Dawn held the phone in numb fingers, tears welling and concern soaring.

Now trouble had begun in earnest.

Life got more complicated beginning early Tuesday morning. A woman reporter from the *Dispatch* in a stylish suit, tape recorder in hand, showed up at the front desk. Of course Peter wasn't in yet. So Dawn had to handle Ms. DiNotello—and her flagrant ambition—alone. She started out smartly: "The paper's received several anonymous calls about three women having been murdered here.''

On the defensive from the start, Dawn began by explaining that Eloise and Nicole had simply violated clearly posted safety rules and drowned. The police had examined the tanning machine. Because it had been forcibly opened to free Chantelle, no one could say for sure that it hadn't simply malfunctioned and that she hadn't passed out before she could call for help. Ms. DiNotello should understand that there was absolutely no evidence of foul play.

Ms. DiNotello was attentive and sympathetic. Dawn wouldn't mind if she talked to club members and staff people, would she? Watching her stride eagerly into the club's interior, Dawn found herself hoping that whatever she wrote wouldn't be too damaging. There was no real evidence that anyone had been murdered—despite her personal suspicions.

A priest came to the desk and asked for a manager. He was short and thin. His hands were long and very white. Father Harold was Chantelle's only living relative. Moist eyes on Dawn's face the entire time, he talked about God's unfathomable motives, the profound necessity of enduring until his plan was made clear, even if it was to be revealed only in heaven.

In the face of these spiritual pronouncements Dawn's thoughts—shame on her!—turned to purely secular matters. The club would escape a lawsuit a second time. She gave Father Harold the answers to his questions about just how his sister had died. He left with his head down. In the face of his suffering and stoic acceptance Dawn broke down into sniffles after all and used a Kleenex in jerky little movements. She bowed her head. Poor Chantelle! Before eleven o'clock seven members had decided to leave the club. By then Peter had come in. He pointed out to them that the contract required them to complete payment for the promised membership period, even though they wouldn't be coming in. No, that wasn't a rip-off. It was standard health-club procedure.

Dawn strolled around the club: no mistake, many members had canceled their workouts. The crowd was as thin as it had been when she and Peter had first taken over. Her heart sank.

Her former lover, Sam Springs, and his current flame Dinah were having lunch. She had ordered her sandwich before seeing them. They moved over to her table. Sam was all grins when the three chatted. Dawn asked Sam what had made him so happy—and bit her tongue so as not to ask if it was manic-depressive behavior.

"I heard that you had another fatality, Dimples," Sam said.

"Do you mind not calling me that!" Dawn glared arrows at her ex-lover.

"Sorry."

"Another death makes you happy, Sam?" Dawn couldn't keep the edge out of her voice. "Mind if I ask why?"

"I'll get to that one of these days." He grinned. "And before long, too."

Vexed, Dawn carried her lunch back to the office. "The Riddler," she used to call him when they lived together. A character from an old comic book she had once unearthed. Calling him a name hadn't stopped that horrid habit then. Nor would it now, had she bothered to trot it out afresh. How refreshing that he was out of her life.

Or was he?

A call came through from a Mr. Paulson, whom she didn't know. When she took it, it turned out to be Zack Keyman. She stared at the receiver, a crippling rush of emotions coursing through her. Words rose to her lips in waves, then fell away. She knew, no matter what Detective Morgan told her, that the man at the other end of the line had killed three women. And he was still walking around free! Still, she couldn't simply slam down the phone.

"I want to talk to you, Dawn," he said.

"We had one talk in my apartment. Another on the phone. I thought we were done."

"I wanted to tell you how sorry I am that Chantelle died."

She drew her breath in sharply. Impossible to read his words, decode their true meaning.

"And ask when you're going to decide about my getting my job back. Peter said—"

"I don't care what Peter said! We only began to talk about it. And you can be sure, Zack, that I'll *never* allow it."

"You still talking that crazy stuff about me killing those two broads?"

"Very much so!" Her knuckles whitened. She shouted inwardly: I *know* you killed them—and Chantelle, too!

Pause. She heard his breath rustle like an adder. "You know what I could do?" he said.

"What?"

"I could start following you around again. I mean wherever you go. I could spy on you. You know, when you go off with that rich dude in the limo. Hothead Hector. Kinda bother you till you change your mind. How would you like that?"

"I wouldn't. And neither would the police." Damn! Her voice was shaking.

"The cops? They're too busy chasing crack and Colombians to bother with anything I do."

"I wouldn't bet on it!" She slammed down the handset. At once she phoned the police. She couldn't get through to Detective Morgan. As she hung up, a noise came out of her throat that was too much like a whimper. She stared at her tuna sandwich on its paper plate. It now looked as appetizing as a dish of boiled eyeballs.

She couldn't stand to be in the office another minute! She rushed out past the desk staff. She hurried over to the atrium banister, gripped it, and tried to grip herself as well, to clutch some inner rock against the rising force of the tide of Zack's deadly, torturing mischief. As she drew deep breaths and rolled her neck, she sensed that these tides were only harbingers of a deadly hurricane that, when it arrived in full force, would sweep her livelihood and her promising future irretrievably away.

CHAPTER
8

That afternoon Dawn and Peter met and discussed the situation resulting from Chantelle's death. He had taken off his closely tailored double-breasted suitcoat. Above the armholes of his vest, his shirt carried half-moons of perspiration. So the trouble was finally getting to him. No more glib chatter about accidental deaths. He told her that the Gang of Four had come to him, too, to prophesy doom. "They could have just let it go at that, but they had to go on and tell me what trouble they plan to cause if things aren't straightened out right away— whenever that is." He hunched his big shoulders, as though against a blow. "I have a lot invested in this club, D.G. It's my ticket to bigger things. Much bigger. I can't have it pulled out from under my feet by—"

"Zack Keyman."

He scowled. "Or whoever." He opened his desk and took out a revolver.

"Peter, what are you doing with *that?*" she exclaimed.

"Just keeping it handy." He spun the cylinder—*tik-tik-tik-tik.* "I went home at lunchtime and got it, just in case."

"I don't like guns. They make me nervous."

"Not as nervous as the people you point them at."

Peter put the revolver back in the drawer. "Remember where it is. I'd use it for the good of the club. I hope you would, too." He looked intently at her. "So . . . short of starting to shoot people, how do we get control of the situation?"

The first item on their agenda was to hold some confidential meetings with staff members—two had already turned in their resignations—putting them on watch for suspicious behavior by anyone within club walls.

Second, they resolved to push the police, particularly Detective Morgan. To Dawn that meant he would find crazy Zack and arrest him. She considered that decision a victory over her dominating partner and one that would bring this awful business to a speedy close. They chose to make Karl Clausman, he of the wide body, full-time caretaker at the club. He would sleep there and patrol regularly with a steel bar over his shoulder, one he had broken during a vigorous heavy-weight workout.

One good thing did happen that day. Jeff Bently asked her out for dinner. They went to the local Greek diner, which was all he could afford, but he refused her offer to help pay. She tried to be cheerful and kept joking, even after the counterman sneezed on the bread. But whatever topic came up seemed to lead back to one of her problems. Jeff launched several nontaxing subjects—his brief set-to with Mr. Flower Power, as he called Hector, the horrid weather, the Dawn Patrol. None flew. Later, when they were leaving the diner, she shook her head. "I'm really sorry, but this isn't our evening, chum. You have a worried lady on your hands." Jeff didn't own a car, so she drove him to what he called his apartment. It was a single room over a garage. As they hugged good night, she said, "You do have heat up there, don't you?"

He nibbled her ear. "In a way. I use the body heat of sweet young things like you to warm me through the night."

"Not this body. At least not this night." She laughed.

"Can I consider that a definite maybe?"

"Beats me."

True answer. At that moment she wasn't sure how she felt about him.

Initially she had been fond of him and very interested in extending their relationship. Now somber club events were twisting everything in her mind, switching her priorities around. She pondered and mulled a great deal, hardly thinking about driving. The dash clock said 9:30 on yet another night as cold as frozen marble. She glanced in the rearview mirror frequently, a driving routine.

After five minutes behind the wheel she became aware that a car was following her. She flipped the mirror to the night angle and squinted. A battered sedan.

Zack Keyman!

She had just pulled out on a strip of expressway, her customary route home. Zack's car drew closer. Her heart was suddenly pounding. Her wool scarf began to scratch her neck as her pores opened. Dear God, what was he doing? The sedan was so close now that she saw only the glow of its headlights above the Honda's trunk line. She was afraid to slow down, so she hit the accelerator instead. Fifty-five gave way to a "fuelish" sixty, then sixty-five. The Honda shuddered at the higher speeds.

A bumper-against-bumper jolt tore a cry out of her throat. Another! He was trying to kill her! Her knuckles popped as she clutched the wheel. One patch of ice on the damned highway and—

Jolt! The Honda's wheel twisted in her grip. Zack Keyman was crazy, and he was going to murder her right now unless she did something. And the Honda wouldn't go any faster. She pressed the accelerator to the floor.

The sedan loomed closer again, nudging the Honda. Its tires screeched for an instant, and so did she. Her insides lunged like cats in a sack. She was certain she was going to die. Behind, in the lane to her left, about ten yards from the sedan, another pair of headlights appeared. These were set farther apart. As the ten yards closed to five, then three, Dawn saw Hector's limo with shadowy Rudolfo at the wheel.

She heard the frantic blast of Zack's horn, then a second longer, more desperate one, as the limo nudged his left front fender like a whale playing with its young. She saw Zack weave out of control for an instant.

A second nudge sent the sedan hurtling toward the edge of the road. She slowed as Zack's vehicle nosed into the high bank of snow left by the plows. Its rear end swung around to begin the skid that spun it two full circles. It ended with Zack's sedan pointing toward oncoming cars, which somehow avoided a collision.

Farther down the expressway she pulled onto the shoulder. The limo eased up behind her. Hector got out and walked up. She cranked her window down. Hector nodded politely. "I think we'd better talk. Now," he said. He looked toward Zack's car. "I don't believe he'll dare tell the police what happened. I imagine he'll say he skidded."

They left the Honda at her apartment. She was too shaken and grateful to seriously consider refusing to talk to him. She was certain he had saved her life. Then there were all those other confusing, delightful Hectoring memories. She did, however, refuse to go to his pied-à-terre. He took her instead to an expensive Italian restaurant with an intimate dining room, which the flamboyantly mustached owner, Carlo Stefano, opened without charge or delay for "my classiest customer and his equally classy lady," though she had never seen him before.

When the wine had been ordered and poured, Hector sat back with a sly smile. "I can't say much for your young male companions, my sweet. Last Thursday night's string bean who could clearly kill with one hand

and break construction blocks with either foot. And to-night's insanely reckless hothead.''

She didn't want to bother answering. She was too tired, and there was too much to explain. "The guy in the car killed three women at the club.''

His brows rose. "And chose to add you to his list? Why not? But are you sure?''

She tossed her head and drank some wine. "Nobody believes me.''

He leaned forward. As always she was more than merely aware of his presence. "In any case, we've reached the topic I wanted to discuss with you. I had intended to persuade you to talk with me before you walked from your car to your apartment. Luckily I asked Rudolfo to follow you.''

"I don't like being followed.''

"As I've told you, often in life we don't know what's best for us.''

"I hope this isn't going to be another attempt to—''

"I heard today at the club about the latest death. So I thought it best to give you some business advice.'' He sipped his wine, then held the glass up to the light.

"You can't afford me as a consultant, I assure you. But in the interests of friendship, and more, I'll give you my recommendations free of charge. Listen closely.''

She frowned. She hadn't expected this. "All right. Go ahead.''

Behind her a speaker came to life. Music began. The first few bars she knew. It was the Schubert quintet. Not that! Not tonight. She grasped the extent to which Hector and Carlo were coconspirators. She shook her head. "Not that, Hector. It's not that kind of evening. It's not even close. Off, please.''

He signaled, nearly hiding his brief grimace of annoy-ance. In seconds Schubert was replaced with soft Nea-politan songs. "It's quite plain to me that these three unfortunate—occurrences, shall we call them?—are le-thal to the future of the South Harmon Aerobics, Pool, and Exercise club, whether they happened by accident or by design. Shortly SHAPE will have no future." He looked intently at her. "Do you follow me?"

"Some members have quit already, and a few staff, too."

"Precisely. That is why you must sell out your share."

"What?"

"At once. Its value has already been compromised, my sweet. The time is fast fleeing during which you can even cut your losses. Should there be more . . . trouble, you could lose everything you've invested."

She stared at him, aware her eyes were widening. Of course! That was just what was happening. She just hadn't looked at her troubles in a businesslike way. "And your advice is . . . ?"

"I've already given it. Ask Peter to buy you out. Take any reasonable offer he makes." He raised his glass, expecting her to toast with him. She raised hers hesitantly. The rims clinked with less elegance than the paper-thin crystal ones in his pied-à-terre. "Then allow me to take care of you for many years to come."

She put her glass down. "Hector . . ."

"You must!"

She frowned, meeting his black eyes. "The club means so much to me. I can't give it up just like that."

"It will fall to pieces as you watch. I guarantee it."

" 'Guarantee'? That's an odd word to use."

"Some business matters are predictable," he said quickly.

Despite his arguments, which went on till the bottle was empty and beyond, and his irritation, which bloomed into anger like an ugly flower, she stood by her recent revelation: the club had become the most important thing in her life. She didn't intend to abandon it; she would fight to keep it and make it prosper.

"Fool!" he said. "I'm certain you'll be sorry."

"Well, I'm not! And I'm not sure I appreciate your advice."

He shrugged and sat back. "The main problem with sound advice: it isn't taken." They got up to leave. His arm found its way around her shoulders. She was too tired to shrug it off. "No decision you make can be final at this time," he said. "Whether you like it or not, the club's future and your own must remain open."

In the backseat of the limo he kissed her and managed the artful intrusion of his tongue into her mouth before she reluctantly turned her head, battling off both erotic memories and her own desires. He held her covered breast in his hands and pressed a kiss on an L. L. Bean Gore-Tex parka over a Patty Logan wool sweater over a Ship 'n Shore Dacron blouse over a J. C. Penny nylon slip over a cotton Maidenform bra over her chilled and shriveled left nipple. "Come back to me, my sweetest sweet!" Love in the northeastern winter."

"It's time to take me home."

He sighed. "As you like."

He punished her with his silence the rest of the way.

She plunged alone toward her pillow ready for an instant replay of the long and difficult day. She sank like a stone into the waters of sleep.

She knew at once all wasn't well when, arriving at work, she found Peter already there, pacing the office and trying to screw his left fist into his forehead. "The press! The damned press! Read! See! Suffer, too!"

Ms. DiNotello looked to be bucking for a job on the *National Enquirer.* " 'Death Club Claims Third Victim!' " Dawn read. It turned out that the attention-grabber was a quote from a member who had chosen to remain anonymous. Probably Phyllis Melaney of the Gang of Four: Pardon me, Peter and Dawn, while I "Death Club" you to death. She read on. The story was about eighty percent accurate. Not bad for the press. She had gotten all the bad stuff right, sure enough.

Dawn felt queasy, not just because she had skipped breakfast. "What do we do?" she said, feeling weary already.

"We have Glassman pretend we're going to sue for libel. We grant no more interviews."

"I'm not sure that's the right thing to do. Maybe we should be more open, let people know—"

"D.G., that is the dumbest thing you've said this week!" Off went Peter's coat. Up came his pointing finger. "At times like this you have to lie low."

"I'm not sure I agree." Dawn was irritable. His cocksureness bothered her more than usual. "In fact, I disagree."

"Disagree all you want. Just let me handle things."

"Even if you handle them wrong?"

His face turned lemon sour. He raked a hand through his curly hair. "What's with you today, huh?"

"I'm having a bad one—to go with the bad two weeks in front of it. What's your excuse?" She turned and walked out of the office, telling herself as she did that she should have stood her ground and had it out with him.

She checked with the desk staff. Session bookings were down, except for the racquetball courts, still reserved every available hour. They would play through the Second Coming, never mind a death scare. Four more members, all women, had turned in their cards. She looked through the other surrendered cards. All women. Could be worse. The split was sixty-five percent guys, thirty-five percent women. Deep down she felt that maybe, just maybe, they could get through this.

If there was no more trouble.

Detective Morgan showed up later in the morning. He spoke with Dawn and Peter with the office door closed. The police lad had called in the manufacturer of the malfunctioning tanning machine. A technician had come up from New York to look at it. It was pry-barred to pieces, and he couldn't tell about the latch, but he said that somebody definitely tampered with the timer. The juice was supposed to shut off when the timer ran down. "Only it never did." Morgan's lined face twisted, with what seemed great effort, into a tight smile that softened his features. "So even if the first two ladies went down natural-like, there's only one word to describe why Chantelle Carson cashed it in." He raised both hands, index fingers up, like a grade school music teacher. "All together, class. One, two, three . . ."

"Murder," they muttered.

"I hope you'll keep that out of the papers," Peter said.

"Mr. Faldo, if there ever was a time when papers waited for the facts before going to press, it's long over. Did you see this morning's *Dispatch*? They had Chantelle murdered."

"But the reporters will want to talk to you sooner or later," Dawn said.

"Screw 'em!" Morgan said. "If I say she was murdered, whoever did it gets tipped off that the cops are wise. Right now I'm not saying anything."

"Thank goodness!" Peter sagged back in his chair.

Dawn looked at her partner, saw the sweat again beginning to dampen his shirt above his vest. He was extremely agitated, threatened. He wanted badly to defend the club. So did she. They just had different opinions about methods. She wondered if she had ever realized just how important SHAPE was to him, too. Possibly it meant even more to Peter than to her. He was ambitious. His yardstick was financial success and visibility.

Well, there had been a new development that might help them solve the club's problems. She told the men about Zack following her and trying to cause a wreck. Diplomatically she left out Hector and his limo. In her version Zack wiped out, probably because of bad tires. Morgan made a note. "I think it's time to pick the lad up a second time. This time we'll shine some lights in his face."

"It's past time," Dawn said. "I told you. After he failed to run me off the road last night he has to know we're wise to him. You probably won't find him. If you do, all our troubles are over. I just know it. All the evidence points right at the man."

"Not all of it," Morgan said. "We've started asking questions. Chantelle's roomie looks to be a drug dealer. He has a record, and so did she, for dealing. So . . . maybe debts were being paid, other people being warned." He grinned and tipped his hat. "See, Dawn, nothing's as simple as it seems." He said goodbye to her and Peter and went on his way.

Later that afternoon there was another conflict between her and Peter when a TV crew arrived and asked permission to tape. Her partner, with Karl Clausman carrying his steel bar and playing the heavy, rushed downstairs to deny them entry. She tugged on Peter's sleeve as he moved down the stairway, whispering that the crew ought to be allowed in. There was a good crowd in the place; it was peak time, late afternoon. All looked normal. Forget "Death Club." But, no, he wouldn't hear of it. He brushed aside her protest with a few demeaning comments and more than a whiff of bad old chauvinism. To Hector's insight about the business consequences of what was happening to SHAPE she added one of her own: the Peter-Dawn partnership was under its most severe strain to date.

Even a month ago she would have asked herself what she could do to accommodate his wishes and keep the partnership viable. Now things were changing in ways she didn't fully understand. Her old responses were base coin, insufficient to make the strategic purchases needed for this time of pressure and testing. Instead of being more accommodating, she wanted to be less so. Much less so. What was happening to her?

The phone. Hector. He wanted to know if she had approached Peter about selling the club and moving into the pied-à-terre. He rushed on to describe the foreign travel he was planning for the two of them. But first she had to "tear the albatross of SHAPE from around her neck." She said she hadn't spoken to Peter about selling her interest and wasn't sure she ever would. To her surprise he began to shout into the phone. For the first time in their relationship she simply hung up on him. She knew him: that would bring him over in person— for his workout, of course. Then he would manage, sooner or later, to find her alone.

Quite without thinking, she began to pack up her things to leave the building. To run from him. No! She wouldn't. She opened her desk drawer and dropped her purse back into it. She wouldn't run! She would stay and face him, even though she had never known him to be quite so out of control. Yes, he was desperately in love with her. More, though, he seemed to be jealous of the club. The two emotions together could make anyone behave crazily, even Hector Sturm.

She called Beth to see if she could help with the file reorganization that was Dawn's number one priority for the week. Despite recent events at SHAPE, the job still had to be done. She and Beth spread file folders all over the office. Once they were in the correct order, a data entry temp would add the information to the club's computer data base. They had a double reason to do the job. Darlene Sopht, the police clerk, had been careless about refiling after she made her copies. Once they had arrested Zack, the cops could circular-file all their copies, she thought.

Sometime later she glanced up and, sure enough, saw Hector moving across the lobby on his way to the elevator. She saw him twice more glancing her way and fully expected him to bull his way to her side. She and Beth kept working. By the time she looked at the clock three hours had passed. At the desk she went through the names of members working out. Hector's was gone. So he had left without speaking to her.

"I was worried about Hector coming in to bother

me," she said to Beth. "He didn't. Maybe you're a good-luck charm."

Beth said, "I gave him a piece of my mind about what he was doing to you. He knows what I think of him."

"I told you: you needn't have."

"Well, it worked. No Hector," Beth pointed out.

Dawn wondered if a small part of her was disappointed that Hector hadn't come after her.

She found herself still thinking about Hector that evening while watching the local news. She groaned. The TV people had gone away mad. The SHAPE building loomed on the screen, thanks to a carefully chosen camera angle, like the Bastille or the count of Monte Cristo's prison. The announcer explained that the Death Club's management had no comment and had barred "fact-seeking" reporters anxious to determine if the apparent accidents were actually murders, as many club patrons feared. She grabbed the phone and called Peter at home to tell him she had told him so. She got his answering machine and hung up in frustration. Where did he go that he was so seldom home?

The next morning she found that the *Dispatch* didn't seem inclined to forget, either. Reporters had managed to find two members who had left the club yesterday. Word of their fears appeared on the first page of the local news section. On the bright side aggressive Milton Glassman had gone on record, saying that SHAPE was preparing a libel action against the media for "gross actionable distortions."

She went to Jeff's massage studio. He was in session. He had added an answering machine to his new phone line. Business was picking up for him, she hoped. She smiled. What a contrast between him and Hector! Not just years separated them. Jeff was idealistic, simple in his ways, an abstract thinker unconcerned with worldly goods. And he was a sweet, gentle man—unless provoked. Then there was Hector, baroque in his tastes, a wielder of real power, the kind that produced fortunes and affected the lives of others. First she had thought him controlled, even-keeled. Now, as he began divorce proceedings and attempted to invest more heavily in the relationship Dawn was attempting to end, she found him a man of passion, filled with unexpected ruthless desires. Somewhere in the back of her mind stood a possibly significant idea that refused to step forward and be recognized. The elusive idea was one to which she intuitively felt she should be paying greater attention. Just the same it continued to escape her.

Just before noon there was a call for her. She hesitated, asked the switchboard who it was. There were more than a few people with whom she didn't want to speak. Detective Morgan wasn't one of them. She took the call.

"You want to hear the good news or the bad news first, Dawn?"

"I—the good, I guess."

"We picked up Zachary Keyman and *thoroughly* questioned him."

"Oh, thank God! At last! And he confessed, right?"

"Don't forget the bad news."

"What is it?"

"He has alibis for the times of death of all three women. Even for the hours before and after each unhappy event."

Dawn's stomach sank. "He's lying, of course. He must—"

"We checked them all out. He has witnesses."

She eased down into her desk chair. "But—I can't believe this!" She bit off the urge to start babbling, tried to gather her thoughts.

"We're putting the first two deaths on hold," he went on. "Maybe they were accidents after all. We're starting with the Carson woman. Seeing who might want her out of the way. Boyfriend, druggie buddies, personal nutty friend. You know."

"I see."

"Sorry to have to give you the word about Keyman. If it makes you feel any better, he *is* crazy. You want to file charges on the auto thing?"

"Never mind, Lieutenant Morgan."

"Yeah, might as well drop it. You have good sense, lady. I like you. Sorry I can't solve all your problems at once. And I don't think you can solve them by yourself. As a detective, you make a good health-club owner. *Ciao.*"

She hung up and saw Jeff coming into the office. His lanky presence was a much appreciated comfort, considering the hoops her head was rolling. She was too shaky-kneed to rise. Zack hadn't killed anyone! Even if the drownings had been accidents, what about Chantelle? Why hadn't her murderer acted somewhere else? Settled his vendetta in a dark alley or in her apartment? That would have made Dawn's and Peter's lives so much easier.

She blurted out to Jeff what she had just learned. She had expected his sympathy, which she got, but not the faraway look that swept like a fog into his gaze. "Much to think about," he muttered.

"Just what do you mean, Mr. Bently?"

"Why so many dead people? Who done it? Things like that."

Her eyes swept him appraisingly. "If you get any ideas, let me know. Okay?" She looked at him through narrowed eyelids. He did have his odd side, sure enough. Yet, for her, it seemed to add to his charm.

"Dawn, I think I'll meditate on the situation," he said. "Excuse me." His voice had lightened, turned almost dreamy. Off he went, probably to assume the lotus position on the futon in his massage studio.

Zack's innocence—oh, she had such trouble accepting it!—niggled at her all day. That and her slightly strained relationship with Peter kept her on edge. She tried to be the level-headed partner when they spent an hour discussing Detective Morgan's revelation and what it meant to the club, but she knew she was acting sullen in response to his unconscious high-handedness. She hated the moody-woman act, but today she couldn't help it. "Our only hope is that the cops find out who killed Chantelle—and fast," he said. She disagreed, but kept silent. She was putting together a plan of which Peter wouldn't approve. She would act on what she believed, despite his disapproval. And she had an idea what to do.

Having resolved that issue, at least for the moment, she looked forward to an evening of paperwork without inner distractions. She was disappointed. The events of the last two weeks bubbled in her memory. Her mind was busy doing some subconscious rearranging, like a dealer preparing the deck for another hand. She dawdled in her work, and finally gave up completely.

During her 10:00 P.M. workout some of the ideas that had tumbled free all day came together so abruptly that her legs froze on the exercise bike. The digital RPM readout dropped to zero. Despite the warmth of exercise, something icy nestled into her abdomen. She gnawed on her new thoughts through the rest of her workout and shower. Not until she got home for her glass of juice and cup of tea and sat down on her two-person rocking chair did she try to organize them with the help of a pad and pencil. She printed slowly while, outside, a late February wind groaned down the streets.

"Dawn's First Theory," she wrote. "Assume Zack didn't kill anyone. Assume Eloise and Nicole drowned accidentally. Only Chantelle was murdered."

Then . . .

A person or group had it in for Chantelle Carson, and maybe the killer would soon be caught. That was that. It was more or less simple.

"Dawn's Second Theory," she wrote. "Assume Zack didn't kill anyone. Assume all three women were murdered. They had something in common for which they were killed."

Then . . .

With them dead, there would be no worse trouble. Not as simple, but bearable.

She thought for a moment, then went on printing. "Dawn's Third Theory. The dead women had nothing in common, except their club membership. The real motive behind their death had nothing to do with them. They were the victims, but SHAPE was the target. If so, why? And who was behind it?"

Not simple. Ominously open-ended, maybe with worse to come.

Who?

She began to shiver, and knew the reason for her chills.

She had found a name!

CHAPTER
9

Detective Morgan's cubicle wasn't even in the precinct house. It was in the "annex," a partially remodeled grade school a block away. Dawn was waiting for him at nine the next morning when he came in whistling, a container of coffee in hand.

"I have to talk to you," she said. "But it has to be completely confidential."

He led her to a small conference room. After she told him she was going to talk about the deaths at SHAPE, he said he'd have to run his tape recorder.

Dawn was aware her face betrayed great discomfort. "This is all sort of—real personal stuff, you know what I mean?"

He grinned, his best effort yet. Stubborn facial lines eroded, replaced with friendlier ones. If he always looked like that, she thought, his professional image would be improved by the power of ten. "Real juicy stuff, huh, Dawn?" he asked. "Good thing this desk has a blotter, to soak up my drool."

She realized he was teasing her, trying to relax her, she supposed. Nonetheless, she was very much on edge. "These days it seems everything ends up in the papers," she said.

"All the bad stuff ends up in the papers." He adjusted

his pocket recorder. "The good stuff gets forgotten."
He looked directly into her eyes. "If you just listen to
the media, you'd wonder how the human race has endured for thousands of years. Worse than that, you'd
wonder why it even matters."

"It's not just my reputation I'm worried about. It's
someone else's, too."

"I'll do what I can to keep things quiet." He
shrugged. "But we're talking about murder. In the end
you could be in a witness chair talking to the world."

She swallowed. It dawned on her how simple her life
had once been, how it now threatened to run out of
control. Testifying . . .

He smiled, finger poised on the start button. "Still
want to go ahead?"

She knew she did and wondered just why. There had
to be a good reason. She understood it was the club.
Whatever else all this trouble was doing to her, it was
refocusing—and clarifying—her priorities. "Go ahead.
Record," she said.

He sat and sipped coffee, his tape recorder running,
while she talked. She told him about Hector and her,
pussyfooting around the more intimate details. No matter. He got the idea. It took some time. She brought
him up to date right up to their last conversation, in
which Hector had again urged her to sell her share in
the club.

"He got back from Asia just before Eloise St. Martin
died. Since then he's gotten more and more intense and
demanding. I've never seen him behave like this. And
the business about finally divorcing his wife . . ." She
was aware she had flushed all shades of red in the last
hour. Now she just wanted to get through to the end. "He
wants me—permanently—more than I ever thought he
would. He's gone out of control. So much so that . . ."
She hesitated, swallowed, even though she knew Morgan understood what she was going to say. "Maybe he
killed all three women to force me to sell my share of

SHAPE," she blurted. "Once I did that, I'd have no career. *He* would be my new career."

The detective leaned back in his chair. His grin was infectious. "I like it! I like a little passion around a case. A little of the old human element. Passion and desire—yeah! A man gets tired chasing drug savages all the time." He nodded vigorously. "Yes, indeed. If I wasn't a happily married man with four more kids than I can afford"—he looked Dawn over as though he had never seen her—"I'd go to dangerous lengths to get your attentions."

"Look, Monty, it was hard enough for me to come down here and say all this stuff. I told you I'm trying to end the relationship. I don't need—"

"Easy, Dawn. Easy. Men are weak and stupid. Women are women. It's the way of the world. You're not the first woman to get in over her head—just like maybe he has. Despite what you've just said, there could still be a drug connection with the Carson woman's death." He explained he would conduct a two-pronged investigation: drugs and Hector. He told her to say nothing to anyone about their talk.

"What am I supposed to do with Hector?" She was aware of the sudden shrillness of her voice.

Morgan got up and paced. "We're getting on thin ice now," he muttered. "Real thin. Anyhow, if you feel like it, maybe you could playact a little. Maybe you could tell him you're seriously considering taking his advice about selling out, but you need time to think."

Half to herself, she said, "He's not a patient man."

Morgan came around his desk and put his arm lightly across her shoulders. "You play it by ear. You're a bright lady. You'll figure out how. Just don't take any chances, that's all."

She nodded.

"Maybe I can get the captain to put a few more guys on Hector's past and present."

Dawn's emotions were churning in so many directions

she couldn't describe how she truly felt. "Are you going to . . . talk to him?" she said.

"Not right away. First we investigate; then we chat."

At the door he thanked her for coming in, regretted the awkwardness of her having to discuss personal matters and the further inconveniences to come, should they be on the right track. "But in the end, murder has a way of shaking up more lives than just those of the truly unlucky," he said. His smile was that of a man who now had direction and professional purpose.

Then why did she feel so bad?

During the rest of the morning she failed to acquire any of the detective's enthusiasm. Instead she warred inwardly with a strong sense of having been a Judas. She told herself she had acted hastily, driven more by fear than by logic. She surveyed the formidable landscape of Hector's personality. He was a man of strength, not weakness. Sifting through her memories of him, she found far more kindness than hostility, more reason than violence, more imagination than brutality. He simply didn't seem capable of even one murder, let alone three. No, not Hector. Yet . . . she remembered the violent light in his eyes when, despite his protestations of love, she refused to submit to his wishes. She had spurned a man whose strong will and intelligence virtually assured him of maximizing the considerable potential of his life. He wanted her. Enough to kill to get her? She nodded. Yes! Down deep at the heart of the matter it made perfect sense.

At noon Peter prepared to leave the club. He said he would be gone through tomorrow. He wore one of his best suits, tailored to fit like a woolen skin. She asked him if the trip was business or pleasure. "Little of both," he said. "You know."

"Actually I don't. Want to tell me?"

"Not really."

She watched him go down the stairs and out into the cold. What in the world was he up to? He didn't choose to tell her. After he refused to confide in her, causing her to feel like a second-class citizen, she didn't feel guilty about the solo she was about to perform. She went into the office and picked up the phone. She called the *Dispatch*. "Hello, I'd like to talk to someone about holding a news conference."

It was about time she acted on her own beliefs and opinions!

She would have been more convinced about her strengthening spine if she had acted while Peter was in town.

She told Jeff and Beth what she planned. They called some of the smaller newspapers and TV stations for her. Toward the end of the day they set up the small meeting room with a mike and chairs. She asked Beth if she minded showing up tomorrow morning for moral support, even though it was Saturday. The petite woman put her arm around Dawn's waist and gave her a tiny hug. "No problem. I come in early Saturdays, too."

Dawn smiled. "You're a gem, Beth."

"It's little enough," she said.

Dawn rose early to work on her appearance, top to toe. Today she was glad she was a good-sized attractive woman. Even though she didn't plan to smile during her official statement, she decided it wouldn't hurt to show her dimples during the appropriate questions and answers. She wore her best suit. Peter would have approved, if he'd been around. She pushed aside the persistent self-criticism that reminded her she hadn't made it to equal partnership until she opposed him face to face on an issue without caving in.

In the club office Beth put the finishing touches on Dawn's hair, went lint-hunting, and touched up her sparse makeup. "Break a leg!" she whispered on the way down to the meeting room.

Dawn hadn't announced the news conference, except to the media. Even so, in addition to half a dozen reporters and two camera crews, the room was crowded with staff and members. Beyond the lights she saw Karl Clausman, Jeff, and Zack—that horrid man! How had he gotten in again? Oh, there was her ex-lover, Sam, and his classy sweetheart, Dinah. What was he grinning about? She was pleased to find herself relatively calm. I'm going to be able to carry this off! she thought.

"Good morning. Welcome to South Harmon Aerobics, Pool, and Exercise," she began. "My name is Dawn Gray. I'm co-owner of the club and closely involved in its management."

She gave some details about the club and its membership, then stressed its growth and increasing prosperity. She tried to give the impression that it was professionally and safely operated. The two drownings, she said, were accidental; both victims had violated the carefully posted and strictly enforced safety rules. She explained what they were and what Eloise and Nicole had done wrong. No evidence of foul play had been presented.

Knowing that she was going to make Detective Morgan's job harder and maybe turn him from a helpful professional into a cool and distant stranger, she nonetheless went on to the subject of Chantelle Carson's death. "I've spoken with the police, and there is evidence that her death was not an accident. The woman was murdered." Staff and members muttered to one another. She studied the media people. She saw the ambitious Ms. DiNotello, alert and eager as a circling hawk. Only she took notes; the others used tape recorders or cameras. Dawn went on to say that the police were investigating to determine motives and murderer. She thought of Chantelle's drug connection and what kind of hard work that would mean for Detective Morgan. Such information she wouldn't broadcast. She simply said that nothing related to her death had any direct bearing whatever on the club.

She finished up by pointing out that, despite the deaths, club members for the most part continued active participation. In time she was sure Chantelle Carson's killer would be found. That Chantelle had died here at SHAPE was a coincidence that Dawn hoped all reporters would note and mention. There was every reason to think the club was already back to normal, on the track to further growth and prosperity. In closing she said it was very important that word of the real situation she had just described get back to the community, rather than the confusion and innuendo resulting from emotion and careless reporting. She hoped all here would do their part to make this happen. She would answer questions, if there were any, for twenty minutes.

Good heavens! She *was* carrying it off, she thought.

The questions went well enough, too. To the expected ones about the drownings, she reminded them again that both had been accidents. She referred the still-curious to the police, who had so far found nothing strange about the tragedies, except their timing. No, there was no reason to think anyone had it in for the club, either, she said. Except Zack. He stood leering near the door. Then her eyes found Hector. She thought she saw something hard and unyielding in his stance and folded arms. My lover—and my murderer? Seeing him, she was glad she had told Morgan about her suspicions. At that moment she sensed the man was more than capable of taking a life to get what he wanted—her. No matter, she mustered her deepest dimples as the questions turned toward her personal reactions to the tragedies. Time ran out and nobody seemed to mind.

I did it! she thought.

The group began to break up, and the camera crews dismantled their equipment. Ms. DiNotello ambled up and exercised her icy smile. "Good performance," she said.

"I don't know what you mean," Dawn replied somewhat frostily.

The reporter changed the subject to generalities. Dawn knew the woman was fishing for anything that might give her a new angle, the more sensational the better. Dawn carefully reviewed her every word before uttering it. Though she caught nothing, Ms. DiNotello hung close. On the way up the stairs, she said, "Dawn, what's really going on at SHAPE?"

"I just took about an hour to make that clear."

They left the stairwell and entered the lobby. Ms. DiNotello said, "You and I both know—" She stopped talking. Across the lobby in the bar area a crowd was gathering. One of the reporters was lying on the floor by the bar.

The two women hurried over. Crouched beside the fallen man was a club member named Dr. Forrest in spandex shorts and a Jog for Life T-shirt. He was exercising the controlled violence of CPR on the reporter's chest.

Dawn knelt by his head, ready to play the part of second Samaritan by squeezing his nose and blowing hard into his mouth. Dr. Forrest said, "Don't get near his lips!" He bobbled his head toward the bar where a half-empty glass of juice stood. "He could have been poisoned. Close the bar right now. Don't touch anything. Then call the police."

Dawn rose and found herself facing Ms. DiNotello whose foxlike face was brightly lit, as though she had just beheld a miracle. Behind her stood many of the other reporters who moments ago had been heading for their cars. They were waving their tape recorders like wands. "So there's nothing suspicious going on at SHAPE, Dawn?" Ms. DiNotello said. "You've got to be kidding!"

Dawn pushed past her and ignored the questions of the other reporters who attempted to follow her. She rushed for the office to call the police. She hurried in, slammed the door, and locked it. Only then did her eyes sweep the interior.

Peter Faldo was sitting at his desk! His expression was cold. "You've about ruined everything," he spat.

He said he had finished his club business faster than

expected. He had returned during the news conference. Despite his anger, he hadn't thought it wise to interrupt. Then the reporter had died and the doctor suspected poison.

Dawn sat red-faced, worse than embarrassed. All her planning, which had seemed so sensible, had been overturned, strewing her hopes for the club like vegetables from a cart.

"Why did you call the news conference without talking it over with me?" He leaned forward accusingly. "You know I wanted to keep the media out of it."

"I didn't agree with you, and you were too high and mighty to listen to my arguments." She wanted more strength in her tone. It just wasn't there.

Things had gone so wrong!

"I was right to dodge the media! Wasn't I? *Wasn't I?*"

"I just wasn't lucky!" Dawn said. "The conference did just what I hoped it would, Peter. It let everybody know that there was only one real murder and that somebody killed Chantelle Carson for reasons that had nothing to do with SHAPE. Her death may have been drug-related, according to Detective Morgan."

"Fine. And now we have a poisoning."

"We don't know that yet. Dr. Forrest was just—"

"Oh, stop it, Dawn! We've got bigger trouble than ever and you know it." He got up and paced. He took off his expensive jacket, tossed it over the back of a chair, then faced her. "What I want to know is where does this leave our partnership?"

She managed to meet his glance. "I'm . . . not sure."

"What are we, Dawn, partners or adversaries? After your performance today, I'm not sure. Maybe it's time to rethink what it's all about."

"Maybe."

He stared at her expectantly. "I'd be happy to hear your ideas."

"Peter, I don't have any now."

"I'm trying to build up this club in ways you don't even know about, and you're bungling everything."

"I won't stand for that!" She jumped up. "I'm not bungling anything to do with SHAPE. Instead, I'm finding out this place means more to me than—than love!" Was that true? It didn't matter. She was outraged at his accusations. "I'm a grown-up. I don't have to stand here and take your pronouncements like medicine. This morning's been brutal. Let's both take some time to calm down. We'll talk this afternoon about where we go from here."

"Fine." Peter sat back down. On his face was a shadow of his usual expectant expression. "Who calls the cops? You or me?"

"I do. If you're so smart, you can go out there and deal with the doctor and the ambulance."

"I thought it was your turn."

His attempted joke fell on stony ears. There was nothing funny about another human being stretched out, still and dead. She had fled from the corpse and now from the too-familiar routines around its disposal.

Badly distracted, Dawn failed to be on her guard against meeting Hector.

Early that afternoon he cornered her near the pocket billiard tables. The moment she realized he was beside her, she jumped and stepped away. She looked at him now through suspicious eyes. She had beheld the drowned, the burned, and the poisoned—and here was the fiend who had killed them all.

He didn't seem to notice how halting her words were or how cold she was toward him. He was too intent on expressing his dismay at finding she hadn't arranged to sell her share of the club to Peter. This new death—no matter who it was, how he died, or why—reduced the value of her investment by so much. His face, like that of a diabolical actor, was shadowed with seemingly honest concern. She recalled her coaching by Detective Morgan. "I'm seriously considering selling out. I just have to . . . get my head right."

"How long will such a thing take, my sweet?"

"I—don't know."

"If you continue to delay, you may have nothing left to sell. Furthermore, if you delay much longer accepting *my* offer, my interest in you may cool."

"Good! Let it cool." She stepped farther away from him, well out of his personal space. She didn't like standing close to someone who, when she faced the facts, might well be a murderer. "Listen to me, Hector Sturm. I am getting tired of men telling me what I should or shouldn't do! You all think you're so smart. You think you know all the answers. I'm sick of the lot of you!"

"Is that right?" His eyebrows rose.

"Yes!"

He lowered his eyelids. "I want to make love to you—now! Anywhere! Find us a space, a closet, even. I want—"

"No!"

"A spirited Dawn Gray is a new someone whom I want—"

"Stop it!" She whirled away, knowing her face was crimson. Damn him! Monster or not, he could turn her on like a desk lamp. She strode away. He followed. Soon they were in the lobby, among others, thank goodness.

Beth Willow approached them, hugging a long florist's box. The smile on her heart-shaped face made her the only happy person in the club that day, as far as Dawn could see. "From a secret admirer!" she beamed. "Wonder who it is. Aren't I the lucky girl!" She waltzed off.

"A strange woman," Hector muttered.

"She knows about us. She's on my side. That's why she picked a quarrel with you the other day."

"Oh?" Hector's face was impassive. "Was it wise of you to tell her?"

"It's not easy to be silent while being tortured."

Ignoring her stony face, he chuckled. "I would think

you could find better people for your staff. You should dismiss her."

"Because she doesn't like you?" Dawn laughed. "So you don't like her now. Well, someone does. That box was from an expensive florist."

He grunted. "I'm well aware of what flowers cost. Haven't I sent you enough of them?"

"Haven't I loved them?"

"Do you love me?" His hand was on her forearm.

About to jerk away, she remembered Detective Morgan's advice about playacting. She made herself stand still. How different his touch now seemed! Hesitant, heart pounding, she was delighted to see rescue on the way. "Oh, excuse me," she said. "Here comes someone I know: Detective Morgan."

Hector moved off with a swift good-bye. The detective saw only his back.

"That's him!" Dawn whispered. "Hector Sturm. You should arrest him."

"In good time. When we find out more about him."

She turned to look after Hector. He was already gone. "I told him you were the law. He fled."

"Even so—"

She turned quickly back to him. "I want an end to all this!"

He frowned at her. "Maybe that will happen if you cooperate with me. Thanks to your news conference, you've warned the killer we're after him."

She lamely explained the pressure she was under to protect the club as much as she could. She was sorry, but she just couldn't stand by and hear "Death Club" on every channel's nightly news.

"And now another guy is dead, and you invited all the reporters in to see it happen."

"Do you think I knew somebody else was going to die?" She was aware that she was shrieking. "You sound like my partner, for God's sake. I did what I thought was the right thing and—"

He touched her shoulder. "It's okay. Let's close all that up, Dawn. It's a lose-lose situation." He invited her to join him for a private talk with Peter. In the office he told them that the lab boys who had been crawling around the bar had found that all of the juice in the dispenser was poisoned—never mind with what, something tasteless and exotic. Everything else seemed clean. He advised tossing out all the food and every open container, scouring down the bar and all its hardware. "No matter what you do, it'll be a while before business there gets back to what it was—if it ever does."

Peter groaned. The bar was a true money-maker.

The detective brought them up to date. That morning's death had brought the tragedies into focus: SHAPE was the killer's target. Those who had died hadn't been hated, only unlucky. And maybe now the two drowned women should also be regarded as murder victims. He leaned back in his chair and folded hands behind his head. "My question to you, Peter, is: who?"

Dawn was puzzled. Why did he bother quizzing Peter when she and Morgan agreed that Hector was now the prime suspect? Her partner's responses were expectedly vague and unimaginative. The detective was wasting tape. On the way out she asked him what he was up to. He shrugged. "I like the Hector angle a lot, Dawn, and I'm working on it big-time. Just the same, I'm not a man to put all his eggs in one place."

"Well, I am!" Dawn was so vexed she nearly stamped her foot. "Every second you put off arresting Hector is going to cost SHAPE. And you haven't even questioned him yet!"

His lined face softened a bit. "Maybe by the middle of next week," he said.

After Morgan left, Peter went out of the building on personal business. Dawn returned to the office. Her appetite, which had been largely dormant, reared up. She decided to splurge and faxed an order to a we-deliver sub shop. When her Italian cold cuts-hold-the-onions arrived, she ate it at her desk. Between bites she sorted out invoices, keeping busy in an effort to center her emotions.

There were more resignations from the club during the rest of the afternoon. Dawn didn't need to look at the sign-up sheets to know attendance was off by half. Suddenly she had an idea. Each day the names of those who used any club facility were entered into the computer in connection with the monthly graphic exercise profile sent to each member. She hadn't forgotten the dates the three women had died. She brought up the data base and did a search on Hector's name. He had been in the club on all three of those deadly days.

Today made four for four.

Never mind Detective Morgan's methodical approach. She knew Hector Sturm was a man of action who got what he wanted, always. Now he wanted her. He wouldn't hesitate to do whatever it took to get her, including murder. Her intuition whispered like a stage prompter: Hector, Hector, *Hector kills!*

Jeff came into the office and invited her to go snowshoeing in Reservoir Park tomorrow. The day's events weighed so heavily on her—another poor dead soul!—that she had trouble working up enthusiasm, even though she liked Jeff and wanted to see more of him. "Come on, kiddo," he said. "It's called Sunday. People aren't supposed to work."

"I've never been on snowshoes in my life."

He shrugged his sloping shoulders. "We're not talking tightrope somersaults here, Dawn. Two minutes' worth of instruction and you'll be off and running—rather, slogging."

"Should we ask Beth to go, too?"

"I only have two pairs of shoes. Anyhow, some time alone with you would be nice." He did have a cute smile.

They lucked out on the weather: no wind and bright sun. But if Dawn had expected complete relief from her

114

worries about the club, she was disappointed. As they talked, it became obvious that Jeff had been thinking about recent SHAPE events, too. She wasn't about to tell him she was virtually certain that Hector was behind the deaths, but she found his generalizing annoying.

"I'm formulating a theory," he said airily, as though he was playing some kind of game. The sun glinted off his metal-rimmed glasses. Bundled up as he was against the cold, he looked like some kind of gangly robot sent by aliens to irritate her. "But more research and investigation will be necessary."

She invited him to her apartment and fed him leftover soup and quick biscuits. They ended up on the double rocker with her favorite Modern Jazz Quartet tape riffing in the background. She curled up in his arms—and fell asleep. Only when he tried to extricate himself did she awaken, apologetic and cotton-mouthed. At the doorway, she turned her sour lips away from his and offered her cheek.

"I tear myself away only so I can continue my investigations," he said with a smile. He was teasing her.

"Jeff, I'm so sorry I fell asleep! I had a tough week. I hope you understand that my dozing had nothing to do with how I feel about you. I'm really growing very fond of you."

"Vice versa, I assure you." His smile was warm.

"Next time I'll do a lot better than just not fall asleep," she said.

"Watch out! I hold people to promises."

Closing the door behind him, she reminded herself that he was no fool, though he sometimes acted like one. His investigations . . . She placed little worth in his speculations. His flamboyant pronouncements sounded like those of a sincere racetrack handicapper. In the current somber race against death she was certain she already knew the jockey wearing the silks of murder: Hector Sturm.

Or did she?

CHAPTER
10

Monday morning Beth stopped Dawn to ask her how the club was going since the bad media reports of the weekend. "More cancellations. Workouts are way down. Except for the weight guys and racquetball players; they're not afraid of anything. Forget the bar. I checked yesterday and today. Nobody bought anything. I closed it and told the bartenders to stay home."

"Is SHAPE going to make it?" Beth said.

"It has to."

Beth nodded toward a couple ogling in the lobby. "The curious public has arrived to gawk."

The two walked over to the strangers. "Good evenink! Can I interest you in a membership?" Dawn said in what she hoped was a Transylvanian accent.

The slight man with a toothbrush mustache and a retreating hairline looked as startled as though she had stuck his finger into a light socket. "Not just now." He backpedaled, the woman beside him.

All Dawn's troubles seemed at that moment to be beyond ludicrous. This couple became both a symbol of her woes and a target of her anger. "You should consider it. We're having a Death Threat Special this month. Prices cut to the bone—oops!"

The couple fled.

She and Beth managed brief giggles. Before depression returned, Beth said, "I got more flowers yesterday. From Mr. X. Just a card with them saying how he was admiring me from afar."

"Who, who?"

"Don't know who. But I know I like it." Beth's violet eyes were shining.

"Probably a club member," Dawn said. "Somebody who's had his eye on you for a while."

"I brought them to the club. Come on and see them. I have the first batch, too. They're lasting great!"

"I'll keep an eye out. Maybe I'll spot his lusting looks, whoever he is."

On the way to see the flowers, Dawn was stopped by her ex-lover, Sam, a jovial grin on his round face. "It's about time we had lunch, Dimples. My treat."

She looked at him coolly. "I'm not sure I want to have lunch with you. There're bound to be memories on the menu."

"I'll give you other things to think about, concerning the business I promised you we'd talk about. You'd be wise to talk to me, especially after what happened Saturday."

"All right," Dawn grudgingly conceded.

"If you don't mind, we won't eat in the club, Dimples."

"I'm tired of you calling me that," she snapped. "And your jokes are about as funny as nuclear fallout."

"Dinah laughs at them," he said.

"And she seemed like such a bright woman, too," Dawn said snidely.

He glowered at her. "What's with you? You never used to say boo."

"This club is going to come down around my ears. Things like that are starting to make me a different woman," she snapped, her patience at an end.

"Help is on the way," he promised mysteriously.

What kind of help he explained over tapas and beers

at a tiny restaurant around the corner from the club. She heard him out with increasing surprise. He had told her that his employer was Healthways, New England, but he had chosen not to mention that his responsibilities centered on the acquisition of properties. He claimed to be good at his job. His most recent success was the purchase of a struggling Portsmouth, New Hampshire, health club for a nearly discount price. They hadn't been able to reach the level of membership required to keep solvent. Any large enrollment effort would take capital that the owners didn't have—but Healthways did. They didn't want to sell, but in the end they had to sell or go bankrupt.

"How did you find out about their financial condition?"

"I joined, listened to people talk, sniffed the air, you might say."

"Very funny."

"I've been doing the same thing at SHAPE. Very nice operation, Dimples. When I walked in the door a month ago I didn't think Healthways had a chance. Like, SHAPE was a going concern."

"Peter and I worked hard enough on it, I assure you."

"I'll be talking to him next." Sam took a huge bite of one of his tapas, then talked and chewed at the same time—another of his delightful habits. Nonetheless, he still had all that energy, controlled now, that had so appealed to her, and evidently to Dinah. "I started with you because of our, uh, former personal connection. As I said, I didn't think Healthways had a snowball's chance, and I didn't like that." He leaned forward, jaw still working. She saw food. "Because my career depends on my being able to acquire properties and keep on acquiring them, I'm only as good as my last act. So I wasn't feeling so good about SHAPE. Then you started to have . . . trouble. The kind of trouble that affects membership rolls."

"It hasn't really been so bad."

He smiled. "Dimples, I come into the club every day.

118

You're down by almost half on sessions. When membership contracts run out, none of the absentees will renew. Don't be too bright-eyed about the trouble you're in."

Dawn tossed her head. She had scarcely touched her food, and she wasn't going to now. "You want to buy SHAPE for Healthways."

"Uh-huh. Want to sell?"

"No," she answered without hesitation.

Sam sat back, his grin broadening annoyingly. "Too bad that's not all there is to it. There's lots more, though—the lawsuits you have pending, the diminishing income to go with your loss of membership, the capital you have tied up that you'll lose if you go bankrupt. Chapter Eleven is a distinct possibility for SHAPE." He slid an index card out of his inside coat pocket. I've taken a look at a few trends. Want to see?"

"No!"

"Not looking isn't going to change reality. Dimples, you're on the skids. Talk to your accountant if you don't believe me." He raised his palms, the offensive grin moon-wide. "I might not look like it, but I could well be your savior."

She refused to cooperate with him and cut lunch short. He asked her if she would join him when he talked to Peter. At first she was going to say no; then she reconsidered. Their partnership had been dealt some hard blows lately. If it was coming apart, it would happen under the pressure of considering Healthways' offer, whatever it turned out to be. If Peter unilaterally sold out his interest, where would that leave her—and her future?

Driving back to the club, she was depressed by the great heaps of discoloring snow. Spring seemed light-years away. Her career and her future were being torn from her arms like an infant in a tornado.

She went into the office and told Peter what Sam wanted. He agreed to talk to him, and Sam joined them at once. Ever the businessman, Peter not only took notes but also asked Sam questions about Healthways, its assets, management, and long-range plans. Dawn was dismayed to hear Peter ask if, should they sell out, there would be a place in management for one or both of them.

"Peter, how can you even consider—"

"I'm not considering, D.G. I'm fact-finding. Be cool."

As the two men talked, Dawn's spirits sank still further. Healthways was apparently something of a juggernaut, well financed and led by pragmatic men bent on making a great deal of money.

Men like Peter.

And now they were out there lying in wait. Sam, their emissary, had been sent over the crest of the hill with a request for surrender. The discussion dragged on for another forty-five minutes before Peter had enough information. To her pushy ex-lover's question about the possibility of a deal, he said, "Dawn and I, and our accountant, have a great deal to talk about. I can't possibly answer you now."

"When?" Sam said.

Peter looked at him stonily. "I'll let you know."

After he left, Dawn said, "He's been spying on us for a month."

"It's his job."

"How can you be so level-headed, Peter?" I wanted to scratch his eyes out!"

He shrugged. "It's just business. Nothing personal to it."

"He enjoyed every minute of it! He's enjoying the whole damn thing."

"If he is, it's because you chose not to live with him any longer. It's a little piece of his getting even with you for rejecting him."

"Who cares what the reason is?"

"Call Ketty. See when she can come over with the books."

"Peter!"

He got up and put both hands on her shoulders. "D.G., we've got trouble. Maybe we can get out of SHAPE without losing everything."

"But—"

"You have a good head—when you use it. Use it now. The dead reporter could have been the nail that sealed our coffin."

"I'm sorry I held the news conference!" Her eyes were burning.

"That's all over. That's not what I'm talking about. I'm talking about holding up your end of the partnership, the way you used to."

"Don't patronize me!" She was crying now.

"I'm not!" He threw up his hands. His underarms were soaked. Seeing those patches of wetness made her realize all this wasn't easy on him. She steadied herself. Partners. They were still partners. For better or worse. She couldn't help but feel, though, that he was having second thoughts about their arrangement.

She called Ketty. She couldn't get over to the club until tomorrow morning.

"What's the rush?" she said.

"We need to know what SHAPE is worth, building and all. At least on paper. And we need you to run some numbers about our cash flow over the next months. Bring what you have. You can work up the rest after you talk to us."

Dawn and Peter spent the rest of the afternoon over almost as unpleasant a task: reducing the staff in light of the fall-off in participation. They also had to take a look at the possibility of reducing hours. Already morning attendance had reverted to pre-ownership volume: nearly none. The ladies had been frightened off—except, surprisingly, the Gang of Four, led by Phyllis Melaney who had been the first to threaten not only to resign but to go out howling to the media. Dawn had seen them earlier that morning in the intermediate aerobics class, clustered for comfort because only eight of the normal complement of sixteen other women had shown. She guessed why the Gang of Four still came: excitement. Their comfortable lives—complete with husbands, houses, and kids—were boring. If they hung close together and didn't eat or drink, they could safely titillate themselves with the idea of danger lurking all around them. That was a lot more stimulating than leaving and not returning. She wondered if that was wise of them.

After all, why couldn't there be another death?

That idea stayed with her the rest of the afternoon. Something was setting the stage behind the scrim of her consciousness. Props went into place, actors took their positions . . . But what was it that she was supposed to understand?

It wasn't workout night, and she didn't relish spending the evening mulling over cutbacks. And it was snowing again. The first flakes looked as big as Frisbees. That meant more, finer ones in the hours to come. Lots of them. A good night to hole up under the afghan. As she drove home, her Honda skidded, moving her stomach just south of her wisdom teeth before she regained control. Mr. Harnish, the born-again superintendent, had already shoveled the walk for the first time. He liked to keep ahead of the snow. During one storm last year she had seen him shoveling it eight times. Now *that* was a super super!

After dinner she took a long hot shower. She toweled herself dry and put on her down robe. She was ready for the rocker. She pulled the afghan over her legs, turned the radio amplifier down low, and tuned in to easy-listening music.

She wanted to think.

She let her mind wander, allowing it to churn back over the day, the last few days, the deaths, her emotions. She wanted to stimulate whatever was going on behind the screens of her consciousness. She thought of

Hector—once passionate, now angry—demanding, telling her what she ought to do. Hector had killed in an effort to have his way, to have her.

But had he? He had so much to lose! He said he loved her, but how far into craziness would he really go to add her semipermanently to his life. Yet, hadn't he decided to divorce his wife? Before loving Dawn, he hadn't been moved to take that big step. He was the first to say the drownings had been murders. What if . . . he hadn't killed those people?

Then who had?

She turned that one around and around, like a child beholding the swirls of a hand-held marble. If the reporter's death hadn't been caused by some random nut drawn to the club with poison in hand by the earlier tragedies, the murderer's ultimate victim had been exposed: the club. Did someone want to simply destroy it, or . . . What?

When she answered that question a half hour later, she cried out. It was so obvious! What better way to lower SHAPE's value than to drive off the members. Falling membership meant falling income. And that meant bankruptcy and financial collapse. What then? New ownership, of course. After new people took over, the deaths would eventually be forgotten. Profits, which Dawn and Peter had just begun to make, would grow larger and steadier as dark memories faded. Why had it taken her so long to realize that someone stood to gain a great deal if he could buy her and Peter out for an unconscionably low price?

Why, then, couldn't Sam be the murderer?

She examined that possibility. He had demonstrated his instability in the two years they had lived together. Surely chemicals couldn't have completely regulated his damaged personality. If he was the murderer, and if Peter and Dawn chose not to sell out to Healthways, he would kill another person randomly. That would bring wholesale member departure and probably armed police guards into club rooms. After that it would only be a matter of time before the place became a shuttered disaster.

She tossed and turned through the snowy night. It seemed endless because now there was urgency along with uncertainty. Neither she nor SHAPE could endure casual police efforts that dragged on until Sam—or was it Hector?—killed again. Oh, Lord! She wasn't *sure*. Either one could be guilty. No, it was Sam! Well, she wasn't *really* sure, but . . .

She got up and paced her drafty rooms. Pulling a drape aside, she saw the world was a swirl of white. Northeaster. Super. She found herself watching the clock, waiting for the morning hours when she could get over to the police station and tell Detective Morgan that she had changed her mind. Sam Springs was the man the police should be investigating. Not Hector Sturm. From time to time she checked on the storm—still bad. So she cornered herself between two worries that blended into one: she had to reach Morgan as soon as possible.

She was being silly, going into a tailspin. But too much had happened, and threatened to happen, for her to relax. Now her nerves had taken over. She stared up at the dark ceiling, waiting for the sound that meant the storm was over and the city could move again: Mr. Harnish's snow shovel.

In time she heard it as the dawn's gray light crept around the drapes. She got up, dressed, swallowed some coffee, and bundled up to the max. She dug the Honda out from under the eleven inches of snow that had fallen. She got the car started and under way. But the plows hadn't yet been out. Luckily the streets were deserted. Five blocks from her apartment she skidded into a drift. She tried rocking the car out—forward-reverse, forward-reverse.

She stayed stuck.

She clutched the steering wheel in impotent hands and

tried to shake it. She distantly knew she was behaving crazily, but she couldn't help herself. The damned snow! The damned lazy plow crews! If she could afford to live in a better part of the city, the roads would already be clear. She left the Honda behind and went in search of a pay phone. It was cold, that nasty post-snowstorm wind giving the air the bite of a pit bull. She had to slog two blocks back toward the apartment before she found a phone. Then one more to find another with a receiver.

She phoned Morgan's number. Busy. Of course. After a storm, calls to the police increased dramatically—everything from health emergencies to domestic disputes between couples who'd had to spend an unexpected few extra hours together. She tried again and again, the cold gnawing into her toes. She hadn't taken the time to put on heavy wool socks.

She phoned SHAPE. Karl had somehow made it through the snow and opened up, but the staff hadn't arrived. She phoned Peter. They agreed to close the building for the day. Tomorrow she would share her suspicions about Sam.

She tried the police again. Still busy! Leaving the Honda to the mercy of the snow crews, she slogged on home. An hour later she got through to the police and spoke to a sergeant. He told her that Morgan was home sick. No, they didn't give out home numbers. She hung up and beat her fists on her thighs in frustration. Delay in arresting Sam Springs could be fatal to SHAPE. In her fatigue and emotional imbalance, the snowbound day ahead loomed like a massive stone blocking the path of her life.

Then Jeff arrived, snowshoes under his arm. "It's a winter wonderland!" He grinned.

He set about to prove it in the face of her resistance born in anxiety and frustration. He led her into a maze of unplowed streets where winds had whipped the snow into dunelike drifts. Up them they went, knowing that cars lay imprisoned beneath like enchanted fairy-tale monsters. At uncleared major intersections, they stopped where sixteen lanes crossed and made *rrrhumm-rrrhumm* traffic noises. And took time to play dueling breath clouds and make snow angels before moving ahead.

He led her down near the Department of Public Works complex in the warehouse district, to a hole-in-the-wall restaurant where the posted hours were two to eleven in the morning and the coffee came in thick cups that made Dawn think of a 1930s diner in the middle of Kansas. There were no chairs. Plow drivers in sweaters and denim jackets and road crews bundled up in parkas and two pairs of woolen pants with thick, layered gloves stuffed in their pockets stood in groups gobbling sweet rolls and smoking unfiltered Camels.

She and Jeff leaned against the wall, parkas opened to the welcome heat. She couldn't contain herself. First she told him about her reasons for suspecting the new, violently passionate Hector as the murderer—then rushed on to tell him about yesterday's meetings with Sam and her suspicions.

"He's killing people so Healthways can get SHAPE cheap," she said. How much better she felt getting it all out! "What do you think? Is Sam behind it? Or is it Hector after all?"

"Let's go outside," he said. "I'm getting too hot."

As they swayed along side by side, she said, "Well?"

He didn't answer her directly. Instead, he began to talk generally about his travels through the Far East, about studying with masters of one kind of another. Even though snowshoeing and unburdening herself had lowered her stress level and improved her general frame of mind, she nonetheless wasn't all that patient. "Are you making a point, or testing the outline of your memoirs on me?"

"If there's a point, it's that there are two different kinds of thinking, ours and theirs. Eastern and Western.

It's not simple to explain the difference, Dawn. And I'm really not qualified to do it. Here's one way to look at it: we take things apart, they put them together. The Asians are into balance."

"What's that have to do with SHAPE, Jeff?"

"Maybe you're looking at the situation with one kind of thinking and I'm looking at it with another."

"And what's the difference?" She realized how edgy and feisty she still was.

"Beth and I were talking about that the other day. She's been exposed to a bit of similar thinking and training along the way. We figured that we Western people really go after specifics. Who killed Chantelle, for example? Who poisoned the juice? Like that."

"Yes, well, why not?"

"The other kind of thinking might be to soak up all the details . . . and let the answers come by themselves."

Dawn swung along, now accustomed to snowshoeing rhythm. She swallowed her growing frustration. "Well, using that kind of thinking, what answers do you get?"

He looked down at her. "None, yet."

She didn't play fair then, but she couldn't stop herself. She lectured him on the urgency of finding out if Hector or Sam was guilty. Or both, possibly. *There* was an avenue she hadn't explored. Each killing for a different motive. While Jeff could sit back on his futon and give massages whenever it suited him, she had to bite her nails over the whole damned SHAPE enterprise. She didn't have time for philosophies and long interludes waiting for profundities to bubble up from deep in the psyche. Come on, Jeff! So she was being difficult and bitchy. That was everyone's occasional right.

Surprise! He reached out with his long arms and wrapped her in a giant hug. He bent his back and lifted her off her feet. Her snowshoes dangled like duck feet. He showered mini-kisses on her chilled cheeks and brow, then planted a wet one where it did the most good.

They didn't talk about the club again that day. He led her on a trek over a snow-blanketed golf course and then made a long, slow swing through increasingly trafficked streets back to her apartment just as evening fell.

She made fondue, heavy on the veggies, with a little sirloin and a lot of crusty bread. They went from the table to the rocker. Under the afghan they stripped away each other's winter wear and began a serious mutual body exploration, touching, stroking, and tasting. Hours later, twisted, trembling, and spent, she sprawled contented and alone, at peace for the first time in weeks.

By the next morning the streets had been largely cleaned. Dawn, Peter, and Ketty went over the books and came up with a paper dollar value for the club.

It was worth sixty percent more than they had paid for the business—an impressive increment. Ketty agreed to provide figures on potential growth and on the current and projected cost of the falloff in membership. Dawn didn't need a computer printout of that projection: it would cost them the club altogether.

She reached Detective Morgan by phone. As she spoke of Sam her voice rose to match her excitement. She spun out the webs of her suspicions, cast them around her ex-lover like an exotic spider and drew them tight with a *"See?"*

She breathed heavily into the mouthpiece, waiting for his response.

"Interesting," he said in a puzzled voice. "I thought your money was on your sugar daddy, Mr. Hector Sturm."

"Either one could be the killer, Monty. Or, I was thinking, maybe both of them. Maybe each killed for his own motivation!" With no matching enthusiasm from Morgan, her own began to deflate like a balloon the day after a party. She began to feel a bit foolish—and annoyed. "I'm trying to help you solve your case. And I don't appreciate your indifference to—"

"Hold on, Dawn! Give me a break! You've seen four suspicious deaths in the last month. I've seen four hundred since I got into this business. I have a little more perspective than you do."

"So what about Sam? Will you arrest him?"

"*Arrest* him? I just heard his freakin' *name* two minutes ago, and you want him in the slammer?"

"Monty—"

"Today I'll talk to Sturm. Maybe next week I'll talk to Sam Springs. You run your spa. I'll do the detecting."

"Sam could well be the killer! Believe me."

His heavy sigh rustled down the line. "I will say this, Dawn. You got the two classic motives with those two: passion and money. Love and loot, I like to say."

"We have to find out who's responsible. If we don't, SHAPE will be dead on its feet."

"Great choice of words, Dawn. Catch you later." He hung up.

Dawn stared down into the telephone mouthpiece. That conversation had been nothing like the one she had imagined in the horrid night during the northeaster. Amid her tossings and turnings, she had envisioned Detective Morgan as something of a savior, an oasis promising relief from the thirst of anxiety and night thoughts. Now she saw that he was not the dramatic hero of her fantasies, after all.

Clearly she saw that she had to do more to save the club.

But hadn't the faintest idea how to begin.

She and Peter called Sam and arranged a meeting, and in the hours before he arrived she seriously considered what it would mean to her to sell out. Surely it would mean the end of a great deal of stress and worry that mounted by the day. Surrender would banish, too, the mists of the baseless guilt she felt about the four deaths, as well as her deep, persistent sorrow for the dead and their loved ones. The Dawn of three weeks ago—when Eloise had died—would have taken the money and run, particularly if Peter had recommended it. She wouldn't have had the flint in her heart to dig in her feet and fight. Now she was already battling, however ineptly, against the forces bent on destroying SHAPE. She wouldn't quit until she won or the club collapsed into bankruptcy. She understood the reason behind the change. During the last weeks, some grinding had been done on the lens of her personality. The abrasives were the tragedies and their fallout: trying to end her affair with Hector, the support of Beth and Jeff, and beginning to feel more than friendship of the thoughtful, gangly man. Now she focused far more clearly on her motivation. SHAPE had truly become more than merely her career. It was her profession and her identity.

Sam arrived dressed to rival Peter, complete with an expensive leather briefcase as thin as a Swiss watch. His round face was faintly flushed with anticipation and energy. Dawn sensed the old mood swing upward, muted now by lithium, but not erased. As she studied him, a chill as numbing as ice water rolled down her back. Her heart was telling her he could kill—would kill—to add this club to Healthways' booty bag. Like Peter, he had always been hungry for success, and he had all the patience of a piranha.

He was the murderer!

He smiled and bubbled as he ran through the preliminaries. Dawn watched and listened in awe to the audacious monster, as though to the performance of a great actor. He had been in touch with the management of Healthways. Despite the difficulties that the club was experiencing and the damaging media coverage, his organization was prepared to make a generous offer for SHAPE. After some additional stalling for effect, he named the figure Healthways would be willing to pay.

Peter laughed, and Dawn groaned inwardly. Deep down, in a cowardly little corner of her heart, she had been harboring a dream that if the offer was really fair, she could take her share and buy another club elsewhere in the country where costs were lower. Now that hope had shimmered away as well, leaving her firmly on the hard bedrock of SHAPE.

Peter's glance at her brought a shake of her head. He turned back to Sam. "No way," he said.

Sam sat back and smiled. She wanted to scratch his face. "I urge you to take some time to reconsider—"

"We don't need time!" Dawn's temper flared. He was a viper and a sleaze, and she wanted him out of their office.

Sam's brows rose. "Don't be so hasty, Dimples. Be businesslike. My management has instructed me to tell you that any later offer we make will be less generous than the one on the table now."

Peter was pale and sweaty, but determined to be professional far past Dawn's capacity for it. "We'll think it over, Sam. But you can be pretty sure the answer will still be no."

"Unwise, good people. Most unwise." Sam, too, was displeased. He had reddened at hearing their quick rejection. The shelf of his mad desperation was revealed by the receding tide of his self-control. "I hope when you sit down alone together that the Angel of Good Sense will see fit to touch your foreheads. I see it this way: I'm offering to pull you off a sinking ship."

Dawn scarcely heard him. She was looking at his hands and imagining the ghastly things they had done. Peter got up. "Call us tomorrow."

"I can't believe this!" Sam's face was florid now. "This goes miles past merely poor business sense. This is idiocy!"

Peter stepped forward, lowering one arm in a flourish. "The door, my good man. Please use it."

Sam hesitated, his wide eyes darting from one face to the other. "I think you'll be sorry about this."

Dawn's self-control shredded. She sprang up. "Get out of here, you—you dreadful man!"

"Hey—"

Peter jerked the door open. "You've stayed just bit too long, Sam. Better go now."

In the doorway Sam glared at Dawn. "One day you're going to have to come crawling to me, bitch! On your knees you're going to have to lick my shoes."

After he was gone, Dawn was too upset to talk about the offer or any other business matters. She told Peter that any discussions would just have to wait. She was in no mood to argue. She went out and covered the desk while a staff member took a break. She tried to shake free of the fresh worry that clung to her like a leech: what would Sam do next to force them to sell?

While tidying up the countertop, she found an envelope with her name on it and, above it, the date. She was so agitated, she stared down at it for a long moment with distaste, as though it were a smear of fungus. She wondered what the problem was with her. Oh, she knew.

She was afraid.

The deaths at SHAPE and the troubles that went with them were overflowing into her personal life. Threats loomed up like wax figures in an amusement-park haunted house. Her hands trembled as she drove her index finger under the flap, opened the envelope, and slid out a single sheet. She was holding her breath. On the sheet was a drawing. Comprehending what it was, she smiled, then grinned. It was a cartoon featuring caricatures of her and Jeff, both on snowshoes, holding hands and looking smug and self-satisfied. Tiny hearts ascended like bubbles from their heads. She dialed him on the club phone and thanked him. The sentiment and the drawings were both cute.

"When's the next northeaster?" she said. "I can't *wait!*"

"It was a good day for you, too, huh?" She heard the smile in his voice. "Lord knows I worked hard enough to entertain you."

"It wasn't *all* work." She thought of their long interlude on the rocker—and felt a blush rising in her neck.

"Do I get to talk to you today?" he said.

"I—have some things to tell you."

"Let's ask Beth to join us," he said. "We'll see if she's discovered who her secret admirer is."

With the snack bar still closed, they had to order deli takeout. Beth picked it up. They sat in the trainer's room and spread out their food on the covered rubbing table. The petite woman set a Valentine's Day chocolate box beside the pickles. "It came in the mail late yesterday," she said. "Even though the holiday is long past, I still appreciate the sentiment." Her grin was fetching. She clearly enjoyed the attention, wherever it originated.

"Has Mr. Mystery come forward yet?" Jeff asked.

"Uh-uh, but he sent another card."

"Could I see it?" Dawn said.

"I have them all at home. I'll bring them in tomorrow."

Dawn had little appetite, but knew she ought to eat. As she did she brought the others up to date, with emphasis on Sam and her most recent suspicions. She was just slightly distracted by Jeff's presence. He caused a pleasant, warmish feeling in her insides that she liked to think was near the heart.

"So, bottom line, Dawn, do I have to start looking for another job?" Beth said. "Is SHAPE going down in flames?"

"Not yet!" She hoped she was as sure as she sounded.

She and Peter met after lunch. She quickly realized

his level of excitement was still high. They quickly reviewed their position. No, they wouldn't sell out to Healthways. To his jacket, already on a hook, he added his vest. She understood he had something important to tell her. He didn't want to be behind a desk when he got to the point. He led her to a chair and sat facing her. "I feel guilty," he began.

"Over what?"

"Over fast-talking you into providing a lot of the capital for this venture." He waved his hand to include the whole of SHAPE.

She smiled. "You made it clear we were taking a risk."

"I think I wasn't fair in the way I described the risk. I also feel bad about all the work you've put into SHAPE. You could end up with nothing, despite all we've done."

"That's occurred to me, Peter. But the same applies to you."

He shrugged. "I'm a higher roller than you'll ever be. Crash-and-Burn Faldo. Anyway, now that ugly push is coming to an uglier shove, my conscience is acting up. It really is."

She studied his face, imagined she saw earnest sincerity there amid the dark smudges and wrinkles of worry. "So what are you going to do about it?" she said.

"I'm going to offer to buy you out."

"Peter!"

"Listen. Hear me out." He leaned forward and spread his hands, palms up, on his knees. "I was talking to my parents. They're comfortably retired now in Palm Beach. They've joined the golf and sailing clubs. They're realizing they have more than enough money, and I'm going to inherit it in the end. Last week Dad asked me if I could use the money for some kind of investment now, to avoid the inheritance tax. I told him I'd think about it. After our chat with Sam this morning,

I made up my mind. You deserve to get off the hook, D.G."

"I don't want to get off the hook."

"I think you do. You just won't admit it, because you're turning into a hard-nosed broad. Just the same, you should hear me out."

He said he'd offer her twelve percent more than Sam had. It was low, he knew, but something close to what her share was worth. He'd give her a check. She could walk out tomorrow with an eleven percent profit on her original investment. If she wanted to ask Ketty whether that was a good offer, she should do so. He could tell her right then it was.

"Oh, Peter, I don't know. I've come to understand that the club is more than just an investment for me. More than something to keep me busy every day. It's become a very big part of my life."

He nodded. "I understand. I do. Same here. But I can say to you what I wouldn't give Sam the satisfaction to hear." He covered her hand lightly with his. "I believe SHAPE is going to go under, Dawn. I really do. You should, too. Sam or somebody else is killing people here. Come down from wherever your good sense has been hiding and think it through. Working out in this club is like inviting death to walk up and tap you on the shoulder."

"Members are still working out."

He shook his head in vexation. "One more death, Dawn. One more, and we might as well close the door. Admit it."

"Well . . ."

"I'm offering at least one of us a chance to get out of this halfway whole—you."

She sat speechless. In fact at the moment she had no response.

"Go talk to whomever you trust, Dawn. Anybody with sense will tell you to take the money and run. Only don't wait too long."

"I don't want to give up the club." Her voice was tiny.

He got up and towered over her. "I'm advising you to take my offer."

"I don't think I want to. I mean I'm not sure, but I think I'm going to turn you down."

That set him off, sure enough. He cited specific instances and opportunities that would fly out of her life and be forever irretrievable if she went down with SHAPE. As he did so, he became more emotional. When he got past telling her she was not only unwise but ungrateful, she, too, got up and for the first time in their partnership shouted back at him. She told him he wanted to make her a quitter. *He* was quitting if he thought the club was finished. It wasn't. The two of them could make it a success. Their sentences grew shorter, their emotions hotter. Their last exchange was a full-volume shouting match.

"Sell!" he demanded.

"*No!*" she shouted back before storming out of the office.

CHAPTER
11

The next morning Karl Clausman, who had set up camp in the club as designated security guard, came to Dawn in the office. He told her that each night since he had moved in he'd made rounds of the club at different times, padding around barefoot and silent in the dark, iron bar in hand. Until last night he had never seen or heard anything unusual.

"Last night I got this feeling, you know, that somebody else was around. I was gonna turn on the lights, but that would have tipped my hand." Dawn looked at Karl's hands, like clusters of massive sausages. The best kind of hands to catch and hold a murderer. "I could see good enough using the exit lights. I was on the ground level when I definitely heard something. Somebody moving around. I yelled and went toward the noise. Whoever it was went up the stairs."

"You didn't see who it was?"

"No. Not then. Maybe not later, either. Let me tell it. I started yelling. He started running. I went up the stairs after him. I figured I'd chase him up to the top level and corner him. But somehow he slipped by me. I heard him going down the elevator. I ran like hell downstairs again. I thought he'd go out the front, but he went down to the street level and out one of the emergency exits—just a half second before I got there. He flew out fast. I was right behind him. He ran around the side of the building in the dark. And I slipped on some ice and fell on my ass. By the time I got up, he was outta there. I checked the door out later. The latch had been rigged during the day with a little piece of wood so it could be opened from the parking-lot side."

"But you never saw who it was."

"Well . . ." Karl turned his heavy head away for a moment. Then his gray eyes found Dawn's face and didn't blink. "Not sure. Might have. Just caught a half a glimpse. Could be wrong, okay? I could easily be wrong. But I gotta say it. Right? 'Cause SHAPE is hurtin' big-time."

"Yes. Say it."

"It could have been what's-his-name, the massage guy."

"Jeff? *Jeff Bently?*"

"Yeah. That's the guy."

Dawn put her hands on the desk. She hoped Karl wouldn't notice she was gripping the edge with whitening knuckles. She thanked him and said she'd talk to him soon, tell him what she was going to do with the information.

After Karl left she pried her hands from the desk. Jeff? Not Jeff! He couldn't. He was incapable of murder and massive deception. She remembered his fingers on her, inside her . . . She sprang up and rushed to the mirror. Her face had twisted into the mask of a betrayed woman. Oh, no! She whirled from the glass, tried to compose herself. Not caring that she looked a monster, she rushed up the stairs to the massage studio through a fog of betrayal. Jeff *couldn't* be involved in any way.

He couldn't!

The door was closed. A piece of paper had been thumbtacked to the adjacent cork square. Jeff would not be available today. She leaned against the door, pressed her face to the particleboard. No, no, *no*.

She was overreacting. Paranoia tromped on her affections for Jeff. Get it together, Gray, she told herself. Don't be so quick to suspect the increasingly significant other in your life. In time she backed away from the door and went downstairs to see Beth. From the doorway to the trainers' room she saw her petite friend arranging yet another bouquet of flowers. Unable at that moment to face Beth's violet eyes wreathed in delight while she was enduring a battering, Dawn fled.

She phoned Jeff at his garage apartment. No answer. Where was he?

She was too distraught to deal effectively with SHAPE business. The widow of the dead reporter was filing suit. The business manager waved a list of vendors. Which, she asked Dawn, would be the best not to pay? Cash-flow problems had begun. Peter wanted her to set a time when they could talk again about the possibility of his buying her out. He had thought it over, and possibly he could make her a better offer. She glimpsed Zack wandering around the club, along with more "tourists" who wanted a guided tour of the murder sites. She couldn't stand it!

She grabbed her parka and headed for the door. At home she undressed and crawled under the covers. Every half hour she rolled over and phoned Jeff.

At five-thirty he answered. "I want to talk to you!" she blurted.

"Talk."

"In person. Where were you today?"

He said nothing.

Her heart seemed to pause, too. "Why won't you tell me?"

"Maybe it's not your business. What's up?"

"Please come over here. Now."

He arrived forty-five minutes later. By then she had worked herself up into something between a rage and a tailspin, and she was too distraught to be consciously afraid of him. He barely had his jacket off when she said, "Somebody was sneaking around the club last night. Karl almost caught him. He thought it might have been you."

A fleeting pained expression crossed Jeff's narrow face. He took off his glasses and wiped the condensate away with a red bandanna handkerchief. "And if it was?"

"Was it?" Dawn involuntarily backed away.

"I said *if* it was."

"Don't play games with me, Jeff Bently! You can imagine what I'm thinking."

"Not exactly. What *are* you thinking?"

"That you were mixed up in the deaths." The words came out of her suddenly raw throat.

He stared at her for a long moment. His nearsighted eyes looked large and moist. "I know you're under a lot of strain, Dawn. But that hurts just the same."

She shook her head. "Uh-uh! Don't try to turn this around. Why were you sneaking around the club when you can come and go anytime during regular hours with no sweat?"

He wandered around the room, eyeing chairs, but deciding not to sit. He still wore his coat. "I wanted to look for something."

"What? Why in the middle of the night?" She was aware she was shrieking.

He shook his head. "I'd rather not say right now."

"Would you rather say it to the police?"

He put his glasses back on. "Don't embarrass yourself any further by accusing me. I'm not your murderer, Dawn."

"Who is, then?"

"I've been thinking a lot about that. I have some theories of my own."

She glared at him suspiciously. "How about explaining them?"

"I haven't got them together. Even if I did, I wouldn't go into them now. I'm not overjoyed that you'd so quickly think the worst of me. It makes me wonder what kind of woman you are. Especially after . . . snow-shoeing.''

She stood hesitant. Her emotions surged and chopped, like creeks meeting at floodtime. The two of them faced each other, the silence extending itself.

The door buzzer blasted in the quiet. She moved to the intercom. "Who is it?"

"Hector. Let me in—at once!" His tone was unpleasant.

She pressed the latch button, then a moment later wondered if she should have. Well, it was too late now. When she opened the door for him, the two men eyed each other with scant pleasure.

"The Kung Fu Kid," Hector sneered.

"Daddy Warbucks." Jeff turned to Dawn. "I'm leaving." Out he went.

"Jeff . . ." Dawn shook her head, knowing her face spoke eloquently of her confusion and turmoil.

No sooner had she closed the door than Hector grabbed her shoulder—hard. She whimpered and tried to pull away. "You foolish child!"

"Jeff is my—friend, and—"

"He can go to blazes—along with you!"

She shoved at his wrist, wincing with the pain. He released her. "Do you know how I spent the greater part of this afternoon, Dawn Gray? *Do you?*"

She only now grasped the depth of Hector's anger. His face was drained of color. His eyes burned with intensity. "I don't know."

"In the pleasant company of the police! Specifically, in the company of one Detective Morgan!" He sat down in a chair and waved her toward the rocker. "They badly underestimated the person they were dealing with, of course, as well as the extent of my resources and those of my corporation. Nonetheless, before and after my attorneys arrived, the detective bombarded me with the most outrageous and insulting questions—accusations, even.

"It took some time for me to realize the precise direction in which they intended to take me. But when it dawned on me that they suspected I had caused the deaths in your health club, I was outraged. I gave them back, as far as counsel would allow, the same coin they passed to me. Only after some time did I come to recognize the source of their suspicions and flagrant accusations."

Dawn found she was holding her breath.

"It was you!" Hector stood up, clenching his fists. The rage that had recently seemed to diminish returned in greater force. His features were wreathed in a fury that she prayed for her sake wouldn't overcome him completely. "Only when the detective mentioned your name for the first time did I begin to understand what lunacies you had contrived, what fantasies you wove and passed on to the small-minded minions of the law. God knows what dramas you scripted out of the whole cloth of love, romance, passion, envy, revenge!" He clutched her shoulders, jerking her out of the rocker.

She cried out in pain. "If you hurt me again, I'll scream, Hector. Honest to God, I'll—"

He loosened his grip just a bit. "I just want to hear it from your lips, Dawn. That farce I was just forced to play—it was all your doing, wasn't it?"

She screwed up her nerve. "And why not? How badly did you want me? You forget so easily? I remember, even if *you* don't, the price you were willing to pay. Why wouldn't you go just a bit further and take away what few resources I had so I'd be forced to take you up on your sleazy offer."

"Oh, no! Not sleazy. Nothing I do is sleazy, Dawn." He waved imperiously. "Save your rhetoric for your moralistic friends."

She knocked his hands off her shoulders. "You would have killed to have me!"

He burst into laughter, the rage of moments ago gone flying. "*Killed* to have you? Killed to have *any* woman? When there are so many of you? So many young, sweet morsels to be devoured?"

She met his coldly smiling eyes. "I was more than a morsel to you, Hector Sturm."

"Were you? If so, your recent poor judgment and wild accusations have returned you to that group once again." He folded his arms. "You had a predecessor. You'll have a successor."

Something wrenched inside Dawn, like tissue being rent. "You said you loved me!" she cried despite herself.

"It seemed necessary to say it to enjoy your superb body a great deal longer."

Her eyes widened. "A piece of meat, that's what I was to you?"

"That's what any woman is to any man, Dawn. Why else would we put up with any of you, even for a day?"

She croaked with anger that inflated to rage in an instant. "Behind all your elegant talk and your—your *Schubert,* you're just another horrid, woman-hating macho animal!" An unbearable pressure mounted. She whirled, snatched up a vase, and flung it at him. He dodged, and it glanced off the rocker and fell to the carpet. She clenched her fists with fury. "Get out! Never speak to me again! Never dare to call me!"

At last! She had said it at last!

His grin was ice now. "That's precisely what I came to say to you." His level tone strengthened his sincerity. "What a convenient surprise! We part as equals, then?" His cocked brow told her he doubted that at this moment she could match his strength. Well, she could!

"Yes. You and I are through, Hector. That's it!" She commanded her voice not to shake.

He nodded and turned to the door. He paused, hand on the knob. "You know I really have had enough of you."

She went for him, baring her teeth and curling her

fingers to better use her nails. He slipped out, and she didn't follow. She flung herself at the door as it slammed with gunshot percussion.

She stood alone in the middle of the small room. She was rid of him! For so many weeks she had struggled to get to this point. Why, then, were tears beginning to smart in her eyes? She went to her bedroom and kicked off her shoes. Her vision was blurred. She was biting the fingernails on her left hand. She tumbled under the covers and put her head between the two pillows. He hadn't been telling the truth just then—not really! She had once seen real love in his eyes, heard it ring like chapel chimes in his tender words. He was lying, over-simplifying, because he wanted to hurt her. Well, he wasn't going to succeed! She cried until she had no tears left. Some hours later she fell into a restless sleep.

In the morning Sam was waiting for her and Peter at the club. They held a brief meeting during which her ex-lover made a slightly better offer. Healthways was reasonable, he explained, sweat beading high on his forehead as he talked. It would be very much in their interest if they reconsidered.

Knowing him, Dawn caught echoes of the same desperate urgency that had seized him during their initial meeting. There was no doubt that he wanted them to sell. They heard him out. After he'd made all his points, he paused. "So you see, reconsidering your refusal to sell is far and away the wisest course." He drew a document from his briefcase and placed it on the desk in front of Peter. "We'll need your signatures on the sell agreement to get things moving." He drew a gold-tipped Waterman fountain pen from an inside suitcoat pocket with a flourish.

Peter leaned back in his chair and spread wide his arms. "We're not going to sell. Dawn and I are not interested."

"No, we're not," she seconded.

The pen in Sam's hand shook. He seemed startled by

their refusal. "This is crazy! Healthways is throwing you a life preserver and you're reaching out to the shark instead!" He went on in the same vein. Peter and Dawn stood by their decision. Because Sam wouldn't accept their answer, they eventually both rose to politely escort him on his way. By then his face was red, and Dawn saw dancing in the depths of his eyes a quick glimmer of the wildest desperation—and then it was gone.

"Until I get back to my management and hear what they have to say, the matter isn't settled," he said as they reached the front desk.

"We think it is," Peter said.

Sam's eyes swung across them both. Again Dawn saw the dangerous glimmer. Did hate lurk there as well?

"You two drive a hard bargain," he said.

"No bargain, Sam. No deal," Dawn said. She turned away and saw Dinah waiting to see how things had gone. A tiny frown creased Dinah's elegant brow. Dawn wondered what Sam's failure would mean to their relationship, if anything.

Peter invited Dawn back to the office. He studied her haggard appearance. "Up late?"

"I didn't sleep well."

"Thinking about my offer to buy your share of SHAPE?"

She blinked. Her thinking had been about anything but business. In the wee hours of last night, under pillows and sheets, she had both mourned and celebrated the birth, growth, decline, and death of love. "The club wasn't on my mind, Peter."

He stood close to her, hands in his pockets. "Maybe it should have been. My conscience is still bothering me."

"Oh, Peter, don't feel bad. When we took over SHAPE, I went into the deal with my eyes open."

"What I'm saying is that the deal isn't irreversible. I'm offering you a chance to get out before it's—before you lose everything." His brown eyes mirrored an honest concern. "I called my folks the other night. They're willing to up the ante a little.'' He reeled off the new figures, better by another eight percent. He put a hand on her shoulder and looked at her earnestly. ''Whadaya say, partner?''

After last night's turmoil, resisting Peter was child's play. ''I'm pretty certain I don't want to sell.''

''I don't want to sound like Sam, Dawn, but I hope that's not your final word.''

She cocked her head and looked speculatively at him. ''You don't have some kind of—I don't know—hidden agenda, do you? The way you're thinking, your conscience could end up costing you and your parents a lot of money if the club goes down the tubes.''

He looked surprised. ''Nothing like that. I'm just giving you a chance to get out from under while you can. That's all. Please say you'll at least consider my offer.''

She shrugged. ''If it will make you feel better, I'll consider it.''

''You being serious?''

''I think so.'' What was wrong with having a safety valve?

''When—''

''Ease off, Peter!'' she snapped. ''Your pushing so hard really does make me doubt your motives. I wonder whether you're leveling with me. So drop it for now. All right?''

After a curt nod, Peter strode off in silence.

An hour later Dawn had a visitor: Detective Morgan. He took her to an empty studio—much easier to find than a month ago. She told him she had talked to Hector. The cop grimaced. ''I didn't quite realize what a big fish we had in our net. For openers, I didn't know he was a multimillionaire. If we hadn't picked him up on the street, we would never have had the pleasure of talking face to face.''

''We ended our relationship,'' she said. ''Which was precisely what I wanted.''

''Uh.'' Dawn couldn't read Morgan's lined face. ''I

don't think he's the killer. Not just because he's rich and famous. Those kind kill, too. He made a good case for himself. And he really seems to have been elsewhere at the actual times when the three women died." He drew a rasping breath. "Rather impressive, that guy. I can see why you crawled in the sack with him."

She winced. "Sometimes you're not the most tactful man."

He grinned sourly. "That's why I'll never make assistant superintendent. And as long as you've got my personality pinned down, I might as well ask you who else you're sleeping with—if anybody."

"What does that have to do with the case?" Dawn wished her face wouldn't redden so easily.

"Maybe a lot."

"You ought to ask in a way that doesn't make me feel so cheap."

"I get low marks for tact, Dawn."

"I'm not sleeping with anybody."

He nodded, then paused. "What about this Jeff Bently?"

Her memory blew up the briefest shower of memories of snowshoes and knowing hands. "I'm just getting to know him. Why do you ask?"

He told her that Hector had mentioned Jeff Bently during questioning. Then Jeff himself had visited the police station. He wanted to talk about the case to Morgan or anyone else who'd listen. He had some theories he wanted to bounce off experienced cops. Or so he said. Sometimes people who might be connected with murder came forward because they had guilty consciences and were attempting to mislead the law. Nobody at headquarters bothered to talk to Jeff. "I came over to hear what you think of the man," Morgan said.

"I—I don't know. We had a fight about that last night."

"You think he could have been involved in the deaths?"

"I have no idea! Maybe. I hope not. I want to be able to like the guy. But anything is possible. All I know is I want the murderer found before SHAPE falls apart. *That's* what I want."

"We're running checks on Bently and some other people." He thinly smiled. "We're trying."

"I appreciate that." A chill wreathed her spine. "It's just that I'm worried you're not going to get there in time."

Morgan got up to leave. "You'll be hearing from me," he said.

Dawn needed somebody else to listen to her. She was too confused about Jeff right then to face him. She found Beth in the trainer's room working on Karl's left knee, a frequent troublemaker. The two made a curious couple—his bulk and her petite frame. Watching them together, Dawn was aware of their light-hearted camaraderie.

"You oughta just stop lifting for a while," Beth said. "Mr. Knee is making his feelings known."

"Do the cortisone thing again, Beth," Karl growled.

"I gave you a shot two weeks ago."

"I need another one."

"Too much of the stuff, it stops working."

"Do it!"

Beth administered the injection with careful efficiency. After Karl left, she admitted to Dawn that she shouldn't be playing doctor. But she'd had some medical training. "That's the limit of what I'll do. Any worse, off to the doctors I send them."

With the club in its present condition, Beth's modest misdemeanor, if that's what it was, meant little to Dawn.

"You and Karl make a cute couple."

Beth giggled. "He's a beast."

"Maybe he's the guy who's been sending you flowers and candy."

She shook her head. "I'm getting a hunch about who it is, but I don't want to say till I'm sure."

Dawn sat down then and told her about her fights with Jeff and Hector. She tried to keep it brief, but got carried away and rushed on with too much detail. Finally she drew a breath and stopped. "I am putting a real burden on our friendship," she said.

Beth shook her head. "I'm a good listener. It's one of my better qualities." She looked quizzically at Dawn. "Do you want me to react?"

"Well . . . sure, I guess."

"I knew you and Hector weren't going to make it."

"I thought I told you I didn't want to 'make it' with him. I wanted out."

Beth's violet eyes met Dawn's in a steady gaze. "I didn't believe you for one minute."

"Why not?"

"The way you described him. What he had to offer. How he did things. 'Shall we tour Europe this spring, my love?' " She smiled. "Pretty impressive."

"Beth, I haven't forgotten you picked a fight with him on my behalf. You weren't really impressed."

Beth turned to the window. "No, I guess I wasn't, when you really come down to it."

"Hector is history. But what should I do about Jeff?"

"After Hector, does it matter?" Beth seemed to be losing interest in Dawn's problems. She looked at her watch. "We've been talking for an hour. We both have things to do."

Dawn was distantly embarrassed at having taken so much of Beth's time. It seemed an appropriate moment to give her some good news. "Peter and I appreciate your staying on after other staff members have quit. I've suggested we give you a promotion and a raise."

"Thanks, boss!" Beth tossed her head, and her dark hair swirled below the bone barrette. "For me, at least, things are looking up."

Back in the office a few minutes later, Dawn found

Peter had left for the day. His comings and goings were so erratic she found herself wondering what part of their business was occupying so much of his time away from the building. Or was it his personal life that was so demanding? On her desk she found a note from him, saying he had gotten a call from a Mr. Kelso Capozzi, CEO of Healthways. They had an appointment to meet with him tomorrow. She was to meet Peter at 6:00 A.M. for the drive to Boston.

In the car the next morning, Peter said Capozzi hadn't gone into great detail. He wanted to talk to him and Dawn about "the deal." So much so that he had agreed to a Saturday meeting. He had been in a rush and hadn't provided much background. To her suggestion that they shouldn't bother to meet with him, Peter countered by saying that there was nothing wrong with being polite, cooperative, and businesslike. Maybe Healthways was ready to break down and offer them what the club was worth. When she reminded him that neither of them wanted to sell, he said one should never close a door or burn a bridge. It took her prying to make him admit that his real reason for making the trip was to take pointers on how a successful fitness empire was built and on the personalities who did it. "I'm going to get there, too, D.G. I want to see what it's like in the executive suite." His jaw was set. He was deadly serious.

Kelso Capozzi wore a leisure suit with an open shirt. Around his neck hung gold chains thick enough to raise battleship anchors. On his right stood the vice president, Daphne DeCouture, her tan like a flag of prosperity flying over the winter landscape. She was trim and sleek, no stranger to workouts and self-discipline, Dawn guessed. Capozzi had the sloping shoulders and massive thighs of a weightlifter. Some of the couple's obvious prosperity had thickened his waist. Six golf trophies in a case in their small boardroom spoke of other challenges and successes.

A tray on the table held champagne flutes. The neck of a Moët & Chandon bottle protruded from a silver ice bucket. "Celebration first, then business." The CEO's voice was a booming baritone.

"We can't tell you how much we've looked forward to meeting you under these circumstances," Daphne said.

Capozzi popped the cork and filled the crystal glasses. When each of the four held a flute, he raised his. "To Healthways and SHAPE—joined for the greater good." Up went Daphne's glass. Dawn and Peter half raised theirs, then hesitated.

"Maybe we should talk business first," Dawn said. "I'm not sure either Peter or I know what's going on."

Daphne's frown split the center of her forehead like a vertical blade. "We're about to toast the acquisition. After that we'll work out the very best terms we can for both of you."

Dawn's stomach dropped as though her 707 had just hit an air pocket. She spun toward Peter. He had sold out without telling her! Champagne spilled from her glass, chilling her fingers. He had turned to look at her, anger and accusation blooming in his reddening cheeks. "You—"

"I didn't! I was thinking *you* did."

He shook his head. "Someone here is misinformed," he said to Capozzi. "And we don't think it's us."

The story came out. Sam Springs was supposed to arrange for the acquisition of new properties by Healthways. If he managed to line up two acquisitions on terms favorable to the organization, Capozzi would make him a vice president. If he failed, he'd be out on the street again.

Capozzi shrugged. "It was a win-win proposition for everybody."

The first club had been targeted by Kelso and Daphne. Just the same, it had been a tall order to bring it into the Healthways fold. Sam had shown his mettle and strength of will. Yes, Dawn could imagine the energy he would put into the challenge. Her ex-lover would have been at his best. In the end, Capozzi looked uneasy. "We understood from Mr. Springs that you had agreed to our second offer and that you came here today to work out the details of the contract."

"We didn't!" Dawn said loudly.

"Healthways didn't offer us what the club was worth, so of course we didn't sell." Peter looked intently at the couple. "Sam knows that. We told him. No way he could have misunderstood."

"We gave him a deadline," Daphne said.

"He was to close the deal or . . ." Capozzi hesitated.

"Why not tell them, Kelso?" Daphne asked. "At least they won't think we're mad."

They had hired Sam on a hunch more than a year ago. He had carried the earmarks of a master persuader. Capozzi had met enough of them to believe Sam had the right stuff. He knew such men rolled the dice high, win or lose, crash and burn, bet the bundle. He also saw, though not clearly, into Sam's past mental problems. Surely there was some risk in hiring him. So the deal they cut was for Sam to receive a small salary and expenses to keep him going. He had carried it all off. Flushed with that initial success, he had done research and discovered SHAPE. Because it was profitable, he was preparing to pass on it, until he saw Dawn's name listed as co-owner.

"I remember the day he came to me with the list," Daphne said. "His eyes were all lit up. He said, 'This is my old girlfriend! She can be talked into *anything!* "

Dawn reddened. Yes, the old Dawn to go with the old Sam. Both were gone. He had his lithium. She had the continuing annealing fires of dangerous challenges to her career and her modest prosperity. She was no longer Ms. Malleable. She simply couldn't afford to be self-effacing and accommodating any longer. Asserting herself had become a means of survival.

Daphne's grin failed to be completely warm. "I still think you agreed to sell, Peter, because you liked his little friend. The one with the big pointy bosoms."

"Oh, Dinah!" Capozzi chuckled. "Yeah, she's a top-shelf sweetie, all right. I can read ladies like that. She's looking for a guy on the way up, or already up. Ha-ha! No pun intended." He waved a thick arm. "Hey, part of business is making a good impression, however you can. Fine-looking women will do that—better than a herd of shysters, under some conditions." He looked Dawn over, then turned to Peter. "I mean, you're not hurting the team, Ms. Gray."

"Our relationship is strictly business, Kelso," Peter said.

"Sorry to hear it!" He exploded into a basso guffaw that made the crystal quiver.

"Sam's Dinah hasn't made nearly enough of an impression on me to influence my decision," Peter said. "And if she had, Dawn would have hit me over the head with a heavy stick until I came to my senses. SHAPE is a little more professional than Sam might have convinced you."

Kelso and Daphne offered their apologies. They'd be speaking to Sam. They wouldn't make him happy.

Peter asked for a tour. What they found was a centralized operation with a small staff that consolidated data from Healthways' eight locations. Computer terminals and telephones were everywhere.

"We're even getting away from the fan-fold paper," Daphne said. "We use screen readout where we can. We have the same accounting software running at all our sites, and we use well-established reporting and record-keeping procedures."

At the door Peter turned to the successful couple. "I'm going to have something like this some day."

"Good luck. For openers, you'd better stop people getting killed at your club." Kelso chortled at his own humor.

Daphne stepped closer to Dawn. "Remember, sugar, we're still here. You'll get a better deal from us than from bankruptcy." She touched Dawn briefly on the sleeve. "Have a pleasant drive home."

They didn't have a pleasant drive. No sooner were they in the car than Dawn began to review what she had just learned. She began to pick a fact here, another there, piece them together like a quilt-maker. When Sam had first arrived at SHAPE, he found it as stable and impregnable as a castle. He had joined under Dinah's membership and sneaked around for weeks, finding nothing to give him hope as far as a Healthways acquisition was concerned. What happened then connected Dawn's earlier suspicions with the facts just learned from Kelso and Daphne. Increasingly desperate because of the deal he had struck with Kelso, and clearly mentally disturbed, he had drowned Eloise and Nicole, burned Chantelle to death, and poisoned the reporter. Then when the club began to founder, he came forward and made an offer on behalf of Healthways. Owners without Peter's ambition and Dawn's determination might well have sold out and considered themselves lucky. Small wonder Sam had been so upset at their refusal. But he had left the offer open. Dawn now understood why, and a thin icicle of chill went through her. So they hadn't sold, Sam was thinking. Fine!

Then he would kill again!

She had to speak to Detective Morgan as soon as possible. The police would have to fall on Sam at once. Based on the recent information, he absolutely had to be their prime suspect. They had to drag him down and tear away his round-faced joviality to expose the monster beneath the smile. And she had suspected Zack, then Hector—and even Jeff! How could she? *Jeff!* She owed him an sincere apology. After talking to Kelso and Daphne she was certain who had committed the murders. Sam had the motive: a career to be won.

But the police moved so slowly. Morgan had said this

was the year of the felon. Drug-related crimes, in addition to more traditional ones, laid a thousand straws on the breaking back of the camel of law enforcement. If the police dragged their feet and let Sam walk around free, Dawn was certain he'd find another victim.

She and Peter simply couldn't allow that to happen. She explained her somber suspicions to her partner. To her satisfaction he didn't pooh-pooh them. His set jaw told her he was taking them very much to heart. For the rest of the drive home they discussed what could be done and came up with a simple plan.

Back at the club Dawn phoned Sam. Dinah answered and told her Sam wouldn't be back for a couple of hours.

Dawn left a message. "Tell him we want to discuss Healthways' latest offer as soon as possible." In a surge of sisterhood she nearly added that a classy lady like her could do better than live with a murderer. Restraining herself, she asked only that Sam call them immediately once he got home.

She and Peter stayed at the club into the evening. After eight Sam returned the call. Peter told him to come right over. Peter and Dawn then went to Karl and swore him to secrecy. They invited him and his steel bar into the office. He was to be a witness. He was to do nothing unless Sam acted up—a strong possibility.

Sam arrived in a rush. His round face was wreathed with expectation. They put him in a chair facing their desks. They wanted to look into his eyes. Karl sat behind him and to the left.

"What's he here for?" Sam asked.

"He's a witness."

Sam frowned.

"Do you wonder why we asked you to come over here?" Dawn demanded.

"Dinah said you wanted to talk about selling."

"We told her that. The truth is we had a long chat in

person with Kelso Capozzi and Daphne DeCouture earlier today." Peter paused. Sam opened his mouth, then closed it. "They thought we wanted to sell. It seems you gave him that idea—"

Sam interrupted with the beginnings of an explanation. Peter waved his words aside. "Save it for now. We got a clear idea of the kind of deal you cut with Healthways, and we know what you stand to gain if we sell out to you."

"So?"

"You were so desperate that you told them we had agreed to sell even though we hadn't!" Dawn said. "If you were that desperate, Peter and I are certain you were desperate enough to kill three club members and a reporter to help persuade us to sell."

"What the hell!" Sam heaved his beefy bulk off the chair. His face grew red. Veins rose up in his forehead and temples. Behind him Karl stirred in his chair, muttering wide-eyed at what he had just heard.

"You think *I'm* behind what's been going on here?" Sam exclaimed.

Peter and Dawn nodded. "We're almost certain. Only you had anything to gain by the club being in danger of going out of business. It doesn't help anybody else, does it?"

"Wait a minute!" Sam made patting, calming gestures.

"Yes?" Dawn even managed a hint of smile. "Want to defend yourself?"

"I won't bother!" Sam's face was wholly flushed now. "That is so off the wall that—"

"We want you to know we're going to the police with our suspicions," Dawn informed him. "So if you were thinking of killing another person to kind of hurry us toward Healthways, I don't think you'll dare do it now." The whole point of the meeting was made clear now. Sam would be stopped in his lethal tracks.

"I cannot *believe* this!" Sam cried.

"Believe it," Peter said. "And act accordingly. It's

about over for you," He slid open his desk drawer and removed his revolver. He rested it gently on his desk blotter.

"What the hell is that for?" Sam asked.

"You've heard of a fire extinguisher? This is a murderer extinguisher. Instructions: In event a murderer appears, point and pull trigger. The extinguisher does the rest." Peter smiled coldly. "Think of this demonstration as a warning."

Dawn hated to see the revolver, nor did she normally make threats or like hearing them made. In this situation, however . . .

Sam whirled toward Dawn. "You're behind all this, you airheaded bitch. Trying to punish *me* for a failed relationship!"

Sam didn't listen to her begin her denials. He snarled and started toward Peter. "And you're another crazy asshole! I'm starting to put my life back together, and you two loonies start stabbing me in the back. Trying to ruin me before I ever get really get started. Listen up, you crazies! I didn't kill anybody. This place is a snake pit, but Sam Springs has nothing to do with it!" He lunged across Peter's desk, hands outstretched for a grip on any part of him. "You gotta believe me!"

Then Karl was on him, wrapping him up in arms as strong as hawsers and calling for calm.

Dawn read a killer's desperation on Sam's sweaty face. All three of them escorted him to the door and out into the cold parking lot. "We'd appreciate it if you stayed out of the club," she said coldly.

"You can't make me! I haven't done anything. I'll see Healthways' lawyer. I have rights as a member that you can't just take away!" A snow squall blew up suddenly. Flakes powdered their clothing. Dawn shivered. She, Karl, and Peter retreated into the warmth. Sam stood where he was. Dawn took a last look at him through the glass panels.

He was weeping.

CHAPTER
12

Saturday morning Peter called Detective Morgan to bring him up to date on Sam and request a speedier investigation of him and his likely crimes. He was on the phone for rather a long time, which he reported to Dawn when she came in to catch up on paperwork.

"What did he say?" she anxiously demanded. "Is he—"

"He said we have a new suspect every week. None of them have been right yet." He looked as upset as she suddenly felt.

"I can't believe that! I warned him about Sam even before we found out what kind of deal he cut with Healthways." Her knees were shaky. She sat down.

"He gave me some cop philosophy about needing facts, not suspicions. He said he'd continue to check out Sam along with all the other people he's working on."

"He told me they're going through the list of all the members and staff."

"He just told me that includes us, too, of course."

"I guess that figures, doesn't it?"

"Yeah, but I don't like it much. Standard procedure probably. Why doesn't he concentrate on just Sam Springs? When I said that to him, he said I was lucky he bothered to go in on a Saturday to work on the SHAPE case, never mind doing what I wanted." He got up and shifted from foot to foot. Today he had dressed down to only a sport coat and slacks. But the knot in his tie was as taut and well shaped as ever. His expression grew still more unhappy. "I have a feeling that by the time anybody gets to the bottom of all this, the club is going to be bankrupt."

"But we *know* Sam—"

"We *think* Sam's behind it all."

"Oh, Peter, he *is*. It's so obvious."

"And if he isn't, what then? Somebody else dies? More members head out the door." He walked over and squatted beside her chair. He held her hands lightly. "D.G., let me buy you out. Right now. Today. Before something worse happens. I'll have Milton draw up a sale agreement that'll bind me no matter what happens from here on out. That way at least one of us will get out of SHAPE clean. What say?"

She looked away from his earnest face. She was ashamed to admit to herself that for the first time she was sorely tempted to sell out.

Last night she had slept well and felt great relief because she was certain Sam was the murderer. This morning doubt, like a battering ram, again hurled itself against the fragile gates of her peace of mind. She scanned her partner's features with fresh eyes. She had been so obsessed with achieving equality with him in the face of his assertive personality that she had lost sight of his virtues. He wasn't her opponent, really. It was her own faulty mind-set that caused her problems. She was now making some strides toward a more effective personality. Just the same, everything seemed twisted together this morning. "Oh, Peter, I just don't know what to do!"

"Sell! My conscience is torturing me, D.G. I got you into this. I want to get you out with something more than just your smooth white skin."

"Give me the rest of the weekend to think about it."

"You oughta decide now."

She shook her head. "I can't."

She went home, planning to spend the rest of the weekend in deep thought, but two Saturday afternoon hours alone in her apartment were enough. She simply couldn't concentrate. The decision to sell out or not seemed big as the moon, and as unapproachable.

She procrastinated by calling Jeff, who wasn't home. She tried Beth, who was—and likely bored her further with a half hour of theorizing about Sam as her principle suspect, no matter how skeptical Detective Morgan seemed to be.

Suspect of the Week indeed! She got a call from Karl, who asked about the rumor he'd heard—police running checks on all the staff members. He didn't sound happy to hear that it was true.

"Don't tell me you have something to hide, Karl."

"Me? Nah. No way!"

After he hung up, she wondered if he *did* have a little secret, something that might bear on what was happening at the club. Loyal Karl? As he said: "No way!"

By Saturday night she was stir-crazy. She called her friend Judi Mirthson. She and her husband happened to be having a party. Did she want to come over? It was all couples. She went anyway, then spent the night in their guest room.

The next morning she insisted her hosts go out for brunch. She'd watch the boys. She sat on the floor with them. They crawled over each another, playing Tickle! She acted the friendly but scary monster and sent them toddling and shrieking for safety. When they began to feel housebound, she bundled them up and took them out on their sled. Pulling the loop of plastic clothesline, she thought about her own childhood. Not that long ago in years, in her recollection at that cool crisp moment, it seemed like centuries. She looked back at the boys, scarved and hatted to the max, and knew they wouldn't be children very long. Time flew, whether you were having fun or not. *There* was an item she had kept on the back burner long enough: marrying and producing a few like the two in tow. She felt that procreative urge, strengthening like a current at the change of tide. Making babies was easy. It was finding the right man that posed problems. She wasn't quite ready to take on parenthood single-handed, though she knew at least two women who had cut out the middleman, so to speak, and gone right to the designated donor. Talk about unappealing! Gray, you're a hopeless traditionalist, she told herself.

That night she called Jeff again from her own apartment. He was at home, but cool. She labored over the conversation like a field hand under the debilitating sun of his one-word responses. She made him understand that Hector had shown up at her apartment to terminate their relationship. Period. No longer was he in her life! Nor was he a murder suspect anymore. Maybe he was pleased to hear all that. It was hard to tell. She asked him if he wanted to come over for dessert. He declined.

She couldn't stop herself from telling him all about Healthways and Sam and how he had become Peter's and her prime suspect. She added that the police were continuing to look into his guilt. He listened without responding. When she had run down, he said coolly, "Does that mean I'm not one of your Ten Most Wanted anymore?" Clearly his feelings were still hurt.

"I'm sorry about that. Please understand my situation, Jeff. My career, my future, and my economic position are all threatening to collapse. I'm not myself. I tend to overreact. Part of that overreaction was suspecting you were the killer."

"Is that an apology?"

She imagined him with his longish head tilted expectantly, that little grin on his face. "It is." She hurried on. "Now will you tell me what you were doing sneaking into the club and visiting police headquarters?"

"I told you, Dawn: I have my own ideas about what's going on."

"I imagine they've changed now that we've figured out what Sam's been doing."

"No."

"Jeff!"

"But for the moment I'm keeping my who-done-it thoughts to myself."

"I need all the help—"

"You're doing fine, Dawn. And right now I don't have anything concrete to tell you."

"You don't think Sam is behind everything!" It came out an accusation. Didn't he understand she wanted all this wrenching trauma over? She had no time to indulge his distanced musings. He wasn't in the Far East anymore. This was New England, and both she and Peter needed to plunge quickly into the dark heart of their troubles. Oooh! He could be so annoying!

"Maybe when all this quiets down we can go back to being friends again," he said.

"So what are we in the meantime? Wary opponents?"

"I'll see you at the club. Thanks for the apology."

As she showered and got ready for bed, she found another Dawn taking possession of her mind. That Dawn, utterly unfettered by emotion, wondered if Jeff might be practicing awesome cunning and devilish deception—taking the daring chance of making love to her one moment and, the next, adding another bloody brick to the pile threatening to crush her life. Instead of detached, the man was sinister. No, no, she was doing it again! Jeff was a good guy. Jeff was on her side. Falling asleep she remembered his tongue on her skin, gliding on its wet track like a snail into her intimate pits and folds. She shuddered at the remembered ecstasy and hugged herself until her groaning sigh rose like a spirit into the darkness. Jeff! *Jeff!*

*   *   *

Monday morning she was in the club lobby when it happened.

In the corner of her eye a blur of motion winked, and then she heard the sound of the impact. Her head whirled toward the center of the atrium where ferns and tropical plants grew amid studied rock arrangements. Almost before it dawned on her that someone had plunged down from the third level, she heard the screaming from there: "He jumped! Oh, God! Oh, God! He jumped!"

She flung herself toward the atrium and looked up. In a moment Beth's small face peered over the side. Even at the distance Dawn could see her friend's features twisted with the beginnings of hysteria. Her dark hair swirled as she flung her head back and forth in horror.

Others rushed to the fallen body. Mutters and screams arose. Should we touch him or not? people wanted to know. On spaghetti legs Dawn tottered over. Face down with a twisted neck and a stone embedded in the side of his head, Sam Springs was dead. There could be no question.

She staggered, a red roar rising around her. She reached out, looking in her moment of greatest despair for Peter or Karl. Neither was among the crowd. She staggered, the faint rising up like a beast. She fell into a woman's arms and held on. A moment later she found herself looking into the face of Phyllis Melaney, leader of the Gang of Four.

"I hereby resign from SHAPE, today and forever!" she screamed hysterically, a mist of saliva wetting Dawn's cheek.

"Suicide!" Dawn hissed. Finding the strength somewhere, she tore herself from Phyllis's grip. "It was suicide!"

"I don't care what it was!" Phyllis raised an accusing finger. "This place caused it somehow. My friends and I are out of here!"

Despite her unsteadiness, Dawn turned her back on

the woman. She doubted they would quit; the Gang of Four had enjoyed the titillation too much. She almost wished one of them would get—*no!* No, no, she didn't. She circled the crowd and the body that had fallen less than a minute ago. He lay so still! Energetic Sam would never move again.

Another wave of dizziness swept over her. She leaned against the wall and heaved air into her lungs. Head clearing, she looked around again for Peter. She needed him to take charge. She wasn't up to it at that moment.

Finally Peter appeared, white-faced but not hesitant. He gave orders. Once again calls went to the police and ambulance. On shaky knees Dawn hurried to his side, trying for a show of professional self-possession in the face of a new tragedy. At the sight of a familiar pale face, she called, "Beth, we have to talk to you. Now!"

She and Peter took Beth into the office. She was badly shaken, her voice quavering. As she spoke it became clear that, really, she hadn't seen Sam jump. From the other side of the level she had seen him walking close to the waist-high banister, then out of her direct view.

"He went around that little corner, you know? Right after that I saw his arm and part of his back as he went over." Beth frowned. "I guess I didn't see him jump, start to finish."

Dawn looked at Peter. "You know the spot? It's like a little alcove there. And you know what's set in the alcove?"

He hesitated a long moment, as though with an effort to recall. "A door to the stairs."

Beth pursed her lips. "So what?"

"So maybe somebody called Sam over to that spot. And when he got there, the killer hiked him up and over."

"Come on! Who could do it? He weighed about two-twenty. Me? At ninety pounds? If you think—"

"No, we don't think you did anything, Beth. Maybe he didn't kill himself is all."

Beth sat back and folded her arms. "You two have let the last weeks go to your head." She pointed at Dawn. "On the phone last Saturday you told me you had exposed Sam completely. You knew he wanted to acquire the club for Healthways. You wouldn't sell. He was going to lose his job and his chance to be a vice president. He couldn't take it. He was unstable anyhow. He killed *himself*." She nodded vigorously. "Just like in the psych books. He came down right out there where you'd see him, Dawn. It was an 'I'll show you!' type of suicide and you know it!"

A grim-faced Detective Morgan arrived with a half-dozen officers who began to take witnesses' statements. Officer Daniels, who had first appeared the morning Eloise had been found drowned, had been assigned to assist Detective Morgan. They took Beth up to the third level and had her show them just what she had seen. The door got a lot of attention. It opened and closed with the faintest metallic clatter. Morgan asked Beth if she had heard it before or after Sam had fallen.

She wrinkled her nose and smooth brow, thinking. "Maybe after. But I'm not *sure,* okay? It wouldn't be fair to say I'm sure."

The detective asked Daniels to stand at the banister and look down into the altrium. Then he asked Beth to try to push him over.

"What? *Why?*" The petite woman looked alarmed. "Are you accusing me of trying to—"

The detective shook his head. "Just checking. Go ahead. Give it a real try."

"Hey, Monty . . ." Daniels looked hesitant.

"You can resist, Daniels. You can resist." He waved Beth forward. "Go ahead, get a running start."

"I don't like doing this!" Beth protested.

"You're first. Dawn's next."

Beth wore sneakers, so had no trouble getting up to speed quickly. But when her slight bulk crashed into the two-hundred-plus-pound officer, he was merely shoved against the banister, still very much on his feet.

"Dawn?"

"I was downstairs when he fell. I couldn't possibly have been involved!"

"What we're looking for here is what it does take to push him over," Morgan patiently explained.

Dawn was heavier than Beth, but Daniels had no reason to be nervous. His weight and strength easily kept him well out of danger.

Morgan then seemed to lose interest. "Even a guy would have trouble getting him over the railing. First they'd have to knock him out, then drag him up to the banister and get him over a little at a time. You know what I mean?" He shrugged. "I think he did himself the Roman way."

"You sure?" Peter asked.

"Sure? I'm not sure of anything." Morgan's sharp glance caught the younger man's eye like a hook. "Mind if I ask you where you were when Springs took the plunge?"

Peter was clearly startled. Dawn remembered waiting for him to show up after Sam had fallen. He had arrived several minutes later. "I was down in the pool area. One of the desk people paged me."

"Any witnesses to your presence there?"

Peter's face paled with sudden anger. "Are you accusing me? If you are, come right out with it!"

"Everybody's a suspect. Why not you?" There was little humor in the detective's smile. He wrote in his book while Peter fumed. Then Morgan looked up and said, "Deep down I got another reason for voting suicide beside him being too big to go over easy."

"What?" Beth said.

"He went over and down real quiet."

Because so many members had quit coming to the club, there weren't any witnesses on the third level except Beth. "I almost wish I hadn't been there, either!"

she complained. "I don't like even being close to somebody dying."

Fingerprint men went over the relevant doorknob.
They'd find plenty of samples there, Dawn knew, but
who could say if any would be useful. Morgan asked
that all club staff be fingerprinted. When he wanted to
go ahead and fingerprint members, too, Dawn and Peter
threatened to go to Milton Glassman to see what right
they had to refuse to allow it. Morgan shrugged their
refusal aside. "We can do it now, or we can do it later—
after somebody else gets killed."

"Please don't talk like that!" Dawn said.

She hadn't realized that Dinah, Sam's lover, had also
been in the club all morning. When she appeared, Morgan's eyes lit up. "*You* I want to talk to right away!"
he said.

He and Daniels took her off alone for an hour. She
tottered from behind closed doors with tear-smeared
eyes and a sagging mouth. Yet somehow her beauty
was heightened by her grief. A comely but dangerous
woman, Dawn decided. Dinah had backed a loser.
Maybe she had gotten *very* impatient with Sam's
failures. . . . Now hold *on,* Dawn, she told herself. Not
everyone who was in the club at that moment should be
suspected of murder.

Later Dawn talked to Morgan about what he had
found out from Dinah. He wasn't satisfied with her explanation of her location at the moment Sam went over.
But that didn't prove anything. He wasn't satisfied with
Peter's location, either. If Dinah wanted Sam out of the
way, she could have collaborated with a man who actually did the dirty work. She claimed Sam hadn't said
anything to her about thinking of suicide, but Morgan
knew that happened as often as not. She'd let the police
know if she found a note.

"She cried when she talked about him," Morgan said.
"But I've talked to bereaved people for decades. On a
bereavement scale of one to ten, where ten is tear out

your hair and nail-gouge your skin, she was a real strong two." He shrugged. "I think she got lucky. He killed himself or somebody else did her the favor." He smiled sourly. "Of course I'm not sure." He lowered his voice. "You want to tell me about that big ox who walks around here with the steel bar over his shoulder?"

Karl? He's a sweetheart," Dawn began.

He took notes. She told him he was wasting his time. Karl could be trusted. Morgan looked grim and said nothing. He walked her toward the bottom of the atrium where photographers inside the police tape were finishing up around a chalked outline. A wag had sketched in a smiling face where Sam's head had lain. Morgan gestured at the scene. "That could be about the finish of this place."

"It was a suicide! It wasn't— It didn't have anything to do with the club. You about said so yourself."

"You must have noticed it's the fifth death in"—he checked his notebook—"a little less than a month. I don't think your members are about to cut it too fine about who died maybe by accident, maybe by murder, and maybe by suicide. And I didn't even go to Harvard."

Dawn made fists, held them against her sides. "Instead of being smart, why don't you find out who did all this?"

"Like to, Dawn. Like to."

"Can I help?"

"Maybe." He extended his index finger and touched the tip of her nose. "Smell out who else will benefit if the club goes out of business."

Even though Peter knew their nerves were raw he asked Dawn to have dinner with him. The day's events had worked new lines into his face. His curly hair was unruly and his expensive suit rumpled. "We both need to get out of this place and talk." She agreed. They picked an inexpensive Middle Eastern place where they had met in earlier times for informal business conferences.

They talked about all that had happened and about their suspicions. "What do you think Morgan really believes?" Peter anxiously leaned forward across the table.

"I don't think he'll tell us. He says he suspects everybody," Dawn said. "That seems to include everybody but me. He suspects you, too."

"Well, he needn't!"

Why did she think he was overreacting? Did he really have something to hide? Tonight he was teased by impatience. Not until they sipped Turkish coffee at meal's end did she find out what really was on his mind.

"I gave you the weekend to decide about letting me buy you out, D.G. Now I'm sure you wish you hadn't put me off. The club's worth less tonight than it was this morning."

Her memory served up poor dead Sam lying amid crushed ferns. "I wasn't thinking of what happened in quite that way."

"It's reality, D.G. And it's one that's torturing me, to tell you the hard truth. Or rather it's my conscience that's doing that. It's shouting louder than ever that I've taken the worst kind of financial advantage of you." Clearly vexed, he jabbed his hand through his curly hair. "After today I'm not sure what SHAPE has left in terms of value. Just the same, I'm going to make my offer again. And I'll make it a little better." He named a figure two percent better than his most recent offer. "D.G., I want to get you out safe and clear."

"If I sell my interest to you, what are you going to do to turn the club around? What's to keep you from losing all your parents' money? My selling out to you won't solve those problems."

"They'd be all mine then, sink or swim. I wouldn't feel that I'd taken advantage of you, which is how I feel now." He reached out and squeezed her hand. "Be smart, D.G. Sell. What do you say?"

Dawn sipped her coffee and tasted the bitter grit at the bottom of the tiny cup. She looked down into that black smear and kept her eyes away from his until she had centered herself. Then she looked up. "The answer's still no."

Then the argument started. He exercised all his considerable assertiveness, backed it up with logic, facts, numbers. He painted the grimmest picture of SHAPE's future. When she still didn't yield, he criticized both her business sense and her common sense. He advised her to drop it all and let him take the risks. She could walk out with a bundle. Yet she knew it wasn't that simple. Something unknown and possibly unkind, no matter his generous nature and concern for her, lay at the bottom of his offer.

To her surprise, as they quarreled it occurred to her for the first time to suspect Peter of being the murderer. Morgan had asked her who would benefit if the club went out of business. Maybe that question wasn't phrased quite right. The real issue might be, what good was a club down on its luck and near bankruptcy? It must be *some* good: Peter wanted to control it badly enough, didn't he? Then there was the matter of Morgan not being satisfied with Peter's explanation of his whereabouts when Sam went over the railing. Was Peter guilty? How could she know at that moment? One thing was certain: something wasn't right in all he said and did.

The more she successfully resisted his persuasiveness, the stronger she felt. As his expression darkened, hers lightened. She was doing it. She was facing him down! Never mind that her motives were unclear and the future a dark puzzle, she was standing up for herself one hundred percent!

When he realized she wouldn't change her mind, he

muttered a bitter curse, his expression set between sullen and resigned. He paid the check and walked out wordlessly beside her. They had driven their own cars. He drove off without a good-bye.

She wondered where that left the partnership. And the club. How could it not fail financially? When it did, what would she do? The future had never seemed darker. She got into her Honda and tilted the mirror so that she could see her face.

Her grin stretched from ear to ear.

She studied her joyful expression, gloated over it. I am crazy, she thought. I am absolutely crazy!

By morning, though, the glow she had felt over her tougher, more assertive personality had faded. She bought a paper on the way to the club and turned to the local news. Ms. DiNotello had been busy with fact and innuendo, combining investigative reporting with gossip-mongering. She wrote that the latest fatality at "Club Death" could be the last of the tragedies there or just another in the continuing string. She'd discovered that Sam had worked for Healthways and had sought to buy SHAPE. Had he killed to lower its value? If so, when his offer was refused, had he committed suicide in despair or was he pushed?

Kelso Capozzi and Daphne DeCouture had spoken to the media at length. Between the lines of their regrets and condolences regarding their employee's death—oh, no, they wouldn't speculate about suicide versus murder—Dawn read that their interest in the club was stronger than ever. Now that its reputation was further on the rocks, the Healthways team suggested its value had undergone a parallel decline. Only under entirely new management could it go forward as a viable operation.

Dinah stood by her man, at least as far as the media were concerned, by assuring all that "Sam Springs was too much *hombre* to take his own life."

To Dawn's surprise she saw Dinah in the club that

morning. She wasn't exercising, just hanging around. She had combed out her red hair till it shone and tied it up with an elaborately knotted blue scarf. Dawn repeated her sincere regret over Sam's death, which Dinah graciously accepted. No smudges under the eyes marred her beauty. She seemed to be reacting as serenely to her lover's death as Dawn had last night to realizing she was square in the middle of utter disaster and grinning about it. Possibly Dinah, too, saw a chance for personal growth springing from the ashes of ruin. Remembering Detective Morgan's assessment of her lack of deep grief, Dawn felt she was possibly being too kind.

As they talked, it was Dawn who felt the stirring of old emotions. She had lived with Sam, happily sometimes, for eighteen months. More than once he had held her in his big arms and told her she was the best thing in his life "by mega-light-years," as he put it. They had shared life and intimacy. She had hung in there with him through all his mental problems and the resulting abuse. She had despaired when the time came for her to leave him. Yesterday she had been so tangled in her own concerns that the Sam who had been part of her past life had been eclipsed by the aggressive business competitor he had become. Now his death had capped so many other recent disasters. Today she couldn't help paying the tearful tribute she truly owed the dead man. And in the presence of her successor. Well, it certainly wasn't planned!

Dawn's good cry found no resonance in Dinah's emotional tuning fork. It was pitched differently, as she understood the rest of the woman was as well. Dinah gave her a Kleenex and a pat on the back. When Dawn was in control again, the redhead leaned close, cupped Dawn's neck in the cool curve of her palm, and whispered, "Don't go overboard, love. In the end he didn't have the right stuff."

After that she wasn't inclined to think too highly of Dinah, putting her in a critical mood that got further exercise later that day when she saw the redhead at poolside in close conversation with Hector Sturm. Her tank suit was even more revealing than her exercise outfits. She might as well have been naked. Dawn's heart wrenched weakly at sight of the piercing gaze he was fastening on Dinah's face. She recognized the same intensity that had so flattered—and dominated—her. She turned and went about her business. She had no wish to see if he was successful with Dinah. Was she to be Dawn's successor with him as well as with Sam? She winced. At that moment events once again seemed to sustain the common wisdom that what goes around comes around. Hadn't Hector replaced another woman with her?

Am I having a bad morning or what? she asked herself. She needed companionship. She found Beth kneeling amid the ferns in the center of the atrium greenery, repairing yesterday's damage as best she could. She had scrubbed away the chalked figure and reset the stones that the police lab men had scuffed aside. "I wanted to replace the crushed plants," she said. "But Peter told me there wasn't money anymore for frills."

"I'm afraid he's right."

"Want to have lunch?" Beth asked.

Dawn closed her eyes for a long moment. "My appetite isn't what it used to be. I've lost eight pounds since Eloise died."

"Want to talk?"

Dawn hesitated. "All I've done is talk at you, Beth. I'm such a wreck that every conversation turns into a monologue."

They did talk, in an empty studio, sitting with their backs against the mirrored wall. At first Dawn made an effort to turn attention to her petite friend's agenda. What would she do if the club failed and she lost her job? And of course had she found out who her secret admirer was?

"I've got some ideas. I think the time's coming for him to step up and face me."

"That's what you said the last time we talked," Dawn reminded her. "What makes you think so?"

"He's up to a gift a day now."

"My God!"

"Nothing cheap, either. All good stuff."

"He has to be somebody shy, right?" Dawn said. "Or somebody who doesn't think he has a chance with you."

"Oh, I don't know about that."

"Who, Beth? Karl, maybe. Or . . ." Where the idea came from Dawn never did guess. "Peter!" she blurted.

Beth grinned slyly. "Could be."

Dawn remembered her partner's frequent absences from the club. He had told her he was away on business, but she had never wholly believed him. Peter was fond of women and had likely been keeping company with one. Maybe that relationship had come to an end and he was courting Beth, teasing her with gifts and suspense. It could be. It could very well be. "I think you've guessed who he is, Beth."

She giggled. "If I have, I'll never tell! Not until I know for sure."

Despite her determination not to, Dawn couldn't help telling Beth about the media coverage of Sam's death. The situation seemed even worse in the telling. At that moment all seemed lost, as it had last night after she continued to refuse Peter's offer to sell. Now, though, she felt no glee at her liberating newfound strength of character. Control seeped away from her, like water under a child's dam. She sank into a choking blubber at the end of which she could only croak, "I—I think SHAPE is finished!" she sobbed. Her back slid off the glass. She lay on the floor and drew her knees up, like an infant in both position and tears.

Later she looked up. Her friend's violet eyes gleamed down on her with unspoken sympathy. Dawn didn't care that she showed emotion as raw as sores. After a long while she was aware that Beth had despaired of offering consolation and had slipped off in silence.

The Gang of Four was waiting for Dawn at the desk. She looked them over: Phyllis, the leader; Claudia, second in command; Stick Dawson; and tiny Cynthia. Each had a membership card in her hand.

"We're giving up on SHAPE," Phyllis announced, oblivious or indifferent to Dawn's haggard appearance. "Just as I told you yesterday. We're going to join Racket and Fitness across town."

"Why not hang around for a few more days? That way you won't miss the murder of the week." Dawn's face was stony.

Phyllis turned to the others. "I *told* you Springs wasn't behind the killings. She's just about admitting it."

Dawn jumped to the offensive. These people weren't like Beth, ready to hear her worst fears. They were members, entitled to the truth. "I have every reason to think Sam Springs *was* responsible for all the deaths. He was the only one to benefit by the club having troubles. When his schemes didn't work out, he killed himself. I was with the police yesterday, ladies, and it was pretty clear that Sam threw himself over the edge entirely on his own. So we can be sure that our troubles here are over, even though great harm's been done." She paused, a bit breathless from her little speech.

"We don't agree," Phyllis said. "We don't think the deaths will stop until . . ."

"Until what?" Dawn asked.

"Until this building is closed and boarded up!"

After Dawn had added the four women's cards to the ever-growing pile of those of former members, she pondered her own words, spoken from her rational heart. They made a great deal of sense. No longer did she see any point in the task Detective Morgan had given her, along with a touch on the nose: find out who would profit if SHAPE went out of business. Sam had been the only possible beneficiary. As she went through the motions of management that afternoon, she pondered her conclusion, turning it this way and that. At four-thirty she called Detective Morgan, told him she thought the club's troubles were finally over, and explained her reasons. "We're home free, Monty. Even though all the harm's been done."

"I gotta disagree, Dawn."

"Why?"

"It's my CI acting up again."

"What's that?"

"Cop Instinct. It's kept me sniffing all around the Springs death."

Dawn smothered her annoyance. "So have you made any progress in other directions?"

He told her the checks on SHAPE staff and members were moving ahead quickly, thanks to computerization. He had already found out "some stuff" about the staff but wouldn't let on just what, only that it was "interesting." Having tantalized her, he said he was busy and had to hang up.

Dawn looked over some printouts and checked with the desk. She found hard data to prove what was already painfully obvious: participation continued to decline. Word of Sam's death must have spread rapidly, thanks to word of mouth and the media. She found Ketty's figures in the office and did some rough projections. Without any influx of money from outside, she guessed the club would have to close in six weeks or less. She began to ponder what that would mean to her. Possibly she should be less concerned now with trying to save the club than with her own post-SHAPE future. That idea, once it took root, niggled at her for the rest of the day.

Before her private workout at ten she found she was beginning to mull over Peter's offer: sell out and get out. She kept turning it over through that invigorating hour-plus, during which she drove herself harder than usual until her breath came in rasping gasps and her muscles trembled to failure.

Recovering, she summarized where she stood at that moment. She had fought to keep the club viable in the aftermath of the deaths, but after Sam's suicide yesterday, the situation looked hopeless. It was only a matter of time before SHAPE would be out of business. The club still meant a great deal to her in terms of defining her own life, but what would it mean to her as a bankrupt hulk? In the last troubled month she had grown stronger in her quiet way, but now it seemed that struggling on longer would prove a vain effort. Armies were allowed to surrender when they had been beaten, to avoid having soldiers slaughtered to the last man.

After showering with her favorite oversized sponge, she rinsed away the lather and watched it swirl down the drain. It was not hard to imagine her own life spiraling down like that as well—unless she acted.

Driving home she made her decision.

She would take Peter's offer.

She emptied the mailbox and made the long climb up to her apartment, legs weak from the long workout. She threw down her purse and exercise bag and went through the circulars, catalogs, and bills. Among them she found a first-class letter in a plain envelope with no return address. She opened it and unfolded a single sheet. On it were pasted letters cut from computer fanfold paper: "Dawn, We have destroyed the club. Now we are going to kill you for what you have done to us."

CHAPTER

13

In his office at the police annex Detective Morgan shook his head. He had made a church with the fingers on both hands and peered over it at Dawn. "Uh-uh! I don't buy it. It's the classic red herring. Put yourself in the place of the killer. He has to figure we're getting close to him. We know he stands to benefit somehow when the club goes down the tube. His motive is economic. So to put us off, he sends you the old 'Tomorrow you die' note and implies that he's a whole team. Come on, Dawn!"

"But—"

The church shifted into two pointing fingers. "You just took twenty minutes to tell me you don't have any enemies. Right?"

"Yes, but . . . these could be people I don't know! People who hate me because—because they're crazy." She was aware her voice had grown strident.

Fear would do it every time.

"The next thing you'll say is it's aliens," he said.

"That's not fair!" Dawn jumped up with her hands on her hips. "And don't treat me as if I were stupid. I'm not!" It was her turn to point. "You don't even know if poor Sam killed himself or was murdered. That's how smart you are!"

Morgan pressed his palms to the sides of his face. His

178

features shifted into a distorted mask. "Police work I picked. 'Murder,' I said. I shoulda been a priest the way Ma wanted. Then I could have a grate between me and women's problems." Before Dawn could blast him again, he went on. "I had Springs's body sent to a forensic pathologist. You know we got a coroner system in this city. Our coroner's a politician with an M.D. He takes care of the run-of-the-mill autopsies. Sometimes you don't know what kind of doc's doing the autopsies, if it's a doc at all. Could be an intern. This way maybe I'll find out something I can use."

"When will you get the report?"

He shrugged. "They said she was busy. Should be less than a week."

Dawn sat back down. "I'm telling you that note has me spooked!"

"Take it from me. According to what you said, you have nothing to worry about."

Easy for him to say, Dawn thought later as she climbed into her Honda. She looked around for anyone who appeared to be following her. Not since crazy Zack had decided he needed to keep her in sight had she spent so much time looking over her shoulder. She stopped at a vending machine and bought a newspaper. Mistake. She spotted another article on "Club Death." The Gang of Four—blast them!—had found their way to the *Dispatch*'s Ms. DiNotello, who had made the most of their enthusiastic condemnation of SHAPE and its management. "You could smell fear mixed with the sweat," she had written, quoting petite Cynthia DeForrest's hyperbole. And lots worse than that.

She threw the paper onto the passenger seat and drove the rest of the way to the club. She had scarcely slept last night, getting up every two hours to peer down at the street and check the apartment's locks. During the interludes when her fear subsided to mere anxiety, she thought about the threat, the club, and the month of dreadful deaths and worries. Her chat with Morgan had wildly churned those inner waters. Was the personal threat bogus? Was it just a red herring, as he had guaranteed? Or was it dreadfully real? How could she know? Now suspicions and dread rose from the whirlpool like drowned bodies and bobbed high for macabre attention. Last night she couldn't sort it out. Today was scarcely different. Her nerves were as tattered as a death row Bible. It was difficult to organize her thoughts, to project ahead to plans, reactions, and schemes to counter those unknown enemies of SHAPE, or possibly only of her. When she drove into the club parking lot she felt she was mooring her lifeboat to a sinking ship.

On her way to the office she scrutinized those few members and staff she passed. Which of you wants to destroy me utterly? Then she reconsidered. Why them? Why not others beyond the walls of the club whose motives were unknown and therefore more frightening? And above all, why were they killing? Was the true target of the attack the club, as Morgan had assured her, or was it Dawn herself? Her head spun with anxiety and worry thickened by lack of sleep. She whimpered softly and swallowed hard against tears of self-pity.

She wanted to tell Peter what had happened. As usual he was late. She was too nervous to sit still. She went looking for Jeff, but he wasn't in his massage studio, nor was hardworking Beth to be found. Maybe her secret admirer had declared himself and they were swimming elsewhere in seas of love. She held that idea for a while: Beth having a lover. Then, as she had yesterday, she wondered if it could be Peter. Her imagination danced away from little Beth and stayed with Peter.

Peter, who wanted to buy the club because it bothered his conscience to think that she might lose her substantial financial investment. Peter who had taken the humiliating step of going to his parents to ask for the money to buy her out. If he had an ulterior motive, what was it? What good was a club with diminishing membership and an increasingly shaky financial future, not to mention the reputation of a gulag? *No* good, that's what. Maybe there was oil on the property, or perhaps the city was going to put a highway through the site.

There was yet another complicating condition—her partner's sexism. Oh, he covered it with a thin patina of even-mindedness when she was concerned. Her recently successful efforts to stand up to him had made that necessary. Deep down, though, he imagined he handled business matters better when she wasn't involved. He could be up to something he wasn't yet prepared to reveal to her. He would do so when he thought the time was ripe. He had done so on several occasions previously.

Her suspicions grew and took root. Suppose that for some reason getting control of the club was what he wanted, no matter that it might by then be on its last legs. Maybe several months ago he had found himself stymied. He wanted control of the club, but couldn't figure out how to get it. Then Eloise had died, truly by accident, and maybe Nicole, too. It was possible that two people could drown without any deadly assistance. Seeing it happen had given him ideas. If another person were to be murdered, the drownings would appear to be murders, too. Whatever he had to gain was so significant that he took the desperate chance of tampering with the tanning machine and poisoning the juice. After that he had offered for the first time to buy her out. She remembered she had surprised herself with her unwillingness to sell. Then she had begun to understand how much the club meant to her, how much it was tied up with her growing self-esteem and assertiveness. Of course she couldn't sell! So he had been forced to turn up the morbid pressure a notch.

Yes, yes, it was falling into place now. Whatever was valuable about SHAPE Sam had discovered and told Healthways. That was the real reason Kelso Capozzi was willing to offer Sam a vice presidency in exchange for bringing SHAPE into the fold. By killing Sam, Peter had eliminated the immediate Healthways threat and further diminished SHAPE's value. On reflection she grasped that all the roadblocks were out of his way now—except her. She had stubbornly refused his steadily improving offers. He had two choices. The first was to frighten her so badly that she would sell out and move away. The second was to murder her. The note had been the next-to-last step in his campaign. Either she would be spooked and would flee, or he would kill her. And he would do it in the club, where her death would tie up all his schemes like a package with the red ribbons of her blood. She gripped the edge of the desk and stared at the door. He could come through it and kill her right there!

She fought for control. No, not with people at the front desk. Not when she could scream. He would have to get her alone. That could be easy. Then, when she looked away for an instant—no, no! Not yet. He wouldn't do it so quickly. Not before he was convinced that the note hadn't done its job. Without realizing it at once, she was on her feet and pacing around the desk. It all fit together. Where she would take it from there she'd have to ponder with great care. One small detail, though, bothered her more than its seeming importance. Why had he used "we" in his note?

She would explain all this to Detective Morgan. She rushed over to the phone. With the receiver in her hand she hesitated. How many other times had she called the lieutenant, crying wolf? She had been so sure each time. Zack and Sam had *seemed* like logical suspects. So she had been wrong. But not this time! Not with Peter. He had the best motive—a pile of money. Loot, not love, as Morgan would put it. Still she hesitated. Be bold, she told herself. She knew she could persuade Morgan that Peter was a far better suspect than the other two men. It wouldn't take the veteran cop long to assemble the evidence needed to arrest and prosecute her partner.

Yes! She would call. She dialed the precinct house. Morgan wasn't there. She left a message to return her call.

Then she thought about her own safety. She would stall Peter when he again raised the subject of buying her out. That would keep him at bay for a while. After that . . . She thought first of carrying a weapon, but couldn't trust herself to use one effectively. Of course she would avoid being alone with him. But in the club he could manage to get her alone, regardless of her evasive action.

She needed a bodyguard.

Whom could she trust? It boiled down to two: Karl and Jeff. Or was it just one? She had to admit that her relationship with Jeff was strained. To her great shame she still wasn't positive he wasn't somehow involved in all her difficulties, even as she assembled Peter's motives. Karl, however, was simpleminded in his loyalty to the club and, in a sense, to her. She could trust him. She would give him an edited version of the reasons for her anxiety. He could easily meet her when she entered the club, hang around her for the day, then see her out. If he wasn't available, she'd stay home. And she would keep it up until the police arrested Peter.

Yes, Karl was the much better bet.

She found him in the weight room, bench-pressing metal disks lined up like Life Savers on the bar. A buddy hovered over him in case his arms suddenly gave out. She didn't interrupt until they had finished. Karl sat up red-faced, sweat darkening the yoke of his tank top. She took him to a private corner and proposed that he be her on-site bodyguard. She realized as he frowned, the wrinkles working up his thick forehead till it furrowed like a washed-out road, that it hadn't occurred to her that he might refuse.

"How come you aren't asking Jeff?" he growled. His light gray eyes dug into her face.

"Jeff? Well, I . . . thought you'd do a better job."

"I noticed you and Mr. Skinny are pretty thick."

"Not as thick as you seem to think, Karl."

He stepped closer. "Anybody tries to touch you, I'll kill him!" His low tones were more threatening than a shout.

"I don't want you to misunderstand—"

His loglike arms went around her and pulled her against him. In the instant before he kissed her she understood his dogged loyalty and his long hours at SHAPE. His devotion wasn't to the club. It was to her! She didn't turn her lips away as soon as she should have. She supposed there was some attraction there, as far as she was concerned, but not enough. His sweaty bulk meant a degree of safety. When she finally freed her mouth, she continued the request that her actions had already rendered counterfeit.

"Don't misunderstand why I'm asking you this favor."

"I'm not misunderstanding anything." His heated glance told her he was indeed.

Dawn's face reddened. She hadn't intended to lead him on with even the vaguest unspoken promise, but it seemed she had done just that. And it wasn't fair! She didn't intend to keep any "promises" to Karl whatsoever. It wasn't her fault she had misled him. She wasn't thinking clearly.

She was afraid.

Going back upstairs, she understood she had complicated her life. The man had admired her from afar but had kept his distance when she was sailing along happily. Trouble had somehow either lowered her standards or raised her opinion of him. Or maybe trouble had reduced their lives to a simpler level: she was the endangered female; he, the loyal brute. Karl was more than loyal. She would have had to be utterly naive not to see that he had been hoarding love for her like the most committed miser.

Color fading from her face, she understood that she had contracted for more than safety. Quite against her will, she had made a deal for still more trouble, though she couldn't then guess how it would come or what part adoring Karl would play.

Rather than being comforted, she found herself more frightened. She sensed that a net had been cast for her. Earlier it had been made up of distant unconnected patches. Now it was being drawn up. Its strands grew thicker. Unless she or the police quickly figured out what was happening, the net would ensnare her completely. She would be dragged into the core of threatened violence and crushed.

So intent was she on the looming dread that she turned a corner and nearly bumped into Hector Sturm and Dinah. She heard the redhead saying, "I'm sorry. I'm not interested. Sam's only been dead—" She cut her words short until Dawn passed. Dawn's eyes caught Hector's, saw the old intensity burning bright. She was delighted that his gaze had absolutely no effect on her. To be sure her personal problems had something to do with that. Yet there was more behind her coolness. Her mind had fully processed how he really felt about her, and about all women: he saw them as pleasure toys. Oh, but didn't he know how to play the game of romance! He knew all there was to that dance—except the deep, true heart of it. Now he had discovered another woman to be his partner, but Dinah was demurring.

Dawn smiled wryly. The ambitious redhead was playing a cunning game. She had tried to ride poor Sam up to fame and fortune. Hard luck there! At the moment Sam was of more use to her dead than he had been alive without the "right stuff." He was her excuse for putting off panting Hector. When the gray fox's appetite was whetted to a fine edge, Dinah would modestly consent to his attentions. Unlike Dawn, who had asked for little from the man, Dinah would go into the relationship wearing a miner's helmet, ready to dig all the gold she could carry.

At the office door Dawn came to a halt. Peter had come in. His well-groomed head shrieked menace; his sharply tailored gray suit might as well have been executioner's black. She should have asked Karl to go on duty five minutes ago.

Peter glanced up. "We've got to talk about more staff cuts," he said.

"If you want."

He nodded toward the door. "You want to close that?"

Fear darted like a scurrying animal into her chest. "No. I don't. I'd rather talk somewhere else."

"About staff cuts?" He frowned. "Where people can hear?"

She swallowed. Did fear have a taste? "Not here," she breathed. "I don't feel like being closed in." She found she couldn't take the chance that he would wait until he was sure she wouldn't sell the club to kill her. From this moment forward she would panic at his presence.

As they talked, she studied his face: the rapid eye movements, the solid cheeks set above the square jaw. One could read nothing there about his murderous tendencies. Like that of a baby-faced killer on TV, his lethal nature was curled in the curving coral of his brain. She couldn't bear being in his company. He would have to be exposed and arrested as soon as possible. Luckily he was in one of his officious moods, when the shell of his equal-partnership mode cracked away to reveal his demanding business side. He laid out a last-ditch holding action in terms of staffing and scarcely noticed her distracted state. She answered in monosyllables, aware that tiny beads of sweat dotted her upper lip. At the earliest practical moment she rushed off.

There was a page for her: Detective Morgan had returned her call. Before she had spoken four sentences, he said, "You better come down here. We have some things to talk over."

She hurried outside and got into her Honda. Protesting yet another sub-freezing day, the car refused to start. She ground away at the starter. Just as the battery was about to die, the ignition caught. She arrived at police headquarters vexed, nervous, and chilled.

Morgan took one look at her and sent a clerk after coffee. "Make it black, heavy sugar," he said. To Dawn: "And you're going to drink it. It has therapeutic value."

She burst into her news at once. "I've figured it all out: it's *Peter* who's behind everything! I had to sit beside him and— Small wonder I'm upset!"

"Hold it, hold it!" He held up his hands. "Now *I* need coffee."

She sipped the black brew and relaxed a bit.

He leaned forward. Under his lined brow his narrow eyes were bright with excitement. "I think we're finally getting somewhere in this case, Dawn."

"So you think Peter is guilty, too? How did you figure that out?"

"I didn't say I did. Let's hear your thinking, start to finish."

When she had finished, he nodded with satisfaction. "That jibes with what I've found out. I think we can safely consider him one of our suspects."

Dawn blinked. "*One* of the suspects. Who are the others? Why do you—"

"Easy!" He raised his hands again. "Give me a chance to talk."

"I can't help it! My nerves are a wreck, and I don't do Valium." She held the coffee mug in both hands, warming them. "So . . . talk."

He leaned back and smiled. "Have you ever thought what great gadgets computers are, Dawn? Great tools for gumshoes. They work fast, they don't make mistakes, and they don't forget. We ran all your club people through a few law-enforcement networks. You'd be surprised how many of them have come to police attention one way or another. Most of them in ways that have nothing to do with your club and its problems."

"But some that do?"

He drank coffee. "Three of your staff, to be precise."

"Who?"

"Your partner, Peter Faldo, first."

Morgan explained that Peter had been connected with a semilegal stock fund. It had turned belly up, and hundreds of retired people had lost their money. Century 22 Investments had been designed from the start to do just that. Two of the swindle victims had committed suicide. Many others were ruined. Peter and his pals had taken refuge behind a hedge of securities laws and were narrowly acquitted. "The whole scheme was nasty, Dawn. Mean-spirited and wicked. How far is it from there to killing to get control of a profitable health club?"

Her partner! The man she had trusted with her inheritance. How could she have been so naive? "You've got to bring him in here for questioning!"

"Not just him." He picked up a sheet torn from a fan-fold printout. "We also have some stuff on a . . . Karl Clausman and a guy called Jeff Bently."

She gasped. Karl! *Jeff?*

"Clausman went fag bashing—literally. He and some buddies worked over a gay guy in New York. The victim didn't take it the right way. He died. The D.A. must have been on vacation and sent law clerks to prosecute the case. Clausman got eight years, but was out in four. Many words here on 'the viciousness of the crime and the remorselessness of the criminals.' "

And she had tasted his kiss! Dawn thought. And asked him to be her bodyguard. Nice to know he would kill to protect her—or kill *her,* if he was the one who'd made the threat. She sank down in her chair, felt as though it was swallowing her up.

Was no one she knew the way he appeared? She felt as though she might pass out from the weight of dark revelations. "And Jeff?"

"He has a long, long record as an anti."

"What's that?"

"Anti-everything. Anticapitalist. Antibusiness. Antiprofit of any kind. He was a demonstrator, a saboteur, maybe a bomb-setter."

"Oh . . . no. He told me he had been a stockbroker!"

"No way!" Morgan laughed and checked his sheet. "He was the opposite of a stockbroker. Antinuke protester. High up in one of the antinuclear organizations. At a sit-in some of his people got roughed up by counterdemonstrators. He went cuckoo, did his Bruce Lee thing. By the time six officers pulled him down and pounded him silly, he had dished out broken legs, chests, jaws, skulls. One guy died." He looked sharply at her. "When they tried to send him to Slammer City, he squirmed out. The shrinks said he was a nut. He got sent to a country-club mental institution. When things quieted down, he got released. That was . . . uh, five years ago. So he washed up on your island."

Dawn's mind raced, overloaded with this new information. What did it all mean? Did it mean that Peter wasn't the killer? But he was! She was certain of it.

Morgan picked up another sheet. "Preliminary forensic tests showed some drug traces in Sam Springs's body. No pills. No needle marks. They're still working on it."

Dawn let her arms dangle limply. She knew she didn't want to try to stand just then. "How in the world am I going to live my life?" She heard the petulant edge to her voice and didn't care. "Someone maybe wants to kill me and I'm surrounded by amateur murderers. My partner is a con man. I mean *what the hell am I going to do?*" The detective made soothing noises. For a moment Dawn felt her self-control slipping. Uh-uh! Time to suck it up. She was *not* going to play Weeping Wanda. Things were bad, but she would get through them. She took a deep breath, made herself stand, and exhaled slowly. The distant urge to cry faded. She asked

Morgan if their chat was about over. When he said it was, she told him she was going back to the club.

"I'm not sure that's a good idea," he said.

"Well, I'm going there anyway."

Once at SHAPE she prescribed the best medicine she knew for shaky nerves: aerobics and a Nautilus circuit. She pushed herself hard at both, until good fatigue descended on her like a blanket. She stayed long under a hot shower. Home at last, she descended into the oblivion of healthy sleep.

Morgan had asked that she call him the next morning to tell him how she was feeling. After she told him she felt just fine, he told her she ought to stay out of the club until the murders were solved.

"How long will that be?"

"Dunno. Weeks? Days? Beats me."

She hesitated. The rest had cleared her mind. She felt less oppressed, more capable of helping determine her fate. "I want you to answer me honestly, Monty. After all your computer told you, do you still think the death threat I got is a red herring?"

"Do Clausman and Bently have anything against you?"

"I don't think so."

"Your partner's a shady mother, but he's not a killer."

"Oh, yes, he is! I know it! He'll kill me to get control of the club."

Morgan paused for a long moment. "I don't think I'm wrong, Dawn, but I'm not going to argue with you now. Why take a chance? Stay out of the club."

"It's my club! It's not dead yet. I can help keep it going by being there at work until you find out who's killing people and why."

"I don't recommend it," he advised.

At another, earlier time Dawn would have done as she was told. Madam Wishy-Washy, sure enough. That Dawn was history, thank goodness. The current model was a little more daring and a lot more willing to confront her enemies.

For that reason, immediately after arriving at the club she corralled Beth and with her went to Jeff's massage studio. He was in session. Beth wanted to know what was going on. "You're my safety valve and witness," Dawn said to the small woman. "What you're going to hear is confidential. Got it?"

"I didn't know the confessional opened this early."

When Jeff emerged, Dawn rushed at him and blurted out his history in disordered fragments. Beth's eyes widened when Dawn got to the mental-institution segment. Jeff grew paler with every moment, his long face twisting with discomfort. "I want everything between you, me, and SHAPE out in the open," Dawn said. "I want to know where your head is after all you've gone through."

"I don't really have to say anything," he said. "I could tell you both to beat it."

"Things need to be cleared up," Dawn said. "I think this is the time."

"I could lie."

"I know you well enough to tell."

"Do you?" What did that little smile mean? Dawn wondered. Jeff closed the door and began to talk. At first he drew out the words with a hesitancy suggesting each caused him pain. Then they came faster.

His eyes met Dawn's. She understood that he was speaking to her heart, a long overdue unburdening. He had been everything the police had told her. During recent years he had been busy, though, making himself into a largely different person. Counseling, therapy, and reflection, not to mention aging, had mellowed him. He had regained stability, and he felt confident that it would continue. Yes, he remained an outsider, but that wasn't necessarily bad. His efforts to start a business under SHAPE's umbrella had been a bigger step for him than she knew. Harboring hatred and a grudge against her?

Quite the opposite. He thought that during certain private moments with her he had made that obvious.

Carried this far by her determination to eliminate him as a suspect, Dawn now felt her face redden. It occurred to her what inner price he was paying to answer her request. She could no longer meet his gaze. She turned to Beth, who was already looking at her. The smaller woman's violet eyes blazed with an intensity difficult to interpret. Was that anger? Had her illusions about Jeff been brutally dashed? Possibly she thought he no longer deserved to be part of the health club or the Dawn Patrol. For a fleeting moment Dawn wondered if Beth had hoped he was her unknown admirer and found his confession of affection to Dawn painful.

Dawn felt then that she owed her two friends an explanation of her behavior. From her purse she took the message threatening her life and gave it to them to read. "Do you wonder why I'm a wreck, guys? Huh?"

Jeff and Beth looked up from the note with startled expressions.

After swearing them to secrecy she revealed her suspicions about Peter, his motivations, and his possible role in the deaths. She left out nothing, not even the revolver in his desk. She felt the note was his handiwork. What did they think?

Jeff surprised her when he said, "I told you earlier, Dawn. This whole business isn't what it seems."

"Your theories again," Dawn said. "I'm still waiting to hear just what they are."

"I'm not ready to tell you yet. Everything you've just explained has to be worked in."

Her old annoyance surged. "I hope your mental computer runs to end-of-job before I get killed!"

Beth said, "Why should you be the only person in danger, Dawn? Maybe the murderer will kill a few more people before he gets to you. This place is getting positively scary! I think it's time for me to find a job somewhere else. I'm the loyal type, but this is ridiculous!"

Dawn and Jeff took time to try to talk her out of leaving. Eventually they were trading gallows humor, gibes, and friendly insults. It simply wasn't possible to continue forever in a dark emotional mood. They splurged on a pizza, had it delivered, and sat in the office gorging. Some of Dawn's tension evaporated. She believed what Jeff had told her about himself. At least he was one person she could now trust, no matter his mysterious, irritating theories. She kept what she knew about Karl to herself. How to handle *his* past was unclear. She was certain of one thing: she wanted him nearby when Peter was in the club.

The next day Karl sat down next to her while she was forking up lunch pasta from a take-out container. "Mind if I eat my apple with you?" She glanced up. Since she had allowed him to kiss her, their previously business-like relationship had suffered. She wasn't sure what that meant to her. She didn't believe there could ever be a romantic connection between them. At the same time, she suspected she had sold him short as a dim-witted muscle man. She was beginning to understand that his mind was active, but that he generally chose to keep silent. She wished he'd show some of the flashes of wit and humor that characterized Jeff's interaction with her. She shook off such thoughts. What was she trying to do—make up an ideal man from the parts on hand?

Karl bit into his Golden Delicious. He had large white teeth that crunched the fruit's flesh. Flecks of juice flew. "I want to talk to you about some things, Dawn."

"Go ahead."

"Not now and not here."

"What kind of things?" She studied his wide, solid face set on a neck so thick it looked as though his head grew straight up from his shoulders. She felt confirmed in her choice of bodyguard.

"The kind of things that go better slow and someplace else." He told her his parents lived in Maine, about five hours north. He had talked about bringing a guest up for the weekend to go ice fishing. His father's fishing shack was out on the lake. His arthritis was bothering him, and he hadn't used it much. She should come. She needed to get away from the club.

He didn't know just how true that was. Without hesitation, she told him about the threatening note and dug it out of her purse. She didn't tell him she thought Peter had sent it. And wisely so. As before, his expression darkened at the thought of someone wanting to harm her. "Come with me this weekend and you won't have to worry, at least for a couple days."

Her conscience made her determined to be fair. "If I say yes, Karl, I don't want you to misunderstand."

He looked baffled. "About what?"

"That if I go, I go as a friend. Nothing more."

"What's that mean, Dawn?"

"It means no love stuff."

"Oh, yeah?" His grin convinced her still more that he wasn't a lug. "Love-shlove, we got to talk," he said.

She then agreed to spend the weekend with him and was surprised when he told her she didn't have to take layers and layers of clothing with her. "There's ice fishing. Then there's *ice fishing*," he said.

No sooner had they made final arrangements and parted than Jeff found Dawn. He wanted to take her to a rock concert on Saturday night. She told him why she couldn't go. To her surprise, his face reflected displeasure. "I wouldn't think you two had too much in common."

"He's a good-hearted guy, Jeff. He cares about me. It won't hurt to go home with him for a weekend."

"I can't believe that gorilla's my rival now that Hector's history." He was leaning forward into her personal space. "Just for the record, I don't approve."

Her nerves and patience weren't what they once were. "Just for the record, I don't care," she snapped back. "The last time I checked, nobody was supervising my personal relationships. I don't remember asking you to, Jeff."

"I thought I meant something to you." Behind his metal-rimmed glasses his eyes carried a hurt look.

"You do." She touched his arm. "Look, Karl said he has some important things to talk to me about. I think they're about what's been happening here at SHAPE."

"I don't think you should go with him."

"Why?"

"I don't think he can be trusted."

"You have some proof of that? Maybe part of one of your theories that you won't tell me about?"

"Just a gut feeling."

"Sometimes I don't think you can be trusted, either, Jeff." She turned and hurried away. He didn't follow. What she said was true. Yesterday she had thought that, despite his past, she could rely on him. Today she wasn't sure. What she was sure of was that she couldn't continue to live her life this way. Off again, on again. It wasn't fair to her friends, and it was hell on her nerves—never mind her social life. Not all of them could be guilty. Or could they? The threatening note had said "we."

The route to Karl's home was a straight run up interstate and turnpike, then a few wiggles along side roads. Though it was March, winter kept its solid grip on the state of Maine. Graying snowbanks still lined the roads like dunes. As they hadn't been able to leave the club until late afternoon, they made most of the trip in darkness. The distance they traveled from the city comforted her. She hadn't been away since Eloise had died more than a month ago.

After getting out of the car in front of Karl's parents' sprawling white frame house, she stretched and drew deep breaths of the crisp air. Above, stars showered the clear sky like spilled sugar.

Mrs. Clausman welcomed her like a daughter. She was a round-faced, energetic woman who kept house with Germanic enthusiasm and care. Karl's father was a graying version of his son, with arms or thick as trunks and shoulders wide enough for plow harnesses. They had held dinner in Dawn's honor. Now they all sat down to hearty beef, potatoes, and dark beer. Mrs. Clausman had made strudel from scratch, dough and all. Dawn had to have a piece. She rose from the table, drowsiness descending like a curtain. Karl led her up to one of the many bedrooms, furnished with down-filled comforters and knickknacks. Later when she was nightgowned, scrubbed, and ready for bed, he came back to tell her that she had impressed his folks.

"Tell them thanks," she said. "Thank you for bringing me up here. I like the change."

She saw the earnest affection on his heavy face. She gave him a light kiss on the lips. Gratitude for relief, however temporary, from her tensions and fears, she supposed. He touched her shoulder briefly, then said good night.

The fresh air sent her quickly into the soundest sleep. She started awake sometime during the deepest part of the night. Dream or dread had demolished drowsiness like a bomb. She sat up, coverlet clutched in her fingers. She strained to hear anything in the silent house. She rose, dragging the coverlet with her like a train, and walked to the window. She opened the heavy curtains.

The moonlight shone down on the snow-covered lawn. At its rear edge a distant stand of pines rose in shadow. For a moment she thought someone stood there amid snow-bent branches. No, no! There couldn't be! Not here. She blinked and looked again, and saw no one. She jerked the curtains closed and went back to bed. Instead of sleeping, she thrashed until dawn. She heard Mrs. Clausman rise and begin the day's household rituals. The moment Dawn smelled coffee she was up to stay.

Ice fishing, Clausman style, was nothing like roughing it. Their property backed up on a vast windswept lake bounded by expanses of pine. A quarter mile offshore stood their ice-fishing "shack," as Karl called it. As far as Dawn was concerned, it was more like a lodge, complete with wood stove, a bunk, table and chairs, and a Coleman stove. An ice auger, powered like a lawn mower, stood in a corner. Racks held rods, reels, and other fishing paraphernalia. A wide bin was loaded with stove-size oak logs. As Karl knelt to start a fire, she told him what she might she have seen from her window.

"No way, Dawn," he said quickly. "You're in Clausman Land now. No need to sweat it."

"I really might have seen someone, Karl! Honestly."

"You didn't. Not up here. Relax."

She thought it over and supposed he was right. "I really wasn't sure anyway."

Was she trying to convince herself? Who would stand out in the bitter Maine cold at 4:00 A.M. some 250 miles from SHAPE and stare up at her window. No one sane, that was for sure!

She and Karl spent the day fishing and talking. She found herself trying to determine just how bright Karl was and how much he knew. It was a playful game that she thought she might continue all weekend. She asked him leading questions, which he obligingly answered for the sake of conversation. He filled her in on his past: junior college, modest ambitions, and the importance of SHAPE to his life. She saw through his lies of omission, but forgave him. She made him sit beside her on the bunk.

"I know about your involvement in a murder, Karl," she said, "and I know you went to jail for it."

He couldn't look at her. His eyes fell to his boots. "Who told you? The cops?"

"Yeah."

"I paid for that, Dawn. Society and me are square. I don't do any of that wild stuff anymore. I learned my lesson." She read his affection for her amid his embarrassment as clearly as a billboard announcement.

"I believe you. People make mistakes." She didn't want him glum. "You're not the only one, either. I happen to know Jeff Bently lost his head once, and the result was a death."

Karl's thick shoulders heaved with surprise. His glance rose and met hers. His eyes were wide. "Then what I said I wanted to tell you makes even more sense."

"It's about Jeff?"

He nodded, rose, and went to the potbellied stove, where he busied himself with poker and wood. "Remember that time I almost caught him sneaking around at night?"

"He admitted to me he did it. He just wouldn't say why."

"Well, since then I've been keeping my eye on him." He turned to Dawn, the poker like a stick of black spaghetti in his huge fist. "I've seen him snooping all over the club. He's been places I don't think he belonged."

"Like where?"

"He was on the third level when Springs took the plunge."

Dawn gasped. "Are you saying—"

"He was up there. I was sort of keeping an eye on him. I'm not saying he was near where Springs went over, but I'm not saying he wasn't, either. I lost track of him."

Dawn was quick to understand that meant Karl was up there, too. Her mind made a quick leap: only he had the strength to overcome Sam's resistance and heave him over the banister. Hold on, Dawn Gray! She told her paranoia to take a vacation. Karl was too straightforward to practice the kind of criminal deceit it would take to carry off this weekend, never mind construct the deadly web in which she sensed herself ensnared. He had absolutely no motive. He was a good-natured muscle man with a crush on her—and nothing more. Of course, she was discovering him to be quite a bit brighter than she had first thought . . .

"Where else did you see Jeff that you didn't think he belonged?"

"Snooping around the Jacuzzi and the tanning machine before they came and took it away."

"This was after Eloise and Nicole died?"

He nodded. "And I saw him in the trainer's room when Beth wasn't there."

"What was he doing?"

"Messing with the medicine and stuff she keeps in there. Maybe stealing some of it, I thought."

Dawn sat back on the bunk. Medicine? Drugs? Beth wasn't a doctor. She couldn't have much of anything like that on hand. Nonetheless, suppose Jeff had stolen something. . . . She found herself beginning to suspect him again, and only hours before, she had felt he was the one man she could trust. She vexed herself with her vacillation. She wanted to apologize somehow to Jeff; it was fear that made her so paranoid and capricious. At that moment the only man she trusted seemed to be Karl.

Contributing to that trust was their relative isolation on a Maine lake, staying warm and comfortable while pulling up an occasional fat perch. She wanted this idyll to go on and on. Wanted to keep her ever-increasing fears for her club and her life at a distance as long as possible. I'm safe here, she thought, and I love it! "I want to spend the night here, Karl," she said. She started issuing warnings against misunderstanding her intentions.

He cut her short. "Whatever you want is fine with me. I'm just glad to be with you."

Mrs. Clausman cooked their fish and served a heaping platter of batter-fried fillets that the four of them couldn't finish. Dawn helped with the dishes. As her hostess chattered, Dawn absorbed the warmth and tidiness of the kitchen, the house, and, when she thought of it, the whole Down East life-style, or at least that part of it practiced by the Clausmans. Even so, Karl had once left this wholesome nest and gone on to kill a man and do time.

Mr. Clausman roused himself from his mostly silent style and sent the couple back to the shack with a half-gallon of "glog," his own recipe mixing wine and spices. They were to heat it on the Coleman stove, sip slowly, and enjoy. The back door of the house would be open, in case they needed to use the bathroom. There were flashlights in the shack. He sent them on their way with a chuckle.

After a few small cups of glog, Dawn and Karl discovered they both liked to sing. Under the light of the hanging kerosene lanterns they ran through their patchy repertoires. They sang duets with increasing enthusiasm as the glog supply dwindled. He had a solid untrained baritone. Her unreliable alto had been the bane of more than one church choir. They crooned, belted, caroled, and chorused. When finally they grew hoarse, they curled up fully clothed under a comforter and fell asleep.

Dawn woke later and looked at her watch. It was 2:00 A.M., and she had to go to the bathroom. She slipped away from Karl's bulk, slid into her boots, down vest, and gloves, and quietly left the shack. The lake was windswept. A sliver of moon did little to light her way. She switched on a flashlight as she made her way over the ice toward the house. The heavy sheet groaned beneath, startling her. It was far too thick to break. The sound, though, had a human voice tone to it. She walked faster, feeling herself becoming unnerved over nothing.

After using the bathroom, she thought for a moment about not going back to the shack, instead curling up in the soft bed she had so enjoyed last night. She hesitated. Karl hadn't asked much in exchange for his kindness and concern. The least she could do was finish out the night beside him.

Bundling up again, she stepped out of the house and

headed for the lake. She had nearly reached the shore when she recalled seeing—or imagining—a figure the previous night. It would have been in the copse only a few yards from where she now walked. She hadn't thought about that on the way to the house. Now it bothered her. She walked faster. The wind was blowing off the lake. She held up a gloved hand to protect her face. The ice groaned again, and she gasped. She broke into a clumsy run in the direction of the shack.

From somewhere behind her, tossed like a leaf on the wind, she heard a high, eerie cry: "Da-a-a-a-wn. Da-a-a-a-wn!"

She bleated with surprise. Trying to run faster, she slipped on the ice and spun down onto her knees. She screamed. "Karl! Help me!"

"Da-a-a-a-wn . . ."

"Karl!" Ahead, the shack door stayed closed.

She scrambled up and ran with panicked speed over what now seemed like a thousand yards of ice. She flung herself at the door and tumbled into the warmth and yellow light.

Karl wasn't there!

Certain that someone was coming after her, she looked for a lock.

The door didn't have one.

She clutched the smooth cast-iron latch, knowing she couldn't hold it against a determined push. She stood there panting, feeling foolish that she couldn't figure out what else to do. Her panic soared. She was alone, defenseless, and someone was stalking her. Where was Karl? Had he been disposed of in her absence? Now she was utterly alone and . . .

She heard boots crunching on patches of snow! Someone was walking toward the shack. The murderer was coming for her!

She let go of the latch, whirled, and snatched up the poker. The footsteps paused at the far side of the shack for several moments. She stood with the poker over her head, arms quivering with anticipation. Her heart pounded, and her breath came in shallow gasps. She wasn't going down without a fight!

The steps came doorward. The latch was raised. The door swung open. She swung the poker down. Halfway into her blow she saw she was going to smash Karl's skull. She tried to stop herself. The poker glanced off his wool cap.

"Ow!" Rage flashed in his gray eyes. He twisted the poker from her two-handed grip with frightening ease. "What the hell are you doing, woman?"

"Where were you?" she shouted. "Why weren't you here?"

He frowned, looked at her and then at the poker. "You woke me up when you left. I had to take a leak, too. I didn't bother going to the house."

"You all right?" Her voice was kitten-weak.

He took off his cap and brushed fingers across his scalp. "No blood. Guess I'm okay. You mind telling me what the hell you're doing hitting me?"

"Somebody's out there, Karl. They're after me."

"Come on!"

"I heard somebody call my name by the house!"

"Who?"

"I don't know. It was a high, crazy sound."

"You sure?"

"Yes! Stop looking at me as if you think I'm crazy!"

He sagged down on the bunk shaking his head. "I think your imagination's working overtime." He touched his head again. "Good thing you can't hurt a German by hitting him on the head."

"I don't need jokes!"

He raised his wide shoulders in an expansive shrug. "What *do* you need, Dawn Gray?"

"No more comments about my imagination, for starters. Next, you stay right here with me until morning. And don't budge."

"You got it. I have to say I really don't think there's anybody out there."

"Fine, you said it!" she snapped.

Neither of them slept much. In the end they lay awake waiting for morning light. Karl wanted to leave the shack at dawn, but she insisted they wait until it was bright.

They stepped out onto ice ablaze with sunlight. Dawn squinted and took Karl's arm. "Morning never looked so good," she said. A few yards from the shack she turned back to look it over for the last time. She and Karl had agreed they would spend the rest of Sunday touring the area before the drive home. She saw a bit of paper clinging to the wall of the shack. She went back. Out of the wind, pierced by two rusting nails, was a note written in pencil in block letters: "NEXT WEEK WE ARE GOING TO KILL DAWN GRAY."

CHAPTER
14

The rest of Sunday was ruined. Dawn had to contend with the icy chill that invaded her spine, making the bitter Maine March seem mild in comparison. Once there it wouldn't be dislodged by the elder Clausman's optimistic pronouncement that the note had been a prank. He didn't know the long, somber prelude leading to it, nor could he grasp what its appearance meant: that someone had followed her Down East to this idyllic spot to terrify her. The willingness to trek up in her wake and hover outdoors through at least parts of two cold nights illuminated the determination of her enemies as effectively as the moonlit snowscape. "We" are going to kill you. She had glimpsed only one solitary figure among the trees. No matter. They were closing in on her and had given her a week to live!

She would have liked to have Karl comfort her, but the note had cast its dark power over him as well, sparking in him an incredible rage against those who wished to harm her. He seemed to swell up like a rooster. Neck cords stood out, and color rose in his face. Never loquacious, he could scarcely speak even hours afterward. When he did, it was to mutter a long litany of promised revenge that rolled on like the landscape along the road south. He felt no bewilderment about who stood behind the note and all the trouble that had come before it—Jeff Bently.

Despite the morbid funk in which she swam, she managed a flash of annoyance. "Jeff isn't the one you should be angry with, Karl," she said sharply. The reason was that she suspected Peter far more than Jeff. Peter had a motive: he wanted the club for whatever reason. Not so, Jeff. Why, then, for heaven's sake, didn't she trust the man completely? Squirm as she did, she had to admit she didn't. Her intuition again—and what had that been worth? Peter was the guilty one. He was the man they'd soon arrest. She sighed aloud and decided that it was appropriate to defend Jeff. "He and I are close friends. He has no reason to wish me harm."

"I didn't tell you everything about him," Karl said.

"What did you leave out?" More tension crept into her neck.

"He loves you. He told me once when we went out drinking together. He was almost trashed. That's when he said it. He also said that he'd never really mean anything to you as long as you had the club in your life. He's sorry that you're the kind of woman who doesn't need to be taken care of. You take care of yourself."

"That hardly proves—"

"He said he'd do anything to get you."

"Karl, some people want to *kill* me. If I'm dead I can't be loved by anybody."

"You're making sense. But Jeff Bently isn't about sense. He was in the loony bin, you know."

"Well, at one time he had problems, but—"

"So why couldn't they come back?"

"Karl . . ."

"If you want, I'll stay with you twenty-four hours a day."

She shook her head. "I know how you feel about me, Karl. I just don't think that would be wise. In the club, though, I want you near all the time."

"I want to be there when Bently tries something!"

Dawn didn't bother to caution the big man about over-reacting and jumping to conclusions, at both of which he was unhappily proving himself an expert. Jeff guilty? That was absurd! Peter was the murderer. She had to keep reminding herself. But . . . could Jeff . . . ? Despite herself her memory served up yet another slice of their intimate hours together. She stifled a groan. Could he do those things with her one day, then want to kill her the next? It couldn't be! Peter! Her suspicions should be concentrated on Peter.

Of all Karl's suspicions about Jeff, only one really seemed to have caught in her craw. It concerned his having seen the massage therapist rummaging in the training room medicine cabinet. The loose end that she hadn't earlier in the weekend been able to grasp now came readily to hand. Detective Morgan had said drug traces were found in Sam's body.

When she called Detective Morgan on Monday morning she didn't talk first about drugs. She told him about her trip to Maine and the note and asked him what she should do. He said she should avoid being alone, stay in the company of trusted people.

"I can't do that all the time," she said. "What about when I have to be alone."

"Be careful."

"Thanks!"

"I gave you advice. I told you to stay away from the club."

"I did this weekend, didn't I?" she snapped. "How much good did it do?" They came two hundred fifty miles to threaten me." Her voice rose despite her effort to control it. "Are you going to find out who wants me dead—or what?"

"We're working on it."

"I want police protection!"

"You and fifty other people I could name without thinking about it. You got your own friendly ox there, right? The fag-basher?"

"He's much more than that! Anyhow, he did his five years in jail. He's paid his debt."

"Take it easy, Dawn."

She asked him if he had found out anything more about the drug in Sam's body. The lab was still working on it, he said, but it looked as if it belonged in the family of muscle relaxants, possibly taken orally. The pathologist hadn't yet had time to go over the body again. He'd let her know when he knew more.

She went downstairs to the trainer's room to ask Beth what kind of medicines and drugs she kept in the cabinet, but she wasn't there. Karl hovered outside the door, standing guard. She was surprised to find the two-door medicine cabinet unlocked. Couldn't be anything very dangerous in there if Beth didn't bother to lock it. She opened the doors and peered in. Plenty of recognizable over-the-counter painkillers, an array of liniments, stomach soothers. There were some prescription containers with Beth's name and the club address on them carrying drug names she didn't recognize, but they weren't marked as being dangerous. As she was about to close the cabinet, she noticed a small collection of gift cards stacked in a corner.

Oh! From the presents Beth had received from her unknown admirer. That was not Dawn's business, really, but her petite friend had already told her about the gifts.

She shuffled through the cards. They were in chronological order, the first dated five weeks ago. The messages were brief. Each praised Beth.

The last few promised a revelation of the name of their writer. As she stood reading through them, she realized she had seen the fine-lined block printing before. It replaced handwriting for the author.

She recognized the hand because she had received similar notes.

They had come from Hector Sturm!

She put the cards back and closed the cabinet. Back

in her office a few minutes later, she nearly choked on her outrage. Her former lover was chasing two women! Dinah could take care of herself; she and Hector were two of a kind. But Beth! Someone like Hector would sweep the gentle girl away—to disaster.

She could understand Beth's pale elfin beauty appealing to Hector. Oh, yes, she knew something of his tastes. Dawn had barely survived Hector with her emotional health intact. Beth would have no chance. Dawn knew she had to do something to protect her friend without hurting her feelings. At that moment she didn't know just what.

That evening, due to staff cutbacks, she had to fill in again at the Tiger Aerobics session. She swallowed her dismay at realizing that over the last weeks the size of the group had been reduced by three-quarters. Ketty's figures said that only a month stood between SHAPE and bankruptcy. On top of all the rest, for the second time Dawn had been threatened with death before the end of the week! Even though she had told Detective Morgan that she thought she was in deadly danger, deep down she wondered if the threats were real or were actually designed to frighten her away from the club and her business interest in it. In short, all that was entirely Peter Faldo's work. She couldn't smother her morbid hunches about Jeff. Everything was so confused! She was looking forward to the distraction of a heavy workout. Her mind and body both needed it.

A latecomer arrived during warm-ups—Dinah. The redhead was stunning in a skintight outfit. Because of her, Dawn found herself pushing the workout to nearly unfair levels, hoping the woman would drop out a panting wreck. But she kept up. It was some of the others who couldn't. They sagged down to rest with dazed, hostile looks.

By the time the group had reached the cool-downs Dawn knew how she was going to handle the Beth-Hector problem. She caught Dinah on the way to the showers. "Meet me after. I want to go somewhere and talk to you."

Dinah's eyebrows went up, but she agreed.

They went to a sub shop not far away, sat in the fluorescent glare, and drank overpriced orange juice. Dinah was kind enough to ask about the club's troubles and if there had been any improvement. Dawn explained there hadn't, but didn't bother telling her about the death threats. She didn't want to distract the redhead from matters she was about to raise.

"I hope you don't want to talk about you and Sam and me," Dinah said. "You and he were ancient history before I even met him. Now *he's* history. Whatever wild ideas you had about him were wrong, too."

Dawn sighed. She supposed she had been unfair to Sam with her suspicions. It seemed unlikely now that he had been involved in the deaths—but of course that wasn't certain. Nothing seemed certain anymore. No matter. He was dead. A brief surge of depression rose and fell away. "I have some things to tell you. I hope you'll hear me out, Dinah. It's all about you, me, Hector Sturm, and someone else. In the end I'm going to ask you to do something, so it would be nice if you'll listen up front. Okay?"

"Well, sure. Go ahead." Dinah seemed like an intelligent, reasonable woman, and for some reason that annoyed Dawn. She explained that Dinah was following her not into one relationship, but into two. Hector had ended a previous affair to make Dawn his lover.

Dinah's green eyes widened slightly. "He didn't tell me that." She looked Dawn over from that new perspective. "I guess you're attractive enough, aren't you? And I'm certain you're no airhead." She sipped her juice. "I hope you aren't making this up."

"I most certainly am not!" Dawn explained that she had taken the initiative in ending the affair. Now Dinah was her successor—or hadn't that quite happened yet?

Dinah smiled coyly. "I've let him talk me into having dinner at his club. He took me there for drinks once."

"Nice place, isn't it?" Dawn said. "I liked the fresh flowers in the middle of winter."

Dinah blinked. "I kind of . . . gathered I wasn't the first woman he ever took there."

"Did he have the Schubert Quintet played?" Dawn asked.

"The what?"

"He hasn't gotten to it yet," Dawn said. "You must seem harder to get than I ever did."

"Okay, you made your point." Dinah's mouth showed a shadow of pout. "I hope that when you say it's over between the two of you, you mean it's over."

"It is."

The redhead leaned forward. "I think you were mad to break up! He has everything—taste, style, money. He's hinted he'll set me up in my own place. We'll travel!"

"Could happen. He and I did a little traveling. Oh, to be at the Puente Romana again!" Dawn wondered whence her smugness. She normally wasn't one to play one-up. Maybe she was sparked by Dinah's grand confidence in herself. Prick the balloon a little.

"So I'm second or third—or whatever." Dinah shrugged. "Who cares? Right now I'm number one."

"That's the problem. You're not. Not quite."

"What are you talking about?" For the first time Dawn had upset Dinah. Her fair neck and cheeks were suffused with crimson.

"While he's been kitchy-cooing with you he's also been working on a friend of mine."

"Who?"

"Never mind who. Someone who's not quite as strong a person as you are—or I am, for that matter. Someone who wouldn't be able to handle getting involved with his type of man, then eventually being dumped." She explained to Dinah the slow, steady increase in Hector's gifts and notes to Beth, omitting her petite friend's name.

"That sleaze!"

"Now we come to what I want you to do. Confront Hector. Tell him you don't appreciate him chasing another woman."

Dinah paled. "Oh, God, have I been playing too hard to get?" Her face twisted with dismay. "I thought that was just the right way to play him, and now . . ."

"So do what I suggest. I think he's more interested in you than in . . . the other party. If he has to pick, I'm confident he'll choose you."

Dinah clenched her fists. "I can't believe this!"

"You'll get him back one hundred percent. And my friend will be spared the anguish of getting involved with him. It's a win-win situation. Will you do it?"

Dinah hesitated, dug her hands into her hair, her face twisting. Then her eyes found Dawn's. "Are you screwing with me, Dawn Gray? Are you playing some kind of head game that will break Hector and me up? Because maybe you're jealous or something?"

"Absolute not! I swear. Now, will you confront Hector?"

"Damn right I will! I can't do it right away, though. He just went away on a business trip. Be back in a few days."

"Where'd he go?"

"I don't know. He didn't say."

"When you do finally talk to him, be sure to mention my name. I don't want him to think he can bluff his way out of this."

"You got it."

They left the sub shop on friendlier terms. "One more favor, Dinah?"

"Big or little?"

"Little. Walk me to my car. You might as well know that somebody has threatened my life."

The redhead looked startled. "And you're worried about your friend being hurt? I'd be on the first flight to France."

"You and I approach life differently," Dawn said. She gave Dinah the details. Then, standing by her Honda, she thought of an obvious question. "You're still coming to the club, Dinah? Even after all the trouble. A lot of members have been scared off. Why aren't you afraid?"

The redhead smiled. "I'm just not."

At home Dawn poured herself a glass of cider. She was still thirsty from the heavy workout, and getting a bit stiff. Maybe a long, hot bath was in order. The phone rang. Jeff. He asked how her Maine adventure had gone.

At that moment it dawned on her that he was the only one who knew where and how she had spent the weekend. Her suspicion about him grew another head, like a Hydra. The faster she disposed of them, the faster they grew back.

She lied. She said her interlude had been restful. "And how did you spend your weekend?" she asked, hoping not too sweetly.

"I went snowshoeing up in the mountains. I meditated, spent the night. I got home about an hour ago."

"Any witnesses?"

"What's that supposed to mean?" An edge quickly came to his tone.

"There were some 'events' in Maine. I thought maybe you—and someone else—might have been involved."

"I have no idea what you're talking about, Dawn. And I don't like the sound of what you're saying. Don't bother trotting out any new accusations to beat me over the head with. I'm not in the mood to listen!" He hung up.

Were his reactions real or bogus? she wondered at once. Was she being fair to Jeff? Suspicion and shame whirled within her like a weather vane in a windstorm. Karl suspected him of being behind the murders. But could she rely on the burly man's judgment when his own lens was clouded with affection for her? She remembered the mighty rage into which Karl had flown yesterday, and how it had continued for several hours. No mistake: that was a killing rage if she had ever beheld one. And Jeff had been its target.

Peter hadn't been in the club today, either. Maybe he was taking the long way back from Maine, fresh from yet another effort to frighten her into selling out to him. She understood that she had long ago reached the hopeless position of suspecting everyone who had the slightest possible motive for being behind the tormenting murders. First it had been Zack, then Hector—both wrong. Then Sam. He was gone, leaving behind a wake of ambiguity. He could have murdered and then, when his scheme failed, killed himself in despair. That would wash, except for the threatening notes. Of course, others could simply have picked up the ball and run with it, pretending Sam's savagery had been their own. On the other hand, if Sam himself was the last victim, Dawn was now left with Peter, Jeff, and Karl as the remaining suspects. Which of them was—Wait! Which two? Or was it . . . all three?

"We." We. *We!*

The next morning Detective Morgan came to the club and announced he was going to bring Karl in for intense questioning.

"You already questioned him, didn't you?" Dawn said.

He looked at her peculiarly. "I know you're a bright woman, Dawn, but this time you're not thinking."

"I don't understand."

"You spent the weekend a couple hundred miles from here, with Karl Clausman. You saw somebody in the woods. Somebody stuck a note on the fishing shack. Don't you think it's obvious that Karl might qualify on both counts?"

"But why? He's fond of me."

The cop rolled his eyes. " 'Tell me you love me. I'll believe anything.' Come on, Dawn! You're not computing."

"I suspect everybody!" Dawn said. "No reason you shouldn't, too, I suppose. Karl? Why not? What about Peter Faldo, too? And Jeff Bently? Why not everybody!"

"Take it easy, Dawn. I've already got the idea this is all hard on you."

"You're taking my bodyguard, you know."

Morgan nodded. "I brought you a present: Charlie Ruiz, a rookie officer. He likes a good-looking woman. He won't mind standing in for Mr. Muscles. See you later."

Ruiz was tall and broad. Handsome as well. Must be the uniform, she thought. As she went about the business of tallying the club's declining resources, he remained at a respectful distance. She was pleased to see he didn't sit down and continued to look reasonably alert. Please, Officer, will you go home with me?

After lunch Beth appeared. Her face was flushed with excitement. "I have to talk to you!" she whispered. She led Dawn down to the trainer's room.

Officer Ruiz trailed at a polite distance.

Beth's heart-shaped face still carried color. At the rubbing table she whirled toward Dawn. "I think I'm in love!" she cried. "Can you fall in love by mail and UPS?"

"Well, I don't—"

"And it's somebody I really don't know. I can't believe myself!"

Dawn felt a distinct sinking sensation.

Beth snatched up a small opened parcel and thrust it at Dawn. "Look at this! It just came in the mail."

It was a long narrow jewelry case. Hesitantly Dawn lifted its lid. She had nearly guessed what lay gleaming on the velvet.

A platinum chain, much like the one she had!

"Look!" Beth's small body was nearly quivering with excitement. "It's platinum, isn't it?"

"Yeah." Beth had forgotten that Dawn had mentioned such a chain as one of Hector's gifts when she poured out her past to the Dawn Patrol.

"I think this is going to be the last anonymous gift," Beth said. "Read this." She gave Dawn a card written in Hector's hand: "Wear this next Wednesday, when we meet." The small woman rattled on about what would happen when they finally met. No, she didn't know who he was, but she was ready to run off with him, if he should ask. She nearly hopped with anticipation.

Dawn's heart sank. She was tempted for a moment to tell her friend that she was headed for big trouble and heartache because it was Hector who was after her. She kept quiet. Dinah would confront the executive with his interest in another woman. She would insist he decide which of the two he wanted. Dawn knew that when he had to make his choice, he would pick the redhead; she knew him that well. The worst Beth would suffer would be brief disappointment.

"I wouldn't get my hopes up too high, if I were you," Dawn said. "Somebody could be fooling around with you."

"What do you mean?" Beth asked sharply.

"Whoever it is has had plenty of time to come forward. He could have done it five times by now."

"I don't like it when you talk like that!" Beth's eyes blazed. Dawn read utter vulnerability in that bright violet light.

Dawn was more certain than ever that she had done the right thing.

Having managed the great favor of eventually getting Hector away from Beth buoyed her briefly that evening. Soon, though, the realities of her hours among Ketty's fan-fold accounting statements weighed her down like a diver's belt. Despite her deep suspicions of Peter, she would have to talk to him about the details of closing down. That thought hurt! But not as strongly as the fear she felt over the note that told her she was going to die next week. Her hands turned clammy at the memory, now never far from her consciousness. By now there was no question in her mind that the threats were real and that she was in desperate danger. Down at the bottom of it was the icy reality that at least two people wanted her out of her club ownership. Which two? She groaned! She suspected everyone, which was as futile as suspecting no one. She got out her day planner. It was Tuesday evening. She had been threatened on Sunday.

That left her four days, five at the most.

Sitting at her kitchen table, she saw her hands begin to shake. The dread she had held largely at bay for so long mushroomed like cancer. She felt herself being centered in death's whirlpool, going around and around faster and faster, powerless to save herself. She gasped and staggered to her feet, the chair clattering to the floor.

She grabbed the phone. She had to talk to someone. Who? She refused to call Peter. Her suspicions about him forbade it. She tried Karl. No answer. Possibly the police had chosen to keep him overnight. She supposed they could do that if he didn't have an attorney around reminding him of his rights. He might not think of getting one.

She was whimpering now like a baby, and hated herself for it. Menace seemed to well forth from the walls. She was going to go berserk unless she could talk to somebody. Hesitating, she overcame her reluctance and called Jeff. As his phone rang she wondered why her intuition told her to trust him, then not trust him, from one day to the next. Her wariness was tangled with her affection for him. Like her, he was a complicated person with as many sides as a cut stone. Was one of his facets the dark and deadly nature of a murderer? She couldn't say. And she couldn't bear to be isolated another moment.

He was cool to her. She had expected that. Only when she told him the whole story about Dinah, Beth, and Hector did he warm up a bit. The bright, inquisitive tone came back to his voice. She tried hard not to dwell inwardly on Karl's reports about Jeff's suspicious snooping around the club—and in the drug cabinet, come to think of it, where she had found Hector's teasing cards.

"So Hector's in the middle of the two women?"

"Yes."

"Could he be in the middle of some other, worse things?"

"Remember, I told you I had the police check up on him. He was in a rage over it. He had alibis for the first murders."

"What about for when Sam died?"

She hesitated. "You know, I didn't think of—"

"And if you're being threatened by someone who uses 'we,' maybe Hector is working with somebody else." Jeff's voice rose with excitement. "That other person killed Eloise, Nicole, Chantelle, and the reporter. Maybe Hector killed Sam and wrote the threatening notes."

"I don't know, Jeff. Was he around when Sam died?"

Jeff paused, his enthusiasm flagging momentarily. "I don't remember seeing him. I guess there always is the possibility that Sam might really have killed himself. There's no evidence that it wasn't a suicide, is there?"

"No." She recalled suddenly that Karl had said he'd seen Jeff on the third level just before Sam fell. But only Karl was strong enough to heave a resisting man over the edge. At the distant corners of her mind were bits and pieces that she should have been bringing together to explain much of what happened. And with that explanation would come the identities of those who were proving to be her implacable enemies. But it was all so complicated and confusing that she couldn't draw those critical conclusions.

She had maybe four days to do so.

"So then where does all that leave us, Dawn?" Jeff asked. "Right back where we started, huh?"

"I guess so."

Jeff surprised her then. "Dawn, I want to help you. With all my heart I want to do whatever I can. I couldn't bear it if something happened to you that I could have helped prevent. Do you know how I really feel about you? Can you guess from the time we've spent together?"

She closed her eyes and clutched the receiver, trying to block out all the ugliness and concentrate on the good. "I hope you're going to say you love me!"

"Yes. I've been trying to all along. But I need one thing from you to make that happen. I think you know what that is."

She hesitated, feeling momentarily unperceptive. "I'm not sure I do," she said.

"Dawn, I need to know that you trust me."

"Jeff . . ."

"You haven't, you know. I'm not easy to hurt, but you've managed to start in on it pretty well."

"I'm sorry." Oh, she meant it!

"*Will* you trust me? From now on?"

"Yes!"

He was silent. She sensed him planning quickly what he could do to help her. "Then give me Hector's private phone number," he said.

"Why?"

"Because I want to talk to him, of course."

"What about?"

"Never mind right now. I'll tell you later. Remember, I'm asking you to trust me."

"I don't want Beth hurt!"

"Trust me!"

218

"Hector's out of town for a couple days—at least that's what I understand."

"Fine. I'll catch him when he comes back," Jeff said. "The ideas you had earlier about what was going on at the club, and with me—have you given up on all those?"

"On the contrary. I just got stuck, that's all. The things you've told me are about the last pieces I need."

"Even if I love you, you're still infuriating with your vagueness," Dawn told him.

"When I'm sure, you'll hear everything. After all, sweet, one person—you—shooting from the hip in all directions is enough." He laughed. "Can I come over? I'd love to see you."

She hesitated. She felt a wreck. It hadn't been a great day. "I don't think so. It has nothing to do with how I feel about you, all right?"

"If you say so."

"I'll see you tomorrow at the club. I wouldn't be good company tonight."

"Have it your way. Looking forward to seeing you. *Au revoir, ma chère.*"

After hanging up, she found herself mouthing a short phrase, like a litany or prayer-wheel scrap: Trust Jeff. Trust Jeff. *Trust Jeff.* He said he loved her! And she had said the same. It seemed true. It needed saying. If only her life wasn't so confused, if only she hadn't been threatened, she could have reacted with proper enthusiasm to the gift of love.

The phone rang. She picked it up. Karl. He was being held overnight in jail. A prisoner had told him he could make a phone call. The only person he trusted was Dawn. What should he do?

"Get an attorney."

"I don't know any." He sounded miserable. "They've dug up every dirty thing from years ago. They keep shoving it at me. That s.o.b. Morgan. He says I dragged you up to Maine and played games with you. He's trying to say I killed—"

"He's trying to do his job. You shouldn't take it—"

"I want to deck him! He keeps picking, picking . . ."

She was abruptly anxious for him. While she didn't love him, she felt tenderness for his concern for her and his kindness. "Don't lose control, Karl! That's all you'd need. It would give them an excuse to keep you longer. I'll call my attorney and see if he can find someone to help you."

Milt Glassman wasn't home. His answering machine took Dawn's message.

After that she found herself pacing her apartment. She didn't feel inclined to sleep until she had helped Karl.

About midnight the phone rang again. She snatched it up. "Milt?"

A distant voice thick with the muffling of disguise: "We *might* give you two days to live, Dawn Gray. *Two days.*"

CHAPTER
15

Peter was at the club office when Dawn arrived, frazzled from lack of sleep. She wasn't about to be alone with the man. She made sure the sight lines between her and Officer Ruiz were clear. Then she went in. Peter's movements were more rapid than normal. He was clearly agitated. When she asked him what was bothering him, he shrugged her off with "Business, business!" She told him they didn't have much business left. He must have studied Ketty's figures, as she had. What was he talking about? And when was he going to sit still long enough for the two of them to discuss the details of closing the club in a way that would minimize their already considerable losses?

"It's always darkest before the dawn," he said.

"Well, it's pretty damned dark right now!" she said. Considering how she felt about him, she didn't care to discuss the latest death threat with him. If he had been the caller, she didn't want to give him the satisfaction of knowing how frightened she was. She studied his angular frame, the face set with fresh lines. She now read sleaziness into every detail of his appearance.

Her partner, thanks to his odd carryings-on and Lieutenant Morgan's revelation that he had been a swindler, had never looked worse in her eyes. She wondered if she was smart to get even this close to him. She glanced out the open door. Officer Ruiz was right there. The police had kept Karl overnight. That meant he couldn't have made the threatening phone call. For a brief time last night she had almost written the big man wholly into the ally column. Then she remembered that she might well have more than one enemy ready to take her life. Karl could be part of a team with . . .

She turned back to Peter. Now that Peter was the prime suspect, Jeff was firmly in her camp, where in fact it seemed he should have been from the start. Face it, Dawn, she told herself. Peter wants to buy me out so badly that he *has* to have a far more rewarding motive than assuaging his guilty conscience. She had originally "hired" Karl as her bodyguard because of her fear of Peter. Why in recent days had she vacillated between him and other suspects? Now it seemed quite clear that Peter was the dark agent behind her deadly troubles. Sitting there staring at him in his expensive suit, it seemed so obvious he was up to something. Weary of bafflement and delays—never mind fear for her life—she blurted, "So you still want to buy me out? From the goodness of your heart, that is."

He tossed his head nervously, "Sure. You said you were considering my offer."

"Peter, will you do me a big, big favor? Tell me what you're really up to. Will you be honest with me this once?"

He looked at her with a thin smile. "What do you mean?"

"You were a swindler! I know about your past. The police told me all about you and Century Twenty-Two Investments. People killed themselves because of you!"

"No one convicted us of anything." His narrowed eyes gleamed like a deadly viper's, she thought.

"You squirmed out on technicalities!"

"We didn't break any laws," he said heavily.

"Answer my question. Are you trying to swindle me?"

He shrugged. "So Morgan has been a busy boy digging through the trash."

"Well? Are you going to *answer me?*"

" 'He that is without sin, let him . . .' "

"That's not an answer!"

"That's all the answer you're going to get right now, D.G. Let's just say I'm too tired to talk about my plans at the moment."

She wouldn't be dismissed. She sensed she was on the edge of discovering something that fit into the whole deadly puzzle. He needed prodding. And she knew just how to do it. "I've thought it over. I want to sell my share of SHAPE to you. As soon as possible!"

He frowned. A faint light seemed to brighten his dull gaze. "You putting me on?"

"Call Milt. He can draw up the papers. I'll sign today. I've had enough."

"I'm not sure I believe you," Peter said.

"Try me."

He got up and took off his suit jacket, then hung it on the hook. "I might do just that."

"I want one thing from you before I sign, Peter."

"It's a little early to start negotiations." He shook his head with annoyance. "What?"

"I want to know why you still want sole ownership. And don't give me that stuff about your conscience. Remember, I know all about Century Twenty-Two and those poor old folks you ripped off."

"Don't you believe in redemption, D.G.?"

"You're avoiding my question completely! Answer me! Why do you still want to buy a nearly worthless club?"

"You're toying with me, partner." His expression turned cunning. "You have no real intention of selling out to me. You're playing games. And I find you a bitch when you do."

She snorted, remembering a day not so long ago when his criticism would have catapulted her into defensiveness. No longer. "What we're saying to each other is that the ship of this partnership has gone on the rocks of lost trust. Right?" She waved her hand around at the office, which was littered with papers, used coffee cups, and other debris. "And it really looks it."

"So clean the place up if it bothers you." He took his jacket off the hook, put it on, and started for the door.

"Peter! We have a lot to say to each other."

"Later."

He left her staring at the door. Everything had come apart in her life: her business was finished, her partnership was collapsing in the face of Peter's still undefined deceitfulness, and far worse, someone was warning her that she had only two more days to live! She recalled the first threatening note, in which her oppressors had gloated over having destroyed the club. They would finish the job by killing her. And it was all happening! Whatever help she had sought from her friends, from the police, hadn't accomplished anything. Just this morning she had called Morgan and told him about the last night's threatening phone call. His advice was still the same: stay out of the club and be careful. What kind of help was that? She felt alone and utterly defenseless. Her head bowed, then dipped down. She folded her arms on her desk and let the tears come.

"Hey, what's up?" It was Beth, peppy as ever.

Dawn looked up, tear-smeared and distraught. "It's what's down, Beth. Everything!" She got up, wiping her eyes. "You want to do me a favor? Sort out the mail and clean up the office a little. I'm going to the ladies' room." Her voice caught and she rushed away, Officer Ruiz drifting along in her wake.

After washing her face and breathing deeply for a few minutes, she felt well enough to tour the club. She felt like a captain surveying her outnumbered troops on the eve of the final battle. There was little activity, save for large men still using the weight room, and obsessed racquetball players lunging and grunting in the sweaty air. She had let more than half the employees go, and the club was still overstaffed. She had *almost* made a career and a success of SHAPE.

She wasn't a fool. She knew she was beaten. The club was a dead loss. But she could still save her own life. She was going to leave the city tonight, alone, well before the scheduled time of her death. She had credit cards. She would use one to book a flight to somewhere warm. She wouldn't wait around to find out whether her enemies were serious. Once away, she would use Milt Glassman as her only contact with the club. He and Ketty could handle the ugly details of its dismantlement, along with that of her partnership with Peter while she sunned, recovered, and planned the rest of her life. She'd contact Jeff, certainly, but not until all the rest was well on the way to being settled.

No, she was no fool.

Beth found her half an hour later. The small woman's face was pale. "I have something to show you. Let's go into the trainer's room." She looked over her shoulder at Ruiz in the near distance. "At least it'll be semiprivate there."

On the way downstairs Dawn realized that her resolution to leave the city had largely restored her frayed nerves. Her anxiety level had decreased as well. She didn't tell Beth that she wasn't greatly interested in whatever she had to show her.

Standing with her back to the trainer's room door, Beth took a letter from her purse and gave it to Dawn. It carried the logo of the Signal Insurance Company.

"Notice it's dated two days ago," Beth said. "I found it among Peter's papers. It was open."

The letter was several pages long. She turned to the last page. The signature was that of Torsten Berman, Signal's senior vice president for human resources. She turned back to the first page and began to read. She read through the four pages twice to make sure she fully understood what the letter was about. It summarized extensive negotiations that had taken place at a lower administrative level between Signal officials and Peter over the last three months.

Signal had purchased the sprawling lot a block away from the club. There, come spring, they would begin building a complex of offices that would hold more than two thousand workers. The new buildings would not contain employee exercise facilities; space would be better used to house operations that directly related to day-to-day business. Therefore, exercise and fitness would be provided through an agreement between Signal and SHAPE. Spelled out were the modification and expansion of the club's existing facilities. The insurance company would provide low-rate improvement loans. The legal details of the agreement were outlined, with further details to be forwarded from Signal's legal department within the month.

The club would provide reduced rates to interested Signal employees, along with an individualized fitness plan for each. SHAPE would also set up and operate an executive conditioning program and create a special workout for recovering cardiac attack victims. The club would expand its presentations on diet and nutrition and make them available to the company's health-conscious management. Despite SHAPE's close relationship with Signal, the assets and operation of the club would remain in the hands of its present owner. SHAPE's autonomy was guaranteed.

Reading between the lines, Dawn saw that something else was guaranteed: a larger, far more profitable SHAPE. Other thoughts wanted to flood her mind like water under pressure. She had to control the valve carefully, give the ideas time to flow smoothly.

She read on. The recent "misfortunes" that had taken place at the club had delayed the signing of the agreement. Signal needed reasonable assurances that the "disruptive incidents" were a thing of the past and that SHAPE was once again a safe, reliable club. Now that Peter had provided those guarantees, there was no need to delay the final decision. This letter preceded the final contracts, but could be considered a formal offer. His acceptance would be binding. Dawn read the pages once again.

Her name wasn't mentioned once.

"I thought you ought to see it," Beth said in a small voice.

Dawn nodded. She sank down into a chair. Her emotions, so calm minutes ago, were rioting in all directions. Her face was flushed. She couldn't at that moment sort it all out, not by half.

While Beth looked on, Dawn phoned Torsten Berman. He wasn't available. She asked the secretary if she knew anything about the agreement between SHAPE and Signal.

"May I ask who's calling?"

"This is Dawn Gray, co-owner of SHAPE."

Silence.

"Yes?" Dawn said finally.

"Why don't you come in here this afternoon?" the secretary said. "I'm sure Mr. Berman would like to meet you."

"Have you ever heard of me?" Dawn's voice carried an edge.

"Why don't you come in and talk to Mr. Berman about that?"

They settled on a time for the appointment and hung up. Dawn turned to Beth. "They had never heard of me." She read the letter again, trying to sort out what it meant in relation to what had happened at SHAPE over the last five-plus weeks. Her mind made leaps in every direction, making it difficult to gather her thoughts—and her suspicions. She was glad Beth was with her to help her make connections.

"Peter conducted all these negotiations behind my back, Beth. I wasn't to be a part of anything this letter says is going to happen."

"But if things go along the way it says here, you *have* to be part of it, Dawn. You own more than half of the club."

"There are two ways that I might drop out of the picture," Dawn said. "First, I could sell my interest to Peter."

"But you refused to do that." Beth jabbed an index finger at the air. "So Peter had to make you want to sell out. And he did it by"—she looked at Dawn with widening eyes—"killing people."

Dawn nodded, squinting with speculation. "The first killing was meant to seriously damage the reputation of the club, but not quite destroy it, and to put me in the position where it made no sense for me to want to keep my interest. When things started to get rough, Peter offered to buy me out. If I hadn't been so determined, if SHAPE hadn't been so important to me, I *would* have sold out. But I didn't. So he killed more people. Then he sweetened his offer. Still I wouldn't sell."

"So he sent the notes threatening your life!"

Dawn nodded. Beth was right. She waved the letter. "According to this, Peter has 'guaranteed' that the trouble here is over. How could he have done that unless he was behind it all?"

Beth nodded excitedly. "I just thought of something else." She walked over and sat on the massage table, her small feet dangling well above the floor. "He still wants you out of the picture—obviously. You won't sell. You won't run from his threats. You were wondering if they were real. I think they were! Now the only way to get rid of you is to kill you. And before long."

Dawn groaned. She felt her knees go rubbery. Yes, it all made sense. While her imagination had soared off in pursuit of one suspect after another, fashioning the most exotic of motivations, the real perpetrator lay much closer to home. His reasons for killing were familiar homespun vices: greed and ambition. She had become an impediment in his upward path. She had to be eliminated.

"You're as pale as paper," Beth said. "Don't faint on me."

"If I haven't fainted up to now, I'm not going to start." Just the same she sank into a chair. Peter! Peter . . . She grabbed the phone. She was lucky. Detective Morgan was available. "Let poor Karl go," she said. "I know who the killer is."

"We weren't getting anywhere with him anyway. I'll take a better offer."

When he had heard her out, she was dismayed that he didn't share her excitement. She asked him why.

"I get the feeling you're using a process of elimination more than anything," he said. "Peter's the only suspect you have *left*. Know what I mean?"

"That's utter nonsense!" Dawn insisted. "I have the Signal letter in my hand. I *talked* to someone at Signal."

"Doesn't sound exactly like damning proof to me."

"What more do you *need*, for goodness' sake? His signed confession?"

"That would be nice. . . . Hey, Dawn, call me again after you talk to this Mr. Berman at Signal this afternoon. Then maybe you and I and Peter Faldo can get together and have a frank and open chat. All right?"

"No. I want you to arrest Peter right away! Before very long I think he's going to try to kill me!"

"Take it easy." His tone turned comforting.

"I'm not joking! You know I've been threatened." At the bottom of her anxiety was the fear that Morgan was frustrated with SHAPE's riddle and more than ready to work on some of his other cases. By the time his interest returned to her problems, she'd be dead.

"If you're worried, take Ruiz with you wherever you go." Morgan turned away from the phone for a moment. She heard paper rattle. "Dawn, I'm finally getting an idea of how the killer handled the first few murders, how they went so easily."

Dawn's attention perked up. He really wasn't losing interest! "What did he do?"

"The pathologist found that the drug in Sam Spring's body was a mild paralytic. So we had the first three victims dug up. It didn't take long to go over them. This time we knew what we were looking for. We still don't know how he got the drug into them, but we'll figure that out sooner or later. Maybe we'll ask your partner how he did it when we have our little talk."

"All right!" Dawn was grinning.

"The three of us will have a chat. That'll give me something to look forward to. It gets boring—murders, murders, murders . . . and no murderers."

"It's not boring for me! I'm to be the next and last of his victims. You'd better start looking for him now!"

"Keep Ruiz with you. Remember to call me when you get done at Signal. You keep safe until we find out who done it."

"We both know it was Peter!"

"So it seems. You sure think so. But your batting average is kinda low, when it comes to finding the guilty party, in case you haven't noticed. I'm gonna keep nosing around. Oh, one important thing. I can't keep Ruiz on you after hours. I'm too short-staffed. If I were you, I'd find somebody to stay around the rest of the time. I wouldn't bother with muscle-man Karl. We sort of tired him out. We went at him in teams and didn't let him sleep much." Morgan chuckled. "You know, we couldn't break him after all. I got a better opinion of him than when we started. Just the same, he's an odd one."

"He's very protective and concerned about me, Monty. And the reason you couldn't get anything out of him is that he didn't do anything wrong. Peter's behind it all. Surely you can see that now."

"Hmmm. Where do you think we might find your partner?"

"I don't know. Try his apartment, though I never have any luck reaching him there."

"Where else does he hang out?"

She frowned. "You know, I don't really know that much about him."

"Strictly business between you, huh?"

Dawn's irritation rose in full force. "Detective Morgan, I think it's only fair to tell you that I expect you to wrap this all up quite soon."

"If we can find Faldo, we might just do that. In the meantime, arrange for company around the clock. Never mind women's lib. I recommend a man."

She asked Beth if she would go with her and Ruiz that afternoon to Signal. She didn't mind sitting with the secretary while Dawn went in to talk to Torsten Berman. The fifty-year-old vice president wore red suspenders and a starched custom-made shirt with French cuffs. His cuff links were gold dollar signs. He admitted not having a clear idea of what the subject of their first discussion should be and to being vaguely embarrassed. He had tried without success to reach Peter.

"He did mention your name during our negotiations, Ms. Gray. He said you were more or less a silent partner."

"Well, I'm not silent, am I?" Dawn said.

Torsten Berman smiled. "Not at all. Neither silent nor invisible. It seems Mr. Faldo's done you a bit of a disservice."

"A bit—"

"If you could step back a bit"—he made distancing motions in the air—"you might see the situation differently. Something like this: Mr. Faldo did all the work, but you reap some of the benefits."

For an instant Dawn was going to blurt out all the details of the murders, crown her explanation with a brief history of the threats on her life, and finish off with the gnawing fear with which she had been living for a month and a half. But something held her back. She supposed it was that Bergen's opinion of SHAPE and Peter somehow remained high, despite the media blasts and needn't be dragged down right then. That would come when her partner was arrested.

Torsten Berman went on to praise Peter's negotiating skills and patience in dealing with Signal and its battery of executives. Even by the standards of a large corporation, the going had been tortuous. The deaths at SHAPE had nearly ended matters permanently. Luckily for the club, the new facility's building schedule allowed plenty of time for the guilty to be exposed, arrested, tried, and convicted.

"Mr. Faldo has assured us that the mysterious violence is at an end." He looked at Dawn, seeking further reassurance.

Dawn flashed a confident smile—where had it come from? "The police will be making an arrest shortly." She didn't bother to tell him it would be Peter. She wondered what that would do to the deal.

"You know, that letter you mentioned was our first official notification to Mr. Faldo that the agreement had been formally approved. After all his efforts, I wondered how he reacted to that good news."

"I don't know. He hasn't been around. And as I said, he didn't discuss any of this with me." The hurt leaked out in her voice.

Berman rose from behind his teak desk and sat on its edge, facing Dawn. "I don't begin to understand the terms of your partnership, Ms. Gray. I've only known Mr. Faldo. But our negotiations went on for so long that I was able to form some opinions about his style."

He was a swindler at one time, Dawn wanted to say, stealing precious dollars from retired teachers. He graduated from running small-time confidence games to murdering five people. That's his "style," Mr. Berman.

"Would I be out of line in suggesting that your partner is a bit of a sexist?" Berman said. "That he believes women should walk a pace or two behind men? That their role, to use the street idiom, is to shop, mop, and drop?"

"You would not be out of line, Mr. Berman."

"He could be called a traditionalist. If that's true, then his wanting to surprise you with the comprehensive arrangement he worked out with us would fit the pattern."

She stared at him, her thoughts rioting with retorts she wouldn't speak. She supposed she appeared thick-headed.

"You understand," Berman continued. "The brave man out hunting, bringing back the spoils to a nurturing woman."

Dawn managed a weak smile. "I understand a lot more than I want to talk about right now."

Berman rose from the desk and adjusted his cuffs. "Would you like some coffee? I'd like to keep you just a little while longer."

When she declined, he went on to talk about how much the Signal-SHAPE arrangement would benefit both organizations. He paid particular attention to the financial details, employees to be enrolled, volumes and discounts, peripheral profits accruing to the club. She remembered some of the details from the letter. He smiled warmly. "You see, your partner has cut SHAPE quite a nice deal—albeit without your input. Some of Signal's human-resources people have also spent considerable effort to reach the agreement." Pause. "I very much hope you won't . . . disrupt the negotiations."

So that's what he was driving at. She supposed she couldn't blame him. Never mind his dollar-sign cuff links, he was shrewd enough to know what he was up against: a woman's hurt feelings versus a slick business deal. Nor did he demean her feelings. He knew they were every bit as real as the bucks that would pass from Signal to SHAPE. She decided he was good at his job.

He couldn't know how involved matters had become. What would happen to the agreement when Peter was named as the murderer and arrested? She knew how lawyers could tangle things up. Delays and expense were their stock-in-trade. The cooperative agreement might never truly go into effect. She supposed Peter had used Milt Glassman's counsel. She would fire Milt the moment her partner was arrested. She wouldn't forgive Milt for keeping all the important developments from her. No matter Peter's pleas.

Clearly this was the time for a holding action. She told Berman she needed time to absorb all she had learned. But for the moment she certainly wasn't going to throw rocks into the gears of what seemed to be a well-designed health-maintenance mechanism. That brought a smile that showed all his bonded teeth. His light touch on her shoulder as they left his office struck the right note of respect and sincerity. "I'll be speaking with Mr. Faldo, Dawn. And I'll suggest that you two put your heads together. There's a great deal on which you'll want to be brought up to speed. Rest assured that Signal is prepared to seriously consider any suggestions you might have, even at this late date. And I apologize for any confusion or distress caused by Signal's unknowing actions. If we'd known the facts, we wouldn't have excluded you. I hope you believe me."

"I do." She thanked him for his honesty. He assured her they'd be in touch.

On the way back to the club she told Beth what Berman had said. They went to the office. "Thank goodness Peter isn't here!" she said to Beth. "I don't want to talk to him. I don't want to be anywhere near him. He's the one who murdered all the people in the club and the one who's threatened my life." Her emotions churned up like a storm surge. "I think he's a horrid, loathsome creature! For what he's done I hope he gets convicted and is given the death penalty!" Through smeared eyes she saw Beth's anxious face.

"Do you think you're going to be safe until he *is* arrested?" Beth asked nervously.

"I should be able to stay away from him. And I'm going to see to it I'm not alone until he's safely in jail."

She hurried up to the massage studio. Jeff was in a yoga position. "How would you like to spend at least one night alone with a beautiful woman?" she said.

"What beautiful woman did you have in mind?"

"*Me*, Mr. Perceptive. That's who."

"I'll check my social calendar." Jeff closed his eyes for a minute, then opened them. "All right. I checked it. I have a beautiful-woman-all-night cancellation. You're on."

On the way home she told him about picking up the phone and hearing Peter's muffled death threat. "I'm not quite frightened enough to forget how to count. Today is about over. That means they're going to try to kill me any time tonight from midnight on!"

"One detail snags my attention, Dawn," Jeff said. "Who's the 'we' his threats talk about? Who's he allied with? I can't think of anyone it might be. How about you?"

"I haven't really thought about it. It must be . . . *someone*."

He shrugged. "Then there are my own suspicions."

"I don't see how they matter now. Peter's the guilty one. Peter and . . . someone else."

"I see things quite a bit differently."

Dawn pounded her fist against the curve of the steering wheel. Oooh, he could be so *annoying*. "Well, I've been waiting to hear them, haven't I?"

"I don't have any evidence."

"This isn't a court of law! You don't have to be right."

"I have to be sure," he said. "If I'm wrong, I could cause some serious hurt."

Dawn tossed her head in vexation. "So you don't think Peter's guilty. You don't think I'm really in danger, then. The personal threats are all bluffs?"

"Oh, no. I think you're very much in danger. But I

intend to protect you, when you least expect you'll need it."

"You are talking rubbish!" She stayed annoyed with him through her broiled tuna and pasta dinner. Even when he insisted he do the dishes and clean up, she continued to sulk. She had too much on her mind to be in a decent mood, never mind his vexing secret theorizing. Peter . . . Peter . . . What a deadly disappointment he had become! She tried to calm herself and sink into Jeff's companionship like a soft pillow. She couldn't! Fearing for her life put a solid damper on business as usual, never mind romance.

She sat on the two-person rocker. In time Jeff came up behind it and asked if she wanted her neck rubbed. She did, but she said no. He paid no attention. Even though he was a professional masseur, he had never done any body work on her. At least not the kind he was paid to do at the club. She tried to relax under the pressure of his wise fingers. The problem was that crazy thoughts roiled up, dragging tension in their wake. Suppose, for example, that Karl was right: Jeff was teamed with Peter to complete her destruction. Jeff could kill her as she slept—at 12:01 A.M., just as the threatening voice had promised. Yet he had asked for her trust, and she had promised to give it. She had to honor that promise. She certainly should be able to. She *knew* Peter stood at the heart of the murders. Anyway, nothing had happened outside of her imagination to give her any reason to fear Jeff. It was her damned intuition that wouldn't quiet. And it had let her down many times in the weeks. Forget her intuition! She had to trust *someone*.

Jeff turned down the high collar of her sweater and worked on her scalenus muscles, which were as tight as bowstrings in the sides of her neck. She groaned at the queer, pleasurable pain. In time she felt the muscles loosen, some of the nervous pressure dissipating. Down under her loose shirt went his fingers, into the pockets of her shoulders, kneading sore tissues there. Then back to the base of her neck. The pads of his fingers eased into the tight muscles. She groaned again. "Hurts good!" she breathed.

"Good and good for you." She heard the faintest catch in his words. He liked putting his hands on her.

His fingertips nosed under the shirt, down to the top of her bra. They slipped under the seam, onto the soft flesh. There he spread his fingers, cupping her, squeezing so gently. She felt her nipples rise between his fingers. She felt vaguely betrayed by her body. She didn't really want . . . Trust Jeff. *Trust* . . .

"How lovely you are to hold!" His whisper was husky with desire.

As slowly as they had descended, his hands left her breasts and slid between skin and cloth, back to the planes of her shoulders. His fingers circled her neck for the first time. She felt his fingertips pressing lightly above the cartilage of her windpipe. "Nice neck to squeeze," he murmured.

Terror shot through her like electricity. He was going to—

The door buzzer sounded. She flew out of the rocker. She whirled to stare wild-eyed at Jeff. He looked hurt. "I don't see why you have to answer it. We were just starting to get you relaxed. We don't need company."

Dawn flung herself at the small panel and buzzed her visitor in. She didn't care who it was! She stood waiting by the door, eyes on Jeff. He threw puzzled looks at her, to which she didn't respond. It seemed to take her visitor forever to get up the stairs.

"What's wrong with you, Dawn?" Jeff said.

"Nerves." Somehow she knew he was going to . . . And she knew how terribly strong his hands were.

A knock. At last! "Who is it?" she said.

"Open up!" Hector's voice.

What did he want? She didn't care. She opened the door. He shoved his way in. The two men exchanged angry glances. Neither had forgotten their earlier encounters. Hector's eyes moved back to Dawn. She knew him well enough to clearly read the fury there. "I want to talk to you alone, Dawn," he said.

"No way!" Jeff cried. "She doesn't end up alone with anybody just now!" He moved a step closer. "If you want to talk, do it in front of me."

"What is this?" Hector grew still more furious.

"My life's been threatened," Dawn said.

"Maybe you did it," Jeff said to Hector.

"Ridiculous!" He pointed at Dawn. "Everything about you has turned ridiculous."

She didn't care what he said. As long as he was there, she wouldn't have to deal with what she sensed would be Jeff's deadly betrayal.

"To get up here," Hector said, "I had to get the approval of the guard you have posted downstairs. A human ox, with a mind to match." White spots of anger blossomed on Hector's cheeks.

"Guard? I didn't . . ." Oh, it had to be Karl. He must have seen her with Jeff and followed them here. She wasn't sure how stable the big man would be after his treatment by the police. Maybe it wasn't surprising he was lurking around trying to "protect" her.

Hector grabbed Dawn's wrist. "I came here to deliver a simple message. Let your karate-loving friend here hear it, too. You're no longer part of my personal life. So stay out of it!"

"I don't understand," Dawn said. "I couldn't care less about your personal life."

"I gave you every chance to continue with me," Hector said. "I came as close to pleading as I know how. You turned me down. Fine! That freed me to find someone else to love. I found one someone—Dinah. Then you had the poor judgment to step into something that was none of your business, and you poured lies into her ears."

"I didn't lie. I just told her—"

"Utter falsehoods about her 'rival.' She has no rival!"

Dawn shook her wrist free. "Oh, no you don't! I saw the evidence—"

"Be damned with your evidence!" Hector raised a fist.

"You want Beth, too! You want Beth Willow, and don't you dare deny it!"

"I do deny it! And I warn you once again. Don't say another word to Dinah about what you believe or don't believe I'm doing. I can make a great deal of trouble for you. So don't—"

"I think it's time you left," Jeff said.

"I'll leave, but not on your say-so. I've said everything I came to say." Hector pointed at Dawn. "Let's hope you remember what I did say." He turned to Jeff. "Perhaps it's a good thing you were here. I might have lost control of myself and done something violent, undeserved by either of us." He opened the door.

Dawn was bewildered and panicked. Hector had lied, but at least he had protected her from Jeff. But Hector had frightened her, too, with his anger. Her heart pounded and she was trembling. She was about to choose Hector as the lesser of two evils and ask him to take her away when Jeff said to him, "I'd like to ask you a question. Out in the hall?"

Hector glowered. "I have no love for you either, fellow."

"One question. And one honest answer's all I need."

Hector pointed at the open door. "After you."

The moment Jeff stepped outside, Dawn slammed the door and turned the dead bolt. After no more than a moment of muffled conversation, she heard a knock. "Okay, Dawn. It's me, Jeff. You can let me back in."

She checked the locks again. They were firmly engaged. She leaned her head against the wood. "Jeff, listen, I want you to go home. I want to be alone for the rest of the night."

"*What?* Did you forget somebody's going to kill you after midnight?"

"I'm an emotional wreck. Jeff, I'm thinking the killer could be you!"

"You told me I had your trust!" The door muffled his voice. Still she thought she heard hurt. Real or feigned, she couldn't guess.

"That's why I'm explaining that my head's a mess tonight. I just—can't trust anybody, I guess, until Peter and his crony are arrested. I hope I'm wrong about you, but I just can't take a chance."

"I found out something important from Hector."

"Jeff, please go!"

"All right!" he shouted. "Don't listen to me. Stay by yourself all night. I'm not sure about everything yet, but I don't think you're in danger here."

"Stop talking and go! Please!"

"I love you!"

She began to sniffle. She heard Jeff's footsteps creak away down the hallway. She went back to the rocker and tried to recover with the help of a few fingers of Grand Marnier from her meager hoard. She stopped her sniffles—just as someone knocked loudly on the door.

Karl's voice: "Hey, Dawn. You okay? I got Jeff right here in a half nelson. He says you're okay, but I thought I'd check. You know how far I trust this dude."

"Karl, you didn't have to— Anyhow, I'm okay. I want to be by myself tonight."

"I never realized just how big an idiot this guy is," Jeff growled.

"You sure you got no trouble, Dawn?" Karl said.

"Absolutely. You can let Jeff go. I don't want anybody with me tonight."

"I'll be on guard right through the night." Karl's tone said he wouldn't be argued with. "You want me by this door or downstairs?"

"Whichever. And thanks, Karl. Really." She added, "And you two should try to be friends."

"I can't be friends with somebody I don't trust," Karl said.

Jeff's retort was a barely audible mutter.

"Good night," Dawn said.

It wasn't a good night. It took four fingers of liqueur before she exorcised the demonic sensation of Jeff's fingers circling her neck. Was he really going to apply the crushing pressure of which his hands were capable? Her attention swung over to Hector's anger and his brutish demands that she stay out of his love life. That had hurt, because he was obviously lying about his interest in Beth. Then there was Karl—loyal and loving, despite her efforts to discourage him. She called his name. No answer. He must have decided to post himself by the front door.

She crawled into bed well after midnight. How could she sleep, knowing that Peter and his accomplice planned to kill her sometime today? She would tell Officer Ruiz at the club precisely how she had been threatened. The police wouldn't allow her to be alone. They might even escort her throughout the whole day. Better than that, they might find Peter and arrest him. That thought gave her some comfort.

She might have slept then, except that all the events of recent weeks descended on her like a horde of demons. She felt a need to try to sort them all out. She understood Peter's motivations, saw clearly how he had orchestrated the murders in an attempt to harm but not destroy SHAPE. All too vividly her memory presented a detailed vision of the three women's corpses, then the contorted face of the poisoned reporter. She wondered if Peter had killed Sam Springs, too. Poor Sam! Maybe he had simply given up on life.

But she couldn't figure out who would be willing to assist her partner in his grisly work. And for what gain? Maybe Peter would make that person his new partner. Together they would ride Signal's bigger and better SHAPE up to profit and prosperity.

After a long while she began to drift off. The telephone blasted her awake. She gripped the covers, hesitating. Maybe it would stop. It didn't. With an uneasy sigh she struggled out of bed. The clock's digits read 4:02 A.M. Her hand was shaking as she picked up the receiver. "It's four in the morning," she said.

"We've changed our minds, Dawn. You're not going to die today." Behind the muffled voice that she had heard once before lay an unmistakable emotion: mad glee. "We'll kill you . . . later. Good night."

As she stood in the darkness, the dead phone in her trembling hand, she imagined that she had misunderstood every recent dark event. She was still lost in fog, as she had been on that dreadful morning almost six weeks ago when she had beheld drowned Eloise, hair halo waving in the water. No matter how many perished, or what seemingly logical motivations burst anew onto the scene, only one constant had hovered ahead through it all like a beacon—a primary victim had been targeted for death from that very first miserable moment beside the Jacuzzi.

Her.

She crept back to bed, thinking she might somehow make the connections that would put facts behind that most recent burst of her overworked intuition. Instead, she drifted off and dozed fitfully for a little more than an hour.

Then the door buzzer wrenched away that meager sleep. She went to the intercom. It was Officer Ruiz. Detective Morgan had asked that he escort her to the club. She invited him up and gave him a cup of instant coffee. She showered and dressed. They got into the squad car together. On the way to SHAPE she told the big cop that the threat had been canceled by the same person who made it. "They're going to kill me later," she said dully.

When she got to the office she found the door locked. That was unusual. Peter and she preferred to leave it open. She dug in her purse for the key. She turned the lock and swung the door open. Peter was asleep at his desk. She turned on the lights. "Okay, partner, time to wake up." Then she saw that he wasn't asleep. The scream rose from her throat with its own overpowering strength.

Peter had blown his brains out with his revolver.

—

CHAPTER
16

Officer Ruiz ordered her out of the office at once. She stumbled out, weeping with shock and horror. Pink tissue and blood had splashed against the wall. The solitary desk staffer, badly shaken himself, was in no shape to offer comfort. Karl appeared. He had followed her to the club.

Beth came in, early as usual. After Dawn told her what Peter had done, they threw their arms around each other. Dawn's tears wet her friend's shoulder. When both had calmed somewhat, they admitted their shock and apprehension. Silently, Dawn wondered how much more she could take before she broke.

Detective Morgan wasted no time arriving. Behind him came the now familiar battery of technicians and investigators. By the time he wanted to talk to Dawn, she had regained enough self-control to deal with him. Karl and Beth had sat with her, talking it all over, speculating about Peter. Morgan put a hand on her shoulder. "I'm damn sorry about this," he said.

"It's not your fault."

He asked the others to leave him and Dawn alone. When they were alone, he said, "He left a note. Wrote it on the word processor, then signed it. He died around four-thirty this morning."

"I got a call from him with his voice disguised just before that. He said 'we' weren't going to kill me today."

"Maybe he's been using the imperial 'we' all along. Anyhow, in the note he mentioned the threatening calls."

"What else did it say?" Dawn said.

"Everything is in there." Morgan's lined face brightened, as though he had just stepped outside on a beautiful day. "He wanted to get the club away from you and make a fortune with Signal's help. He offed all the ladies, poisoned the juice, hit Sam Springs over the head from behind and just nudged him off the balcony before he collapsed."

"What about Maine?"

"He followed you up, hung out in his car hidden nearby. He knew every detail of how the note got on the shack wall."

"It was so cold . . ."

"You'll see the note sometime. It was written by a crazy person. Hunkering down in the cold for a couple days was about the least strange thing he did."

"Why did he kill himself?"

"The note said it was remorse and guilt. He knew we were after him. Sooner or later we'd find him. After that he wouldn't have a chance." Morgan made washing motions with his hands. "I'm glad this one's cleaned up. I didn't like it from the start."

Dawn leaned back and closed her eyes. She heaved a sigh. "It's all over, then? I can go back to a regular life? If I can remember what one was. It's been . . . so long."

"The lab people have to do their reports." The padded shoulders of his suit rose and fell in a shrug. "But what are they going to say? He did a rough-and-ready brain transplant—"

"Please!" Dawn waved a hand. She got up, legs as shaky in relief as they had been in terror. "I want to keep busy so I don't start dwelling on Peter. Where should I start?"

"The body will be out of here about midday. Why don't you call another news conference for this afternoon? Let the world know SHAPE is now safe. 'Y'all come on back here and sweat.' " Morgan's head was cocked, his expression fey, even cunning. "What do you say?"

Before she could deal with that, she had an important phone call to make. She got through to Torsten Berman at Signal. She told him about Peter's suicide and that he had been responsible for all the deaths. He was silent for a long moment. He said he could scarcely believe that the man he had known and liked would commit suicide. It was a great tragedy, for which Berman was so sorry. As to Peter's having been a murderer: "If you don't mind my saying so, that doesn't make much sense."

"Why not?"

"Why should he wreck something he wanted to build up? Those deaths nearly caused our entire arrangement to collapse. If nobody had died, we'd have closed the deal a month ago."

"He wanted to get me out of the picture. I explained that."

Torsten paused. "So the police are satisfied that Mr. Faldo was the murderer?"

"Yes. Lieutenant Morgan urged me to hold a news conference to let everyone know SHAPE is out of the woods at last."

"So my advice is to do it."

"Mr. Berman, will Signal still honor the terms of the agreement, even though Peter was a murderer? Will we still be going ahead with the cooperative venture?" Dawn found herself holding her breath.

"I'll have to talk to the attorneys. I assume you'll talk to your counsel, Mr. Glassman."

"I'll be finding someone else," she said icily.

"I know the agreement pretty well. It doesn't cover any of the ground that's come up in this phone call. And of course this is an insurance company. It's run by conservative people, because that's the only frame of mind for the business. Those higher up might well have finally lost patience with SHAPE and its problems. It's impossible for me to respond authoritatively to your question at this time." He chuckled softly. "Don't ask me what happens if you and the police are wrong. Perhaps a mysterious Mr. X somewhere still has it in for you. And perhaps Peter Faldo was the *next*-to-last victim."

"Mr. Berman!"

"But if that's so, you won't care any more about the contract, will you?"

"I don't find that as funny as you seem to," she said.

"If Signal had foreseen the trouble SHAPE was headed for, we'd never have gone ahead," Berman said. "We're just too conservative for that. For everyone's peace of mind I hope you're right and that the trouble's over."

"It is. I'm sure of it."

She hung up and shrugged off Berman's morbid speculations. After so many weeks of being frightened, she knew it would be a while before her paranoia fully wore off. While she was on the phone, it had occurred to her that even Berman could somehow have been mixed up in the murders—evidence that her head was far from right.

She was grateful for having to arrange the press conference. This was the last time she would have to deal with a death at the club. Even this, the last, had left its mark on her. Her nerves were still edgy from too little sleep. A look in the mirror offered further evidence of what her body was already telling her. Her eyes were puffy and her skin rough and grainy.

She asked Karl to set up the folding chairs in the unused exercise room. She personally made the calls to the media. She made a special effort to reach Ms. DiNotello of the *Dispatch,* who had dubbed SHAPE the "Death Club." Oh, yes, she should be there! To undo some of her earlier damage.

From time to time that busy morning she wondered where Jeff was. She owed him another apology. She had been so paranoid last night! Well, who could blame her? She felt doubly bad about not trusting him, showing the white feather at the faintest hint of peril. How absurd to think he was about to strangle her! If he never wanted to see her again, she would understand. She wouldn't like it at all, but she would understand. She also wanted to talk to him about the subject of importance he had mentioned. She couldn't imagine what he had in mind. After Peter's suicide, it very likely wasn't important anymore.

She rushed home at noon in Beth's car to work on her appearance. She had to look composed and professional. She would wear her best suit again. She held it up to the light. Still clean and well pressed. She had to overdo the makeup a bit, but that couldn't be helped. The shadows under her eyes were nearly purple.

Back at SHAPE an hour later, she was delighted to find the exercise room even more crowded than during her first news conference. Present employees and those who had been laid off had been brought back by the grapevine to hear the club fate. She glimpsed Dinah's bright mop of red hair. And look there! The Gang of Four was back. They had drawn a great deal of vicarious excitement from the club tragedies. Here they were to follow the tale to its end. If all went to their liking, they'd probably rejoin. The good news was that they probably wouldn't be alone in resuming their membership. When she thought about it, Dawn saw her appearance before the group as the first step in bringing the club back to what it had been—and beyond, to what it would one day be. During her preliminary remarks she turned her eyes frequently to Ms. DiNotello in her stylish suit and favored her and her tape recorder with a confident smile. It had been a trying six weeks for the club, she began. She didn't dwell on the morbid events of the recent past. Nor did she attack her poor dead partner. She explained his motivation and the police suggestion that he was mad. Only a madman could have hoped to get away with five murders within such a narrow arena.

Ms. DiNotello wasn't easily convinced. After Dawn had finished her prepared statement, the reporter tried to spark some controversy by attacking the police, who had no representatives present. Why had it taken them so long to figure out that Peter was responsible? Could the suicide note have been a fake? Could the murderer still be at large? What guarantees had the police offered that the case was closed? All these questions she delivered in a friendly, sincere voice. Of course Dawn couldn't answer them. That she couldn't, she supposed, meant that Ms. DiNotello's article would cast shadows on the new, safe SHAPE. Oh, Dawn hated the media at that moment! One had no chance against them.

Nonetheless she maintained her most professional stance whenever the TV cameras swung her way. She'd check herself out on the news that evening to see how convincing she had appeared. When the media people had packed up and left, the events of the morning descended on her like a heap of stone. She tottered off to the lounge and collapsed on a couch. In the worst way she wanted to believe Peter's suicide had closed the door on the weeks of danger and strain. She couldn't shake the possible implications of Torsten Berman's skepticism and Ms. DiNotello's hard questions. At that moment she was too shaken to speculate. She simply closed her mind. She was too utterly weary to turn it all over yet again. She drew up her knees and hugged them. Enough! She closed her eyes. If she could just doze for a little while . . .

She had just drifted off when she heard someone whistling. The tune seemed familiar. She sat up, eyes suddenly wide open. She turned. Dinah stood at one end of the couch, her lips puckered. She was whistling one of the themes from the Schubert Quintet. The sound died, and her face darkened.

"So Hector played the Schubert for you," Dawn said. "I guess that makes you the latest member of his Seduce and Abandon Club."

"No thanks to you!"

"And congratulations on your fine musical ear."

"Stop the wisecracks!"

Dawn realized how angry the redhead was. "What are you so bothered about?"

"After Hector came to see you last night, you still don't know?"

Dawn waved her hand wearily. "Hector and you are the least of my problems."

"I'm here because I couldn't let you get away with trying to ruin our relationship with that story about him trying to score with another woman," Dinah said hotly. The redhead was bent over the couch, looking down on her. Anger had brought red blotches to her pale cheeks. "I'll tell you the truth, Dawn Gray. I came here early this morning to call you on what you tried to do. I would have caught you earlier, but your killer partner blew his brains out, and you got very busy."

Dawn sat up. Her patience wasn't in any greater shape than her nerves, and they were big-time shaky. She found herself getting angry in turn. She sat up to face the redhead. "You have a choice, Dinah. You can believe what Hector tells you, or you can believe what I tell you—the truth, as it happens. Hector goes from one good-looking young woman to another good-looking young woman. Me, you, somebody who comes after you, okay?"

"He's leaving his wife."

Dawn tossed her head. "He hasn't done it yet. While

he was campaigning to sign you up, he was covering his bets by charming another woman—as an unknown admirer, so she wouldn't accidentally spill the beans and enable you to find out."

"He didn't! He told me—"

"He lied to you. He lied to me last night when he warned me to keep away from you. That's the kind of guy he is. Because he definitely has his charm, it wasn't easy for me to wise up to him, either."

"He swore he didn't secretly court anyone else!"

"I saw the candy. I saw the flowers. I saw the gift cards *in his handwriting.*"

"Who—"

"Never mind who!"

Dinah put her hands on her hips. "Dawn Gray, I simply do not believe you."

Dawn shrugged and rose. "So don't."

Dinah said, "Hector and I are going away today. We're going to South America." She looked at her watch. "Oh, he's going to pick me up about now."

"Don't trust him too far," Dawn warned.

"Stop it! Just stop it! Stop trying to undermine what Hector and I have." Dinah strolled away.

Dawn followed her. "I'm just trying to put a little sense into your head. He has a way of throwing fistfuls of stardust in women's eyes."

"You're jealous."

Dawn winced at that. She walked with Dinah across the lobby. "I probably am, just a little bit. Hector and I had some good times."

"He's already talking marriage."

"Maybe you two are a better match than he and I were." At the top of the stairs she added, "You forgot Sam Springs faster than I ever did."

"It's a tough world, Dimples."

When Dinah was halfway down the stairs, Dawn called, "Just don't trust Hector too much."

"I'll send you a card from Rio."

Dawn watched Dinah descend the stairs. She pushed the door open and the mid-March air swirled in. Through the glass Dawn saw Hector's limo, with punctual Rudolfo at the wheel, come heaving like a whale into the parking lot. The rear door swung open for Dinah as it had for her. She glimpsed Hector's arms raised for an embrace.

That tears came to Dawn's eyes were evidence only that she was exhausted and that her emotions were stretched to the limit.

She wandered back to the office. The police technicians were still busy with the space, though Peter with his half-head had been carried away. She would have the office completely cleaned and repainted. She didn't care if that took the last bit of cash in the club's coffers.

She wandered up to the massage studio. No sign of Jeff. Where was he? Possibly it was better that he wasn't around. She didn't want to have to deal with the embarrassment—shame, even—of not trusting him last night. Not today.

She wandered farther, looking for Karl, who had been so helpful earlier. He was apparently out of the club, running an errand maybe, because she couldn't find him. She felt the need to thank him for his loyalty and assistance over the last weeks. She wished they had more in common. He would be a safe person to love. She went to a semiprivate phone and called Milt Glassman. She told him what had happened to Peter and about the crimes he had committed. Milt jumped in with the legal ramifications of it all. She let him babble on and took notes, knowing she would need them when she got a new attorney. He ran on for quite a while. In the end she confronted him with his two-faced silence about the Signal deal and followed up with notification that he was no longer SHAPE's attorney. Satisfying as that was, the conversation took up more than an hour. It was after four. She stowed her pages of notes in her pocket. At that moment having to carry on single-handedly to bring SHAPE back seemed an unachievable task.

She realized she had eaten nothing all day. She sent out for a pizza and began to eat it in the lounge. Halfway through it, Beth appeared. Her eyes were shining brightly, thanks to the careful use of eye shadow and mascara. She had never been made up like this before. And her clothes! She wore a designer jacket and skirt in a soft violet shade that gave still more life to her eyes. The open-necked blouse revealed the platinum chain Hector had given her.

"I'm so excited!" she bubbled happily.

"What happened?"

"Did you forget? It's Thursday! He's coming to introduce himself at last. His last note said we're going to go away together." From her jacket pocket she pulled a piece of paper and gave it to Dawn. "It's my resignation. I won't be working here anymore after today."

"Beth . . ."

"To tell you the truth, I thought he'd be here before now. It's nearly a quarter of five."

Dawn put down the half-eaten pizza wedge. Suddenly it tasted like paste. Oh, no! Hector had told Beth . . .

"I'm absolutely sure he's going to be here any minute." Beth's tone was so enthusiastic that Dawn hesitated to tell her the truth—that she had been stood up for Dinah. But how could she play dumb? She thought of all Beth had done for the club. How she had hung tough when Dawn was down!

"Why are you looking so . . . odd, Dawn?" Beth asked.

Dawn shook her head, appalled at the thought of hurting her friend. Still, if she said nothing, Beth's hopes would drag on and on. She would be tortured for days until it dawned on her that she had been set up and dumped. She didn't deserve that. Dawn patted the couch. "Sit down, Beth. I have something to tell you."

Beth frowned, some of the light in her eyes fading. "What is it?" she asked, sitting down.

"Listen to me, all right? Just . . . listen for a minute. I know who your secret admirer is. I know him because . . . I recognized his handwriting."

"But—"

"Listen. I happened to see the gift cards in one of your cabinets. So I know the man who wrote them is Hector Sturm, the man who was my lover."

"Him? Oh, I'm not interested in him. We had words and—"

"Your disagreements couldn't have been too serious. I saw the candy, the flowers, and that platinum chain you're wearing around your neck."

"So he's the one who's coming to pick me up?" Beth sounded a bit vague.

Dawn breathed deeply. How did you give someone really bad news? "He was using you, Beth. He wanted you only if he couldn't have Dinah, the redhead who used to date Sam Springs."

"I don't believe you!"

This was her afternoon for not being believed, Dawn thought. "About an hour ago I saw Dinah get into Hector's limo. I talked to her just before she did. They're going to Rio together."

Dawn's eyes were glued to Beth's face. The bright light in her eyes dwindled and died. Her eyelids fluttered. Her wrists twitched weakly. She looked to be on the verge of fainting. Dawn put an arm around her friend's narrow shoulders to steady her.

"No, no! I don't believe you!" Beth cried. "I don't *believe* you. You shouldn't make up things like that!"

"I didn't, Beth. It's what happened." Dawn continued to steady the smaller woman, who was now trembling.

"I want to die!" Beth whimpered.

"No, you don't."

Beth heaved against her and wailed weakly. Dawn

kept holding her. After a long while Beth sagged against her.

"I want to get you out of here, Beth," Dawn said. "Where do you want to go?"

Beth's trembling grew stronger. Dawn held on until it stilled. She repeated her question.

"Downstairs," Beth gasped. "To the trainer's room."

"Not out of the building?"

"No."

"Can you walk?"

Beth burst into wild weeping. Her eye makeup made mucky rivulets down her high cheeks. Her face twisted with a new emotion.

"Angry Beth," she sobbed. "I'm Angry Beth!"

"You have every right to be angry. I'm sorry I said—"

Loud weeping silenced Dawn. When it finally died, she put her arm around her friend's small waist and led her slowly out of the lounge and onto the elevator. She walked her down to the trainer's room, led her in, and closed the door. Once in more familiar surroundings, the small woman pulled away and began to gather herself. Some tears carrying mascara had fallen onto the lapel of her expensive jacket, leaving small ugly blotches. She snatched up a towel and wiped energetically at her eyes. "Angry Beth," she mumbled into the terry cloth. "Angry Beth!"

Dawn stood anxiously by. "Can I get you anything?"

"Pill," she said. "I want a pill, but I'll get it." Instead of turning toward the large cabinet where Dawn had found Hector's cards amid Advils and liniment, she knelt at the far side of one of the counters facing the wall across a narrow stretch of carpet. Her sudden wail startled Dawn. She rushed over to her. The small door in the counter had been jimmied open. The wood had been broken from the lock. Beth stared inside, moaning.

"Did this just happen?" Dawn asked.

"Yes, I guess. This . . . afternoon."

"What's missing?"

Beth said nothing. Fresh tears ran down her cheeks.

Dawn touched her shoulder and repeated her question. "What's missing, Beth?"

"Oh, my pills. And some equipment that was stored in here."

"What kind of equipment?"

"I don't know. I never used it." Her knees buckled, and she slid down to the floor. She pressed her face to the carpet, curled up, and sobbed.

"Beth. Poor Beth . . ."

"Leave me alone, please. Just leave me alone!"

"I'll try to find out who broke in here, see if we can get the stuff back."

"Okay. Okay," Beth mumbled through choking sobs. Just leave me alone!"

At the door Dawn paused. "Are you going to be all right? Really?"

"I'll live."

Dawn blurted, "Let me stay. There's so much I can tell you about what kind of man Hector really is that—"

"No! I just don't want to hear it."

Dawn left, pulling the door shut behind her. What we have here is a broken heart, she thought. As she stood wiping away the beginnings of her own sympathetic tears, she heard the door lock. For now Beth was going to gut it out alone.

She sank against the wall for a moment to gather herself. With the sleeve of her best suit she rubbed away the few tears. It had been a bad day for dress suits so far. She closed her eyes and took four deep breaths. When she looked again, Karl Clausman stood before her. She gasped. He had appeared so suddenly! He wore tight workout pants and a Dos Equis T-shirt wide enough to be turned into a pup tent.

"What's with the little squirt?" He waved at the closed door.

"An affair of the heart," Dawn said. "Somebody disappointed her big-time." She cast a sidelong glance down the hall. She wished someone would appear. Damn this nearly deserted club. For some reason Karl was spooking her this afternoon. She moved off toward the lobby. He chose to follow.

"You okay?" he asked. "I mean with Peter killing himself and all?"

"Not okay, Karl. Just managing. I'm an elephant tiptoeing on thin ice. I'm not sure how long I can keep that act together."

"I'll take you home, then. Right now."

She tried to read his thick face for . . . Surely not menace!

In his suicide note Peter had confessed to hanging around in the Maine woods and sticking the note to the side of the fishing shack. Affectionate Karl had nothing to do with it. When one had been paranoid for as long as she, it wasn't something she could turn off just like that. "Thanks, Karl, but I'm going to stick around for a while. I owe myself a workout later."

Upstairs the law was finally packing up and moving out. Detective Morgan had disappeared some time ago, off on another case. Daniels asked her questions about Peter's next of kin and told her where the body would be after the pathologist got through with it. When he seemed to be finishing up, she stepped forward and said softly, "Is it really all over, Daniels? My head says it is, but the rest of me isn't sure."

"It's over. Your partner went overboard to get the club. What lab stuff we got left is just window dressing. Over? Yeah. It's over." He looked speculatively at her. "If I were you, I'd take a vacation, starting in about one minute."

"I can't do that, Daniels. I just about have to start over making SHAPE profitable again."

Daniels rubbed a hand over his tired face. Then he

beckoned to Karl. "Come outside with me. I want to talk to you in the cruiser."

The brief flash in Karl's eyes told Dawn that he and the police were still adversaries. The long questioning Karl had endured, on top of his earlier criminal record, had been hard on his ego. She remembered the proclivity to violence discovering the note had sparked in the big man. The rage with no outlet.

When he came back, Dawn asked him what Daniels had wanted.

"Never mind," he said. This time there was no reading his voice. He wandered off. So much for him.

Where, though, was Jeff?

She stood at the desk herself that evening, counting the house as carefully as any Broadway producer. She compared the figures with those of the last few Wednesday nights. Up a little. Some members who had been in one of the canceled aerobics classes wandered in. They were long-faced and critical—until Dawn offered to lead the session. Broadway indeed: the show must go on! An hour of moderate impact to some of her favorite tapes, a Nautilus circuit, and she would be pleasantly fatigued enough to sleep all the way through to the next day of the rest of her life.

On the way to the locker room, she stopped by and knocked on the trainer's room door. "Beth? You still there?"

"Yes."

"Come out. I'm going to run a pickup low impact. Join us. It'll do you good."

"No."

Dawn wanted to say something comforting. After her friend's earlier reaction, she didn't dare mention Hector's name. Or Dinah's, either, she suspected. Right then she didn't have time to play counselor. After she finished her workout, Beth might be willing to talk to her. She felt bad about being the one who had broken the wretched news about Hector and Dinah. "I'll come back after my circuit, all right? Maybe we can talk?"

Silence.

After the aerobics, she opened up the bar and treated the adventurous to beer and canned juice, all that was available. She'd have to see about getting the food and drink going again. She'd have to develop a detailed work plan, after talking to Ketty. She might have to take out another loan. She and Peter had previously borrowed and proved their creditworthiness. She would do it, if required—and do whatever else it took to reshape SHAPE.

She made herself join the members' conversations about the club's recent morbid history and Peter's part in it. As the agreement had been formalized, she told them about Signal's employees joining next year and about the expansion of facilities and services. Yes, it was all quite exciting—in a better way than the last weeks had been. She wished them a good night and welcomed them back to SHAPE, pressing the flesh. She'd have to do that a lot in the next months and push the staff to do the same.

Before doing her Nautilus circuit, she surveyed the late evening activities. Not a lot was happening, except on the racket courts. She strolled up to the Nautilus circuits where she hadn't been for a few days. She turned on the lights and looked around. The staff could have done a better job of tidying up. Well, supervision, too, would be improving over the next week. Someone had thrown a black plastic sheet over one of the machines, the hip extender. That meant it was broken. She wasn't aware if anyone had arranged to have it fixed. Sometimes Beth, who had a knack, was handy with them. She went to the intercom and paged her. She told her she ought to come have a look at it. The real reason of course was that she wanted to get Beth out from among the training room's four walls. She had pouted long enough. Remembering the depth of her friend's distress, Dawn realized "pouting" scarcely seemed like the right word.

She went to the files and pulled her Nautilus workout card. She was meticulous about keeping a record of the dates, the circuits, the weights for each machine, and the number of repetitions before failure. She picked a pencil from the container. It hadn't been sharpened. Heads were going to roll tomorrow.

She picked the sharpest and put her sheet on one of the clipboards. She entered the date and time, checked off warm-up—if an hour of aerobics didn't loosen her, nothing would. She started the east circuit that began with her lying flat and moving her bent knee up toward her chin, working with the weights, then straightening it out against them. Then repeating with the other leg. She wasn't at full strength, but she toughed out one more rep than last time.

She made her way down the circuit. After each machine, she added data to her sheet. Next came the lateral raise, a shoulder strengthener. She had to lift her bent arms up sideways from her body to the horizontal. Knowing this one always hurt more than the others, she delayed, taking her time snapping the seat belt into place, panting a bit, and sweating. Six more machines to go and already she felt the last of her stress and tension dissolving. She'd make her shower as hot as she could stand it. After that, home to a long overdue good night's sleep. . . .

CHAPTER
17

Her eye caught movement beyond the low wall circling the Nautilus circuits. Someone was coming toward her. It was Jeff.

"Where have you been all day?" she said. "I was looking for you."

"Here and there," he said. As he entered the brightly lit room she saw he carried a paper bag. His long face looked distant, peculiar.

Despite herself, she felt uneasy. "What's in the bag?"

"You're full of questions tonight."

She looked at him sharply. "So would you be if you'd had the kind of day I had, Jeff. Peter killed himself early this morning. Even later than when you left my apartment—"

"What does my leaving have to do with his dying? Why do you put them together like that?" He stood a little distance away, looking intently at her.

"No reason, really."

"Peter didn't kill himself, Dawn. Neither did Sam. They were murdered, like all the others."

Despite her sweat and panting breaths, a chill shot through her. "H-how do you know that?"

"My theories. You know, my theories that I said I

wouldn't explain to you. I just kept finding out more till I figured everything out.''

"And now you *have* figured everything out?" She measured him with her glance, wondering how his mind was working and why she was becoming increasingly frightened.

"Yep. Everything. And in a minute I'm going to show you how everybody began to die." He grinned, holding the bag at waist height. Something heavy shaped the paper.

"Jeff, could we talk about this later? I don't think this is the best time or place."

He stepped closer. "Well, where could be a better place? You don't trust me in your apartment. You proved that last night. And you haven't trusted me implicitly, even though I about begged you to."

"Something told me not to," she said in a small voice. "My intuition."

He grunted. The distant look came and went on his face, like the headlights of a passing car glimpsed from a room. She recalled that he had been mentally ill for a while. She swallowed. She was sweating more heavily now—with fright. "I'd like you to leave, Jeff. I'd like to finish my workout right now. We can talk tomorrow. Maybe with some more people around."

He shook his head. "That wouldn't be a good idea. It would be wiser if you learned right now how the others began to die."

"I wish you wouldn't use that phrase!" she blurted. " 'Began to die.' "

"It's the right phrase. Something paved the way to each death. Something I'm going to show you in just a minute."

"Jeff!" She fumbled with the seat belt release. She was so nervous that she couldn't make it work. She bit off her rising whimper. "You're scaring me. You're scaring me a lot!"

"I don't mean to. Sorry." He smiled warmly.

Why, then, did she read only menace in his face?

He leaned closer. Her fingers frantically worked the belt release. The rotten thing wouldn't let go!

"Looks like your belt's jammed," he said. "Good. Now suppose you're going to be the killer's last victim. And I'm the killer—"

"Jeff! Will you *stop* it? Will you just stop it and go away? Don't you understand that I'm scared of you right now? I'm scared to death!"

"There are worse things than being scared. Being dead is one of them. That's why I have to explain it all to you now. It won't wait."

She lunged against the belt. It held her tightly.

"I was talking about *beginning* to die, Dawn. All of the victims began to die when they were drugged."

She stopped struggling and looked at him. Her memory fed her something Detective Morgan had said about drug traces having been found in all the victims' bodies. What kind of drug was it? She couldn't remember. She did remember him saying there hadn't been any needle marks. Could Peter have made them swallow a drug? Or had he somehow slipped it into their food or drink?

Fear was making it hard for her to concentrate. Jeff was at her side now. Her wits fled. "No! Don't! Whatever you're going to do, don't!"

"Stop behaving like a baby, Dawn. I'm not going to hurt you."

"You *are*. Stop lying to me! You're the one! You're the killer!"

Jeff frowned. "No way! And you're making me angry. You should learn how to watch your tongue, Dawn. Honestly. As I was saying, the killer drugged all the victims first."

Abruptly she couldn't bear his close presence. "Could you please help me to get out of this seat, Jeff?" Dawn fumbled again with the belt. She knew without question now that Jeff was going to kill her right here, so she was on the verge of hysterical babbling.

"Let's suppose I wanted to kill you right now," he said.

She froze. "Jeff . . ."

"The first thing I'd do is sneak up on you or get beside you somehow. Maybe I'd chat or distract you just for a moment, maybe making you look the other way. Of course in your case right now, you couldn't get away if you had to." He grinned.

"Jeff!" she shouted.

"Stop it! You're being silly. I won't hurt you."

She tore her eyes away from the infernal belt.

Jeff was reaching inside the bag!

He drew out a silvery pistol-shaped instrument, but it looked medical, not military. "All I have to do is push this against a fleshy part of your body and—*phttt*—you're inoculated." He moved around in back of her.

"Just like this."

She felt the icy metal against the side of her neck. There was no way she could keep from screaming. Before the sound had died she heard movement, heavy footsteps. She heard Karl's voice. "Got you, bastard!"

She heard the solid thump of body on body. Jeff flew by, feet off the floor. His inoculator spun off in another direction. He fell in a heap and Karl pounced on him, so quick and strong that Jeff could only raise a hand in feeble protection before the big man's hamlike fist smashed into the side of his head. He sprawled motionless.

Turning her head, Dawn saw that Karl had been hiding under the black plastic throw over the "damaged" Nautilus machine. He rose from the motionless Jeff. "Daniels took me out to the cruiser to tell me Morgan said to watch you, just in case," he said. "You told me you were going to work out, so I thought, hey, if I hide, maybe Mr. Killer here will try to finish you off. And he did!" He pointed down at the motionless Jeff. "I knew it was him all along. Something told me."

"Me, too." For an instant Dawn remembered that she

had once thought she was falling in love with Jeff. How could she have been so blind and stupid?

"I got another secret for you, Dawn. Morgan hid his sidekick Daniels in the building." Karl pulled a police whistle out of his pocket. "I was supposed to blow this if somebody tried to get you." He laughed. "I didn't take time for that!"

"Thank God!"

Beth rushed in, tool bag banging against her leg. "Dawn! Are you all right? I heard you scream and—" She saw Jeff sprawled motionless, Karl looming over her seated friend. She hesitated, as though about to break into another run, this one in the opposite direction.

"It's all right!" Dawn called to her. "Karl took care of the 'problem.' "

Beth saw the inoculator lying on the floor in front of her. She picked it up and waved it. "What's this?"

"You might say it's the murder weapon," Dawn said. "Jeff used it on all the victims, then went ahead to drown them or push them off railings, or whatever."

"Jeff was the killer! *Our* Jeff?"

"Yes, Beth, it was Jeff. Forget the Nautilus machine. It's okay, but this belt's jammed somehow. "You're going to have to take it apart, I guess."

Karl dropped the whistle and grabbed each half of the belt. "Maybe a little persuasion is all this needs."

Beth peeked around his bulk. "A little brain might be better," she said.

He heaved, but the buckle didn't loosen. "Maybe if I try once more . . ." He gathered himself for a moment. "Ow! Hey!" He let go of the belt and began to turn back to Beth. Like a puppet with all its strings cut, he tumbled into a heap beside Dawn's feet.

Beth faced her, the inoculator in her hand. Her grin was as bright as sunshine. "Look at me!" she said. "A little while ago I was Angry Beth. Now I'm Happy Beth."

"That was a stupid, careless thing to do, Beth! Playing games with that thing! Karl could be hurt." She looked down at the crumpled man, then up to her friend's face. "You could have killed him! You don't know what's in that thing."

"Oh, Angry Beth knows what's in it, Dawn. It's Happy Beth who doesn't want to think about it."

"First Jeff talks crazy. Now you. Enough is enough! Will you open up that tool bag and help me get out of here?"

Beth giggled. "When Jeff stole my inoculator I saw I'd have to find another way to make you keep very still. You told me you were going to work out, so about an hour ago, I came up and disabled that buckle." She touched the belt around Dawn's waist. "Only cutting this will get you out of there now. And of course I'm not going to do it." She waved the inoculator. "I'm going to freeze you with this. Then Angry Beth will crush your skull with a hammer."

Dawn heard, but her mind refused to process the meaning of what Beth had said. Beth wanted to kill her? *Beth?* "You? You're the person who killed—six people? Not Peter? Not Jeff?"

"Angry Beth did it. There was nothing Happy Beth could do to stop her."

" 'Angry Beth, Happy Beth'? What are you talking about?" Dawn's dismay bloomed like a sinister flower.

"I'm talking about how it is in my head," Beth said brightly.

Seated as Dawn was, she stared straight at the small woman's lovely face. The violet eyes shining brightly now, as they so often had earlier in what seemed like enthusiasm or love, truly reflected insanity. No, no, Dawn was wrong. It was Beth, just Beth. Her *friend* Beth! She couldn't believe what she was hearing! "Why did you kill six people, Beth?" She shook her voice loose from a sandy throat.

"Angry Beth did it."

"Why did Angry Beth do it?" Dawn battled not to scream at her to stop her childlike chatter about two Beths.

Beth stepped closer to Dawn's back, where she couldn't easily try to grab her. "Angry Beth wrote you a note explaining. Don't you remember? We wanted to destroy your club first, no matter what you did to try to stop us. Then, when we had done that, we would finish your destruction by killing you."

"Why?" Dawn shouted. *"Why?* What did I ever do to hurt you?"

Beth stood behind her now. She was silent for a long, long moment. Then she leaned forward until her mouth was inches from Dawn's ear. "You stole Hector Sturm from me!" she whispered.

Dawn sat silent. That didn't make sense.

"I was so happy with him," Beth said. We traveled around the world. He gave me gifts and money. Where do you think I got the nice things in my apartment? And he gave me love. Wonderful love! He told me I was the one woman in the world for him and that we'd spend years together. He'd divorce his wife, and I'd become the once and future Mrs. Sturm. Five years we were together. Then you came along."

Oh, Lord! Beth was the woman Hector had dumped for her! Now she remembered he had said her predecessor was unstable. She had never dreamed that . . . Beth! Then she remembered the day she was certain Hector was stalking her to push his immodest proposals. She had been in the office working on files with Beth, and he hadn't dared approach them. Even he couldn't have handled both women at the same time. And Beth's supposedly giving Hector a piece of her mind had very likely been a rejected plea to be taken back again. Small wonder Hector had wanted Dawn to fire the petite woman.

"After Hector said he didn't want to see me anymore, I didn't know who you were, but Angry Beth rose up strong and found out. She said we'd come to SHAPE to work, be cunning, and labor to destroy you." She giggled. That familiar, once-charming sound now rang in Dawn's ears, as eerie as a scream in a dark graveyard. "And tonight we're almost finished."

"Beth, wait. Hector sent you gifts, notes. I know his handwriting."

"Happy Beth bought the gifts and had them sent. She knows Hector's writing, too—after five years! I'm sure you'd know how to copy it, too, with a little practice. Happy Beth knew Hector would come back to us if you were gone. It was truly written somewhere that if you were dead, Hector was ours again."

"You . . . sent the gifts to yourself." Dawn's voice was leaden.

"Happy Beth did that," Beth said cheerily. "She knew Hector would have sent them to get us back, if it hadn't been for you. And once you were gone, she knew we'd be a couple again. This time for the rest of our lives!"

On top of her steadily mounting fear, Dawn felt incredibly stupid and unperceptive. The only 'we' was in Beth's mind, on her notes, and in her phone threats. "Stop it, Beth! Stop talking about Happy Beth and Angry Beth. You did all this, Beth. Just you! There's no 'we.' "

"Angry Beth hadn't decided when you were to die. Maybe when the club actually went out of business. The day after, maybe." Beth stepped back in view. A muscle moved in her jaw. "But then you told us about that bitch Dinah. We understood it was too late—too late!— for us to get Hector back. The harm you had done couldn't be reversed after all. Angry Beth rose up stronger than ever. You were to die earlier today in the trainer's room." She tapped Dawn's knee with the inoculator. "I was going to use this on you right then, then cut your throat on the rubbing table."

Weakness flooded through Dawn like a drug from the

inoculator. Her voice emerged as little more than a peep. "Only your little toy wasn't there." She made another connection—far too late. "Jeff had broken into your cabinet and taken it, because he had suspected for some time that—"

"He snooped plenty, but Angry Beth said he wasn't quite sure— "

Dawn's hand darted out, trying to grip Beth's slender wrist, but the small woman jerked it away. She was too quick.

"Uh-uh! If you try anything or scream, Angry Beth will kill you now, instead of in a while." Beth opened her tool bag. From it she removed a rag and a hammer. She waved the rag. "This can be a gag. We'll use it if we have to. We want you to understand every last thing before we put you to sleep."

"And after you do?"

Beth held the hammer in both hands. "Angry Beth will crush your skull with this. But we have a little time yet. We won't be interrupted. Even though this part of the club is closed, I made signs and put them in the hall: Danger. Repairs. Do not enter." She giggled.

Dawn panicked. She drew a deep breath, intending to scream. Fast as a ferret Beth was in front of her with the cloth. When Dawn opened her mouth, Beth jammed the rag between her teeth. The scream became a muffled choke. "Mustn't do!" Beth stuffed the rag farther into Dawn's mouth. She could draw breath only through her nose. Beth's face was inches from hers. The violet lakes of her eyes were smooth, undisturbed—and oddly empty. Terrifying!

The rag tasted faintly of massage oil. Dawn raised a hand to tug it out.

Beth slapped her face. "If you try to do that, I'll have to tie your hands," she said.

Beth became loquacious then. She had to reveal the details of just how she had successfully terrified Dawn.

The first two murders were the simplest—Eloise and Nicole had both contributed to getting Zack Keyman into trouble. If there was any suspicion after the two died, Zack would be its target. She helped that along by making a point of saying she had seen him in the club. It took little time to paralyze and slide the women into Jacuzzi and pool. Chantelle was beginning her tanning session. Before she lowered the machine's lid Beth paralyzed her. The latch and timer, which she had damaged, did the rest. Poison in the juice—so easy!

Then she got unintentional help from Sam Springs and Peter. The struggle over the club and its future clouded the waters well. Dawn shouldn't have been so suspicious of her ex-lover. Sam was only trying to do his job, and he wasn't a killer. Beth chose Sam as the next victim because his death would be clouded as to motive and could in no way be connected to her. She had drugged him as he stood beside the waist-high banister, propped him up, and with every ounce of her strength just managed to roll him up and over.

Dawn should have trusted Peter much more, too. Of course he *was* trying to swindle her by buying her share of SHAPE. But when she continued to refuse, he had told Beth before she killed him that Dawn had worn him down. He had made up his mind to tell her all about Signal and to share the profits of a continuing partnership. All he was waiting for was official news from the insurance company. Of course he never knew Signal had finally agreed to terms, because Beth intercepted the letter one day when she was sorting the mail. She put it aside, realizing it was the perfect weapon to apparently implicate him in the murders, further drawing attention away from her. When the right moment came, she showed the letter to Dawn.

The trip to Maine? Angry Beth had been particularly enraged that weekend. She had followed Dawn and Karl all the way up the interstate and parked in the thick woods a quarter mile from the Clausman home. Rage as thick as syrup and the car heater kept her warm enough. She prowled in the night, assuming that slut Dawn slept with Karl, thus adding to her imagined, massive humiliation.

Last night she had summoned Peter to the office, saying that Dawn had decided to sell her share in the club. She wanted to sign at once, no matter the hour, and leave town with the signed sale agreement. She told him Dawn was too suspicious to face him personally. Beth would be the go-between. When he appeared, they chatted about his motives. Oh, he was surprised at how much she knew! Before he tumbled to Beth's having intercepted the letter and committed the murders, she paralyzed him, put his pistol in his hand, and used his finger to squeeze the trigger. It had been messy, but worth it. His death and the forged confession note were her tickets to freedom from suspicion.

The only change in her plans had been forced on her today, with news of Hector's new love. She wouldn't have time to arrange the "accident" she had planned to end Dawn's life without jeopardizing her own through arrest and punishment. Using the hammer, though, would give Angry Beth a great deal of pleasure! She had arranged to fly to California that night.

As Beth rattled happily on, Dawn's heart sank like a cannonball. When she finished with whatever she had to say, which couldn't take too much longer, she was going to use her nasty little inoculator and then . . . the hammer.

Dawn knew she couldn't get out of the machine's seat. The belt couldn't be torn. The buckle was a mechanical ruin. What could she possibly do to help herself? She had hoped Karl or Jeff would regain consciousness, but they sprawled unmoving where they lay. Wisps of resentment over their slow recovery floated through her mind. She swept them away. What could she do?

She looked around, then down. Lying just beyond her

feet was the police whistle Karl had dropped. Her muffled scream hadn't carried. Surely Daniels would hear
the whistle . . . if she could manage to blow it. She
eyed Beth. The petite woman was pacing back and forth
nervously as she spun out the final dreadful details of
her carefully planned revenge—conceived and executed
with the lucidity and single-mindedness that only the
insane could muster. Dawn reached for the whistle with
her left foot. Its sneakered toe fell just short. There was
a little play in the body belt. If she could stretch . . .
just a little.

Her toe touched it! But the rubber made it pop up
rather than roll toward her. She had to try again. Her
body was beginning to tremble with fear. When Beth
finished babbling, she would use the inoculator, then the
hammer.

She reached for the whistle again. Again it popped
up. So vexing! Dawn felt tears trying to fight their way
out. She couldn't cry. She simply didn't have *time*. She
lunged against the belt, gained maybe an inch. Her leg
ached from being extended for so long. Her rapid breathing hissed through her nostrils, thanks to the smelly rag.
She tried for the whistle again. This time it rolled toward
her under the friction of the rubber toe.

She scuffed it closer. Just before Beth turned back,
she rested her foot lightly atop it, hiding it.

Beth glowered at her, hands on hips. A look at her
face chilled Dawn like an Arctic wind. Beth was pale as
snow. Two red spots burned in her cheeks. Worse, her
face was contorted into the mask of a sloe-eyed fiend,
as though the muscles shaping it were being twisted
by . . .

Angry Beth was back.

"Ruining you was fun!"

Dawn gasped, nearly choking on the gag. Beth's voice
was a baritone croak!

"You destroyed my life. I destroyed yours. I'm going
to finish the job by killing you. Now!"

Dawn raised her hands, as though that could somehow hold off her death. She whimpered. Her situation was hopeless. The whistle was at her feet, but it was too far down to reach with her hands. And it was so clear that there wasn't nearly enough time!

Beth raised the inoculator and moved around behind Dawn, who heaved in the seat, trying to turn to protect herself from the device's lethal touch.

"Dawn, when you're asleep I'll use the hammer first on your face!" Beth croaked.

Dawn screamed into the gag. She tried to grab the inoculator. Beth jerked it away. She moved quickly behind the Nautilus unit where Dawn couldn't touch her. She jerked the back of the T-shirt from Dawn's shorts and raised it up to bare a patch of her back. Beth grunted hoarsely in anger when she saw that Dawn still wore the leotard she had used during the aerobic workout. "The back of the neck, then. Wasps know the best way," Beth croaked.

Dawn felt the cool touch of metal, but batted the inoculator tip away with a wild blow. She was screaming uncontrollably into the stifling rag, nearly gagging. Breath hissed like live steam through her nostrils.

"Stop!" Beth smashed the metal device against Dawn's temple. Stars flashed. "Stop now." She hit her again.

Dazed, Dawn tried to keep both hands on the back of her neck, but Beth grabbed one of her fingers. "Get those hands away!" she shouted.

Dawn resisted. Before she realized it, Beth was levering the finger and—it snapped!

Dawn screamed into the gag, nearly choked and vomited with the sudden, horrid pain.

"When Angry Beth says move your hands, you move your hands!" Beth twisted the broken finger. Dawn screamed into the gag. Red light glowed on the edges of her vision, prelude to a faint. "Want me to break another one?" Beth croaked.

Dawn let her damaged hand be brushed away. The deadly inoculator tip sought to center itself on the flesh beside her spine. "I want you to have the hammer as your last thought," Beth croaked, sliding the tip to a precise spot. The terror of helplessness heaved up like a beast in Dawn's brain. This was her last moment!

Across the circuit Jeff groaned. He was regaining consciousness!

Dawn's head spun with terror and the pain of the broken finger. She battled to control her senses. With a grunt Beth stepped away from her and ran over to Jeff.

Dawn tried to reach the whistle, but her arms weren't long enough. She scuffed it between her sneakers. She would have to lift it with both feet high enough to reach it with her hand. She pinned it between the edges of her sneaker soles. Now . . . lift!

Beth knelt beside a stirring Jeff. Like a viper's head the inoculator found bare skin and hissed with compressed air.

Dawn tensed and began to raise her feet. Carefully. She had to do it carefully, or . . . She reached down. A couple inches farther up was all she needed.

The whistle squirted free and dropped back down to the floor. Dawn groaned into the gag. She thought of tearing it out and screaming. But she dared not risk that, because even her most desperate scream might not reach Daniels's ears. The whistle would be louder, more piercing.

Beth straightened up, looking down at Jeff. For a few moments he continued to struggle, then fell back motionless. Dawn imagined herself in the same state. And Beth beginning with the hammer held in both her small hands. . . . Beth stood looking down at Jeff's motionless body. In a second she would finish what she had begun with Dawn.

Whistle or scream, Dawn didn't have time for either.

Stubbornly she centered the whistle again between her feet. Oh, there wasn't time! It would take Beth only seconds to come back. She had just begun to raise her feet again when Beth started back, the inoculator hanging down at the end of her arm like a pistol.

A few inches closer and Dawn would be able to make a try at grabbing the whistle. It shining metal gleamed like a last faint hope.

No time! Beth was coming back.

She stopped, looked down at Karl's bulk. "We don't want him interfering," she croaked. "He needs a booster shot."

As Beth knelt beside him, Dawn used the extra few seconds to inch the whistle higher. The inoculator hissed.

Dawn made a desperate snatch for the whistle with her right hand.

With her damaged left she tore the gag out of her mouth. She sucked in the deepest breath she could, put the cool metal to her mouth, and blew with all her strength.

Beth flew at her, trying to knock her hand away from her lips. Dawn held the whistle with teeth alone and blew it again. Beth smashed at her teeth with the inoculator. Dawn felt some crack and break. The pain was horrible!

But she blew the whistle twice more.

Beth pressed the inoculator against Dawn's straining neck. Dawn felt a quick, burning sting. She went wild with terror. Beth hit her in the teeth again. The whistle and some teeth flew out of her mouth.

She screamed then, wildly, hearing the sound reverberate in her own ears. Then she wasn't sure what she heard or only thought she heard. She knew she wasn't screaming now. She was zooming down a long, dark slide into the oily pool of her own death.

CHAPTER
18

Karl had sorted Dawn's mail and put it on her desk. On top was a postcard, the third she had received from Dinah. It said she and Hector had left South America for business reasons. Hong Kong was next. They planned to savor "the decadence of the East" before the People's Republic took over and cleaned it up. She tore up this gloating card, as she had its predecessors.

If she ever met Dinah—or Hector—again, she would explain just what kind of morbid horrors had been born of the relationships among Beth and the three of them. Not to blame the gadabout couple—after all, Dawn in a sense had once been Dinah—just to let them know that she had almost been the madwoman's final victim.

That terrifying evening four months ago Daniels had arrived at a run with Detective Morgan on his heels. Morgan had been out on another case all day. When he got back he found his cop's instinct still acting up: things weren't yet right at SHAPE. He had tried to set up the murderer by urging Dawn to hold the news conference, but hadn't thought he had succeeded. So he wouldn't have gone to the club if he hadn't found Jeff's note. That catapulted him into action.

Not being able to reach Dawn by phone at home, he had assumed she was at the club. When the desk told him she couldn't be located but her coat was still in the office, he burned up the streets, siren screaming, to get there just as she blew the whistle.

Both he and Daniels had to sweat to get the hammer out of tiny Beth's frenzied hands, her croaking like a frog all the while. She got in one blow that cracked Dawn's cheekbone but did no permanent harm. It had healed itself without medical intervention. Her finger had to be set, but had knitted nicely. Dental work had restored her teeth and her appearance. "Anybody says 'Angry Beth' to me now, the hairs on my neck start dancing," Morgan said.

Beth had been examined by a battery of shrinks and found incompetent to stand trial. She was then shipped off to an institution in the Midwest.

"Probably a country club," Morgan said with a snarl. "Kill one person, you go to jail. Kill a half dozen, you never do a day of time. I catch 'em; the lawyers spring 'em." Later he apologized to her in private for setting her up a bit by telling her he was sure Peter was the murderer. He needed to do that to draw the real murderer out of the shadows. He had put his money on Jeff, but had been hung up on the lack of motive. Beth? He never dreamed . . . He had looked after Dawn's protection, setting both Karl and Daniels out as bodyguards. Even so, he had nearly bungled the case. In fact, he hadn't handled it well at all. He should have tumbled to Beth. He hadn't lived by his own theories. "Remember what I told you, Dawn? There are only two real motives in the murder business: love and loot, with a few variations." He sighed. "I been at this job too long. Maybe I should look into early retirement."

"You?" Dawn said. "How can you retire? You do good work."

He got up and moved toward the door. "Thanks for the kind words. Good luck. If you ever need a cop again, call Daniels. He got promoted to detective." He raised a finger to his lips. "I wrote it up as if he did a lot on the SHAPE case," he whispered. He tipped his hat. "Hang loose, pretty lady."

SHAPE was under new management—Dawn's. To her chagrin, Peter had left all his club assets to her in his will. She still battled with the guilt she felt over having attached darker motives than mere swindling to his offers to buy her out in the face of the club's likely failure. She scarcely felt better about how she had cynically interpreted his frequent absences. The best she had thought was that he was carrying on affairs with a number of women. At worst she of course imagined him skulking about dealing out death and threats to her.

She found out he had been spending his spare time reading to the blind, some of them bedfast and dying. . . .

She had put Karl into a position where he could blossom into an efficient, even imaginative, manager. She told him what she thought the club needed, and inevitably he found an unexpected new way to make it happen. She had intended to have a talk with him about his romantic attachment to her, to explain that for her the spark just wasn't there. Somehow she had never gotten around to it. Maybe she was really looking forward to a few trips to a Maine green with summertime, dips in the icy lake, plentiful meals in the big white frame house, and trail bike rides all over the New England rural landscape. There wasn't really a romance going on, she thought, and probably never would be. Just the same, they made a happy couple. Right then that was about all she could handle.

In a way, Karl had been most kind to her. He had never resented her suspicion that he was the murderer.

Not so, Jeff. He had come to in time to see Beth taken off in a straitjacket. Later that evening, after Dawn had seen a doctor, Jeff had volunteered to spend the night watching over her, to make sure she was okay. Her mouth hurt so badly that she couldn't sleep. She propped herself up on a pillow, swallowed Advils, and they talked. He retraced for her the path of his suspicions.

Initially he thought the first three women had been killed by Zack Keyman. When the reporter drank the poisoned juice, the riddle swung around in an entirely new direction. A random death meant either that someone had killed for pleasure or that another motive existed, supported by the fact that the murders had recurred at the club. Someone had something against SHAPE, possibly. He couldn't imagine what that might be, though he explored the idea a long while. If the murderer's target wasn't the club, he thought in time, then possibly it was one of the owners, Peter or Dawn. That had been a real tangle, with no evidence at all as to which, if either, of them was the bull's-eye. Not until Dawn began to receive the threatening notes and phone calls was that important detail clarified.

Hearing that drugs were found in Sam's body made him begin to suspect Beth. She sometimes gave injections and had begun nurse's training. The problem was her motive. What did she have against Dawn? She and Jeff were Beth's very good friends. He then tried to think what, besides the club, the two women had in common that might provide fuel for the petite woman's revenge. He came up with nothing, which was why he wasn't willing to accuse Beth. Dawn's paranoia was already out of control. A new person to suspect—with no evidence to back it up—would only worsen the situation. When he heard about the notes from Hector to Beth, he understood that Hector was what the two women had in common. During the first moment when he might have spoken about it to Dawn, Beth was in the room. The night Hector came storming into Dawn's apartment filled with denials about any relationship with another woman, Jeff believed him, even if Dawn didn't. Jeff had followed Hector out into the hall and asked him point-blank if Beth had been his mistress before Dawn. He said she had. After he ended their relationship she had phoned him repeatedly, causing him to change numbers. More than once he had turned around and seen her trailing in his wake, a wild waif with nothing on her mind but her mad obsession for him. When he confronted her, she pleaded to be taken back. Refusing her caused a tirade of threats to any woman he chose to replace her. Even so, he was dismayed when she showed up at SHAPE as an employee. Hearing all that, Jeff suspected a motive, but still had no evidence. Did Dawn remember that Jeff had come back to her door, offering what was to be that information? She had declined to hear it, he reminded her with clear resentment in his voice.

He set about then to figure out how Beth had administered the drug, since no needle marks were found. One of his friends was a doctor, but Jeff had trouble locating him. By the time they sat down to talk it was late morning, the day after Peter's death. The doctor told Jeff that inoculations were often given using a compressed-air device that blew vaccines against the skin in a way that caused absorption. It took a practiced eye to recognize the faint marking and to know what it meant. Recently, powered with compressed-air cartridges and fueled with vaccine vials, the inoculators had become fully portable.

If Jeff could find that Beth owned an inoculator, he could go to the police with the information and at the same time prevent her from using the device on Dawn. Because he had unsuccessfully searched the trainer's room previously, he broke into Beth's apartment at noon the day after Peter died and carefully searched it, but found nothing. That meant that if she owned an inoculator, she either carried it all the time or kept it hidden at the club. So he searched the trainer's room again. The only place he couldn't get into was the little closet set into the counter. He pried it open and found what he was looking for.

"What time did you take it?" Dawn asked.

"A little after four."

"You saved my life, Jeff." Why didn't she feel elation at that realization? Likely because she imagined her not truly trusting him made her less worthy of what he had done on her behalf. "Beth was in a rage when I led her down to the trainer's room. The first place she went was to the closet. You had just broken in and taken the inoculator. She intended to paralyze and kill me on the spot!" She groaned. "It was that close."

Jeff had taken the inoculator to the police station, but Morgan was off chasing another case. He waited several hours, left a note, then came back to SHAPE to tell Dawn what he had found out. Then he made a big mistake. He thought that with the weapon in his hands, Beth could do no more harm. . . .

When Dawn recovered from her physical injuries and began to put the shock and fear behind her, she had tried to expand her relationship with Jeff. Though they slept together, something wasn't right. The energy with which he possessed her had something of abuse in it. And one long weekend he used her past all exhaustion, as impossible to satisfy as a satyr.

The next day he came to the club with a huge knapsack on his back. He had moved out of his apartment, sold what little he owned, and was hitting the road. There was a twitch of smile on his face and a glint in his eye that told her he considered the accounts between them settled: Her suspicions and distrust had damaged his pride and affection for her beyond repair. He kissed her on the cheek and left.

To her surprise she didn't cry.

In a way, their barely blossoming love had been Beth's final victim.

She walked to a window from which she could see her parking space. There sat a shiny new Toyota, her reward to herself for having not only survived but prospered. The odometer showed a meager 168 miles. Its interior was still redolent with new-car smell.

She raised her eyes to the foundation and girders of

her building's extension. Construction of Signal's new facility was also right on schedule. The details of the insurance company's sharing SHAPE facilities had been worked out. To be honest with herself, she had to admit that the final terms she had worked out were better for the club than those for which Peter had originally settled. During the negotiations, Torsten Berman had looked up from his papers at her with some awe. "You know, Dawn Gray," he had said, "you're one tough cookie!"